NEW BEGINNINGS IN LAVENDER BAY

THE LAVENDER BAY CHRONICLES BOOK 4

MICHELE BROUDER

This is a work of fiction.

Names, characters, places and incidents are either a product of the author's imagination or are used fictitiously, and any resemblance to actual persons, living or dead, events, or locales is entirely coincidental.

Editing by Jessica Peirce
Book Cover Design by Rebecca Ruger

New Beginnings in Lavender Bay © 2025 Michele Brouder

To God be the Glory.

PART ONE

DeeDee

CHAPTER ONE

When Doreen "DeeDee" Cook was a child, her mother, Louise, used to say that you could run a herd of cattle through the bedroom without waking her up. And it was no different now that she was an adult.

Although it was past noon, she lay on her side on her living room sofa, sound asleep in only her underwear and an oversized T-shirt, a movie playing on the large-screen television across from her. Deep in her slumber, she did not hear the noisy rotation of the fan's blades, set to high to attempt to stave off the sweltering Florida heat; nor did she hear the lawn mowers outside. She didn't even hear the insistent knocking at her front door or the ringing of the doorbell.

It was only when the knocking turned to banging that DeeDee began to rouse, coming slowly out of her deep sleep. Suddenly aware of voices outside, she rolled over, blinked several times, and sat up, her sweaty hair smashed against one side of her head. She felt sticky and thought of a cold shower but dismissed it when she realized that would require getting off the couch and an energy she did not possess.

"She's home—I just saw movement!" The voice sounded a lot like that of DeeDee's oldest sister, Maureen, but that wasn't possible; Maureen lived up north.

"DeeDee, open the door!" Definitely Maureen.

Still operating in a half-sleep fog, DeeDee stood, yawned, and stretched, eventually making her way to the door. Her canary, Peaches, jumped around excitedly in his cage, chirping away.

What was Maureen doing in Florida? Had she mentioned she'd be visiting? DeeDee didn't think so.

Confused, she immediately opened the door of her ground-floor condo to find not only her oldest sister, but the two middle sisters, Nadine and Angie, as well. She squinted against the blazing afternoon sun. It was steamy outside and her breath caught in her throat.

"What are you doing here?" she asked.

"Good afternoon to you too," Angie said.

Maureen opened the screen door, and the three older sisters pushed past DeeDee, into her home and thus, into her life.

Maureen was the first to pull her into a hug. "How are you, DeeDee?"

Her sister squashed her so hard DeeDee could barely breathe, let alone talk. Nadine was next, and her embrace was softer, gentler. Then came Angie, her beautiful strawberry blonde hair styled very short as it was still growing back after her cancer treatment.

Angie wrapped her in a hug. "Come here, you."

DeeDee led them down the short hallway with its cream floor tiles and soft gray walls. Aside from one silver-framed watercolor print of geese flying over a marsh, the space was bare. When they arrived in the open-plan living room, kitchen, and dining area, however, DeeDee saw it through her sisters' eyes and found that she couldn't look at them. If the state of her home indicated her state of well-being, her sisters would figure out pretty soon that DeeDee wasn't doing well.

The dishwasher was full of clean dishes, from weeks ago. The sink was full of dirty dishes, mostly silverware and coffee cups. Cans of soup were stacked on the counter. There'd been a sale. On the stove was the pot she used every day to heat some up. It hadn't been washed in weeks. Crumbs littered the countertops, and there was a dead fly on the floor near the cabinet that had been there for three days. In some places, the floor was sticky where she'd spilled iced tea. Her table was covered with piles of unopened mail, much of it stamped in red with the words "final notice." The garbage beneath the sink was not only overflowing but was beginning to stink.

In the living room, pillows from her bed were at one end of the sofa. Empty bowls and glasses covered most of the coffee table. Beneath the large birdcage, seed and feathers littered the floor. She'd been meaning to sweep that up.

DeeDee finally looked at her sisters. None of them were able to hide their shocked expressions. Eyes wide, mouths open, they took in the state of things. Nadine's gaze traveled to the canary, and she walked over to him. "How pretty," she said of the pale peach–colored bird. Maureen and Angie joined her, and they made chirping noises to the bird, who responded in kind.

"What's his name?" Maureen asked.

"Peaches," DeeDee replied.

"Hello, Peaches," they all said.

"What are you guys doing here?" DeeDee asked. Her voice sounded small, like a child's. A child who was about to be scolded. She hated that about herself, that she could so easily be transported back to feeling like the kid sister.

Maureen spoke first. "Mom's worried about you. Said she hasn't heard from you and when she calls, you don't return her messages."

"I've been busy," DeeDee lied.

"We thought we'd take a road trip to see you," Nadine said softly. She rubbed DeeDee's arm gently.

"You should have called," DeeDee said, realizing her tone sounded snarky. She folded her arms across her chest.

"We wanted to surprise you," Angie said.

"Are you all right?" Maureen queried.

"I'm fine." DeeDee wondered how long it would be before she could ask them to leave. She was hardly in a position to show them the Florida sights. She scratched her scalp. Her hair needed a good wash.

Maureen's gaze landed on DeeDee's head. "You've got quite a bit of regrowth there, kiddo."

DeeDee shrugged. Her dark roots were about two inches long. The contrast with the dyed platinum blonde hair was conspicuous. Not looking in the mirror had been the solution.

"I'm sorry, where are you staying?" she asked. She wanted to add "and for how long," but felt that would be rude. Now that they'd seen her, they could be on their way.

"We're not staying anywhere," Nadine said.

"We were hoping you'd come back to Lavender Bay with us," Angie said. Leave it to her to be blunt.

DeeDee narrowed her eyes at her sisters. This was beginning to stink of an intervention. One she wanted no part of and did not need.

"Now why would you think that?" she asked, her tone spiky.

Maureen's gaze swept around the rooms. "A few things, honey."

"Granted, I might not be getting the housekeeping award this year . . ." DeeDee started.

Angie scrunched up her nose. "And quite possibly not the hygiene award either."

"I've been busy," DeeDee said again.

"All right," Maureen said, taking charge. "First, take a shower, wash your hair, and change your clothes, and then we'll sit down and talk."

DeeDee was about to balk. About to say they had no right barging into her home and ordering her around. It wasn't thirty years ago, and they weren't on Heather Lane in Lavender Bay. But it was three against one and she went, grumbling, off to her bedroom.

Half an hour later, DeeDee reappeared in the kitchen, her wet hair wrapped in a toweled turban. She had changed into fresh clothes: a pair of shorts and a sleeveless T-shirt. She felt marginally better. In that short period of time, Angie had unloaded the dishwasher and was beginning to load up the dirty dishes. Nadine had swept the floor and carried in the dishes from the living room. Maureen sat at the kitchen table with DeeDee's utility bills in front of her, her phone in one hand and her bank card in the other. DeeDee reddened; she did not want her sister to pay her bills. She went to intervene, but Maureen waved her away.

DeeDee stood there, hands on the back of one of the kitchen chairs, waiting for Maureen to finish the call. Sink cleared, Angie pulled out a can of Ajax and began to scrub the sink.

"Angie, that isn't necessary—" DeeDee started.

From the small utility room off the kitchen came the sound of the washing machine starting its cycle, and Nadine emerged, wheeling the vacuum out with her.

"Nadine!"

They weren't listening, and it reminded DeeDee why she lived one thousand miles away from them. Tears stung her eyes.

"Stop!" she shouted.

Maureen disconnected her call. Angie shut off the tap. And Nadine paused in the living room, the vacuum plugged in, waiting to go.

"Please," DeeDee said, lowering her voice. "I don't need you to do all this."

"We want to help you," Nadine said gently.

Frowning, DeeDee said, "I appreciate that. But really, I don't need any help."

Her sisters looked at each other. Finally, Maureen stood and said quietly, "Let's sit down." She cleared the table, moving the piles of mail to a clean section of counter space.

Reluctantly, DeeDee took a seat and was joined by her sisters.

"DeeDee, it's obvious that something is wrong," Maureen said.

DeeDee hunched her shoulders. "I'm going through a tough time." That was an understated way to describe the unforeseeable convergence of events that had sent her on a downward spiral.

"We can see that," Nadine said.

"Why didn't you call us?" Angie asked.

DeeDee started to say that she didn't want to bother them, but the truth was she hadn't wanted her family to know how dismal things were in her life. Her older sisters were all successful in their own right: Maureen had a busy interior design business, Nadine had opened a prosperous inn in Lavender Bay, and Angie had a bustling café. They were no slouches. It was hard to keep up, and it illuminated her own failure. Besides, she didn't think there was any way they could help her.

"How's work?" Nadine asked.

DeeDee stared at the table, unable to look at them. "I'm not working at the moment." After the scathing reviews about her performance in her most recent play, she'd had a hard time securing any new jobs. She'd had no choice but to sign up for unemployment compensation.

"But that last play ended months ago," Angie said.

"I know," DeeDee said.

"Look, why don't you come home to Lavender Bay," Maureen suggested.

"I can't," DeeDee said.

"Why not?" Nadine and Angie asked together.

DeeDee waved her arms around. "Because I might get called for work. I can't leave my house. I can't go anywhere with my hair looking like this." She pointed to her head, forgetting that it was currently wrapped up in a towel.

"Those reasons are all valid," Maureen said, "but we can work around them."

"How?" DeeDee demanded.

"First, if you get a call, you can fly back down the next day and be here for the audition or whatever." DeeDee went to protest, and Maureen cut her off with, "And I'll pay for your ticket."

"You can get your hair done before you leave," Angie said. "Or you can wear a scarf. I can help you there."

That brought a small smile to DeeDee's lips.

"You are getting out of the house, though, right?" Nadine queried.

"Of course," she replied easily. Once a week, there was a quick trip to the grocery store to stock up on soup, crackers, and iced tea mix. And just last week, she'd had a dental appointment, and she had to go to the pet store to get birdseed for her canary. Her home, as messy as it was, had become her refuge. There'd been a time in her life when she was rarely home; she'd been what her mother had called a "social butterfly." But lately even the thought of going for a drive required more energy than she currently had.

Maureen's expression was one of concern. Again, she said, "Come back with us."

DeeDee shook her head. "No way. I don't want to go back home."

"Why not?" Nadine asked. "Mom wants to see you."

"What's going on here?" Angie asked.

"I don't want to leave." DeeDee scratched her eyebrow, even though it didn't itch. Why did she have to explain it to them?

"DeeDee, talk to us," Nadine said softly. She looked around. "It's obvious that something is going on."

"Why don't you let us help you?" Maureen said.

What was it about her oldest sister's tone? Sometimes it was like nails on a chalkboard. The two of them were as different as chalk was from cheese. Maureen was used to telling people what to do; she'd been doing it with the three of them their whole lives. And DeeDee was used to rebelling against that. Nothing had changed in the ensuing decades.

"I feel like you're ganging up on me," she said, trying extra hard to keep the whine out of her voice.

Her three sisters spoke at once.

"No, no, not at all!"

"We only want to help."

"Don't think that."

"What am I supposed to think?" DeeDee asked. "You show up with no warning and expect me to pack my bag and come back with you?"

Initially, there was no comment from her sisters.

Maureen went to speak but Nadine put up her hand. Nadine always had the softer delivery.

"Tell us what's happening in your life, so we can figure out how to help you."

DeeDee was about to protest, but she figured she might as well give them something. Then she could send them on their way. Remembering her manners, she asked, "Would anyone like a glass of iced tea? It's all I have."

She poured four glasses of iced tea, carried them over to the table, and sat back down. "I'm sorry, I have no ice."

"Now tell us what's going on," Maureen encouraged.

Nadine interrupted. "Is it because of the play?"

"I heard it didn't go well," Angie added. "Poor ticket sales."

"The poor ticket sales were due to my poor performance," DeeDee admitted.

"No!" Nadine said.

"I have a hard time believing that," Angie said.

"You're a great actress!" Maureen added with conviction.

DeeDee stood and dug through one of the piles of paper until she found what she was looking for: newspaper clippings of the reviews of the play. She brought them back to the table and started reading the parts she'd highlighted with a yellow marker.

"The play itself is good but the execution is awful, especially that of the lead actress, Doreen Cook. God awful!"

She didn't look at her sisters as she continued to go through the clippings.

"There is nothing salvageable about Doreen Cook's performance. Nothing."

"Doreen Cook owes me two hours of my life; it's time I won't get back."

"Who told Doreen Cook she could act?"

She went to read another one, but Maureen stopped her, placing her hand gently on her arm. "All right, honey, we get the idea."

DeeDee couldn't help it that tears welled up in her eyes. Her shoulders slumped and she looked at her hands in her lap, biting her lip. She did not want to cry. She'd done enough of that.

"Oh, DeeDee," Nadine said. "Please don't feel like a failure because of this one experience."

"Why didn't you tell us?" Angie asked.

DeeDee shrugged. Her sisters had mistakenly assumed that the failed play and the scathing reviews were the genesis of her current state. It certainly hadn't helped, but it wasn't the reason things were all wrong in her life. But she'd happily let them go on believing that line of thinking. It was easier that way. It gave her life a concrete cause and effect. As for the other thing, if she didn't mention it and didn't think about it, then it didn't exist, right? The trick was not to think about it.

Maureen was speaking. "First, stop saying the word failure. It's a setback, that's all, and it happens to every one of us."

DeeDee hoped they wouldn't launch into a lot of inspirational hooey. She wasn't up for that either.

"You've been working as an actress since you graduated from college, correct?" Nadine asked.

"Yes."

"And you've supported yourself," Angie added.

DeeDee nodded. Granted, she didn't live in a big, grand house, but she was proud of her two-bedroom condo. She'd purchased it herself without help from anyone. "You know how much I love acting. I've always had something on the go. I'd be in a play for months on end, then maybe I'd do a commercial or two, and there was always a bit part in a movie, but there was *always* work for me until this last play. Now it's dried up." The speed with which the phone calls and texts abruptly stopped alarmed her. It was frightening to wake up one day at thirty-eight years old and realize your career was over.

"Then like I said, this is only a setback, that's all," Maureen said with an air of finality.

DeeDee agreed with everything they said, but she made no further comment.

They were momentarily startled when a bird hit the window, and they all looked toward it, satisfied the bird wasn't hurt when it flew off. They turned their attention back to each other.

"Have you seen a doctor?" Nadine asked.

"No, what for?" DeeDee said.

"You might be depressed," Maureen said.

"It might be a reactive depression to your most recent performance," Angie added helpfully. When her sisters looked at her, she appeared sheepish and added, "I heard about it on a podcast."

Was she depressed? Or was it only that she couldn't seem to get off dead center? That she was, quite simply, stuck. Did that count as depression? She supposed the increased sleeping and the flat mood might point in that direction. There was a lot more going on than just a poor performance in a play, but did she really want to waste a therapist's time when surely there were people out there with bigger problems?

"Or maybe you just need to regroup," Angie said.

"I don't know if I have the energy to regroup," DeeDee admitted. What was worse, she didn't know if she wanted to regroup. It seemed easier to do nothing.

Maureen gave her a sympathetic smile. "We've all been there. Life has thrown us curveballs and we've been in the same place you are now. Uncertain. Depressed."

DeeDee's sisters had had their own issues. Maureen's son had gotten involved with drugs, Nadine's ex-husband had had a child with his mistress while still married, and Angie had been dealing with breast cancer.

"How has your boyfriend been through all of this? Supportive, I hope," Angie said.

DeeDee's face reddened. "We broke up."

Maureen's face was clouded with concern. "What happened?"

Brad Maxwell had been the director of the play and DeeDee had gotten involved with him, but as soon as the play flopped, he'd ghosted her. It had only served to sharpen her humiliation, making her feel like a scapegoat. She'd wrongly assumed that they'd comfort each other and figure out what to do next. Instead, he'd done a disappearing act, and she'd ended up feeling abandoned. And very alone.

She explained all this to her sisters. This, she could talk about. It was that *other* thing she didn't want to discuss.

Angie spoke up. "Again, like Maureen said, this is only a setback. You've got to pivot and go in a different direction."

"But where?" DeeDee asked. This part scared her more than anything. Not knowing what to do next. It was the stuff of nightmares. The intelligent part of her told her that work was her answer. That she loved her career, and it might help with her current life situation. In theory, it made sense to her; it was the execution of it that was the problem.

"Would you please come home with us? Just for a visit." Nadine said. "Mom would love to see you, and you could spend time at the beach and think and regroup."

"What would people say?" DeeDee asked. What other people thought about her bothered her greatly. She knew it shouldn't, but it did. It was one of the reasons she didn't live in Lavender Bay.

"About what?" Maureen asked.

"My dismal failure."

"First, it's none of their business," Maureen replied sharply. "Second, there is no shame here. You can recover from this."

The thought of leaving made her heart race. Her palms went clammy and there was that familiar but uncomfortable sensation of her racing heart and dizziness.

"I'll be fine," she said. "Besides, what would I do with Peaches?"

"Bring him with you," Angie said.

"Come home, take some time, and then get back on track," Maureen advised.

A thought occurred to DeeDee and she looked around at her sisters. "The three of you have gone through some awful times recently and here I am complaining about my troubles, which pale in comparison."

Maureen was quick to respond. "Please don't do that. Your issues are just as important. It's all relative."

Nadine spoke up. "Remember what Grammie used to say? That if everyone put their bag of troubles in the middle of the room, we'd all go running for our own bag of troubles."

DeeDee could feel herself beginning to weaken. Not that she was convinced that going home was the solution. It seemed to her she'd only be transporting her troubles across state lines. But the change of scenery might do her good and besides, she had the doomed feeling that the three of them were determined to bend her to their will.

"Look, we can leave whenever you're ready," Angie said.

"There's so much I'd need to do," DeeDee said, looking around.

"We'll help you with everything," Nadine said.

"Maybe you'd like to get your hair done before we leave," Maureen suggested.

DeeDee grimaced. "Uh, I don't think so."

Reading between the lines, Maureen said, "Make the appointment. This will be my treat."

DeeDee hesitated and Nadine said, "You know how good it feels when you get your hair cut and colored."

She did know. She always felt like a million bucks afterward. When you were having a good hair day, you were having a good day period.

Angie said, "Go ahead. Call your hairdresser."

DeeDee looked from one sister to another, biting her lip. Finally, she scrolled through her phone until she found the number for her hair salon. After the call, she told her sisters, "She's booked out today, but she's had a cancellation in the morning and can take me at nine thirty."

"Perfect, I'll go with you," Maureen said.

DeeDee drew in a deep breath and said, "Thank you, I appreciate it."

By the end of the day, DeeDee had caved and packed a suitcase for a return to Lavender Bay. She wouldn't stay long, she told herself. Only for a few weeks to get out of her current funk. Maybe they were right. Maybe all she needed was a change of scenery to perk up.

As promised, her sisters helped her get ready to leave. Nadine washed out the refrigerator and threw out a bag of rubbery yellow celery that had seen better days. Maureen dusted and vacuumed the condo, and DeeDee gave the bathroom a good scrubbing and then ran a damp mop over the tile floors. Angie drove up to the nearest pet store and purchased a bird carrier.

As she'd been inert for months, all that activity tired DeeDee out, and she would have loved nothing more than to lie on the couch and watch a movie, but her sisters had other plans. They wanted to go out to dinner, somewhere they could sit outside. DeeDee put up her hair to hide her roots as best she could and put on a blue maxi dress.

Maureen and Angie exited the condo first, followed by DeeDee and Nadine. As soon as DeeDee stepped outside, she froze. Although the sun was dipping toward the horizon, it was still scorching, and the air was heavy. Suffocating. Panicking, she took a few steps backward, almost knocking Nadine off her feet.

Maureen narrowed her eyes and looked at her.

"What's wrong?" Angie asked.

DeeDee shook her head. "I can't do this. It's too . . ." Words escaped her. She shook her head again. "You go on without me. I'll be fine here."

Nadine put an arm around her. "What's going on, DeeDee?"

Maureen stepped closer and asked, "When was the last time you were out of the house?"

DeeDee had to think for a moment. "Last week. For groceries."

Maureen studied her sister for a moment and then said, "Let me rephrase my question. When was the last time you left your house to do something other than buy groceries?"

"Uh, it's been a while."

"How long?" Angie pressed.

"I get out. I went to the dentist last week." As she said it, she realized how weak it sounded.

To DeeDee's relief, her sisters did not rush her. Did not show impatience. In fact, they seemed as lost as she felt. She took a few steps away from Nadine to put some physical distance between them.

"It'll be all right," Angie reassured her. "We'll be with you. You won't be alone."

"Angie's right," Maureen said. "We're here for you. We'll go for a quick dinner and come right back."

"Can you just bring me a meal home?" DeeDee tried. But her oldest sister shook her head. Maureen always thought she knew what was best for everyone.

Nadine stood at DeeDee's side. "It'll be all right. We'll eat, we'll catch up, and we'll come home."

Despite her misgivings, DeeDee nodded. Why did they have to come down here? Why couldn't they leave her alone?

"Come on, let's go, I'm starving," Angie said with a nod toward Maureen's car parked out front.

DeeDee took a tentative step forward. She drew in a deep breath, held it, and then let it go and walked to the car. She had to force herself to do this. How would she handle the drive from Florida to New York if she couldn't go out to dinner?

Angie and Nadine piled into the back, leaving the front seat for DeeDee.

After Maureen buckled up, she pulled her sunglasses down from the visor and asked, "Where to?"

Reflexively, DeeDee was going to suggest her favorite restaurant, but she didn't want to risk running into Brad, so she said the next thing that came into her mind: "Café Bellissimo." She'd never been there, and she hoped she didn't run into anyone she knew.

CHAPTER TWO

Café Bellissimo was situated on the banks of one of Florida's many lakes, about five miles from DeeDee's home. The four sisters asked for a table on the patio and were told it would be a twenty-minute wait. DeeDee was sorry she hadn't called ahead and made a reservation, but her sisters didn't seem to mind. They were given a pager that would beep and light up when their table was ready, and they wound their way to the outdoor seating area and managed to grab four high stools at the bar.

DeeDee looked around and decided she liked the setup. Waist-high black wrought iron fencing enclosed the area, and a triple strand of clear fairy lights lined the perimeter overhead. There were black wrought iron tables and chairs with thick burgundy cushions and matching table umbrellas for times when the sunshine was too intense.

She took a first taste of her piña colada, raised her eyebrows and murmured, "Yum." Angie had opted for a margarita, and Maureen was nursing a vodka martini while Nadine, who'd offered to be the designated driver, sipped from a glass of Diet Coke.

"Look," DeeDee said, pointing up to the cloudless sky. "There's the international space station going by."

Her sisters looked heavenward, watching the shining spark of light slice across the night sky and disappear.

"Gosh, that was cool," Angie said.

It was a sight DeeDee never got tired of. NASA was one of her favorite places to visit in Florida.

Thirty minutes passed before their pager went off. As soon as they were settled at their table, a server appeared, handed them their menus, and took an order for another round of drinks. Although DeeDee felt slightly more relaxed, she glanced at her phone, trying to estimate the amount of time it would take to order, eat their meals, and get back home.

She took a quick sip of her drink. "So tell me what's new in Lavender Bay. How's Mom?"

"Mom's great," Maureen said. "Busy as usual. She and Aunt Gail went away for a weekend. She said they wanted to relive some past times, but she would not enlighten us as to what those were."

"Are those two still joined at the hip?" DeeDee asked, knowing how close her mother and her aunt were.

"Of course, that will never change," Angie said.

They were interrupted by the server, who wanted to take their order. Their menus remained unopened on the table.

"Can you give us two minutes?" Maureen asked.

"Sure," the server said, and disappeared.

All four of them picked up the menus to scan the offerings and snapped them closed after a few minutes, having decided. The server appeared out of nowhere and took their orders.

Nadine leaned forward, her bracelet jangling on her wrist. She looked well, DeeDee thought. Nadine's hair was colored a honey blonde, and her blue eyes shone. The move back to their hometown had suited her well. With a grin, Nadine said, "Angie has a boyfriend."

Angie tilted her head to one side and smirked. "Really, Nadine? How old are we?"

Nadine responded with a laugh. "It's true though, isn't it?"

"And about time, too," Maureen said, lifting her martini to her lips.

"Who is he?" DeeDee asked. They all knew of Angie's disastrous marriage right out of high school and her subsequent vow to never get involved with a man again.

"His name is Tom Sloane," Angie said, "although half the people in town refer to him as Java Joe."

DeeDee frowned, confused. "The guy across the street from your café? I thought you hated him."

Nadine snorted and then erupted in a giggle. "Apparently not."

They all laughed.

A beautiful smile spread across Angie's face. "I never thought I'd say this, but he's perfect for me."

"That is the truth," Maureen agreed.

"I'm so happy to hear that," DeeDee said earnestly. "And how are you feeling?"

Angie set her drink down and nodded. "Good. I'm slowly getting back to my old self. And although it will take a long time to get my hair back where I want it, at least I'm not bald anymore."

"And her last scan was all clear, so that was something to celebrate," Nadine said with a smile.

"That's great news, Angie." DeeDee turned her attention to Maureen. "And how's Everett?"

"Well," Maureen started, drawing it out, "he had a little bit of a wobble a month ago, but Tom and Angie stepped in and intervened and took him away camping for the weekend. That trip seems to have righted him."

DeeDee couldn't imagine the constant worry Maureen must have over her oldest son and his struggles with drug addiction.

"What about Lance and Ashley?" she asked, referring to Maureen's other two kids.

Maureen smiled. "Good. Lance has completed his courses and is now a qualified electrician. Working as an apprentice right now to get into the union. Ashley is enjoying college. It's good to have her home for the summer."

DeeDee turned to Nadine. "And Emma?"

"Good, halfway through college. Great to have her home. The extra pair of hands is a huge help," Nadine said.

The server appeared, set up a tray table, left and returned with a large tray holding their dinners. She set it down on the tray table and passed around their plates. DeeDee had ordered the shrimp scampi, as any seafood dish was her favorite. Maureen had a filet mignon in front of her. Angie had opted for a tomahawk steak, and Nadine had chosen salmon with a dill sauce.

"How's the inn?" DeeDee asked.

With a mouthful of food, Nadine could only nod. Once she swallowed, she said, "Busy. I had two days last week where I had no guests, and I can't remember the last time that happened. It was kind of weird."

"Do you like it?" DeeDee asked curiously.

"I love it!" Nadine's face lit up. "It was one of the best moves I've ever made."

"Any man in the picture?"

Nadine reddened. "Not on your life. I like being single. And the house is always full, so I'm never lonely."

DeeDee smiled, delighted to hear this. She did not ask about Nadine's ex-husband, Richard. Since their divorce, he'd married his mistress. No sense in dragging his name into their conversation, she thought.

Talk turned to the latest Lavender Bay gossip and several times, DeeDee caught herself smiling. She hadn't realized how hungry she was until she put the last bite of shrimp scampi into her mouth. She laid her fork down and pushed her plate away.

"Anyone for dessert?" Maureen asked, finishing her own meal.

DeeDee laid a hand across her abdomen and shook her head. "I couldn't. I'm full to bursting."

She was relieved when none of her sisters wanted dessert and coffee. Now that she was finished, she had nothing to do but sit there, and those pesky, intrusive thoughts began to worm their way into her mind. Her hands went clammy.

"What's wrong, DeeDee?" Nadine asked.

She was aware that her sisters were staring at her.

"Nothing," she lied. "I think I'm ready to go home." She rubbed her forehead, anticipating a headache coming on.

"Are we ready then?" Angie asked.

"I think so," Nadine said.

Once the bill was settled, they headed out of the restaurant and back to the condo. On the way, DeeDee told her sisters they could share the queen-sized bed in her room and the double bed in the spare room. She'd grown accustomed to sleeping on the couch and although her sisters protested, stating they'd go to a hotel, in the end, DeeDee finally got her way about something.

Admittedly, DeeDee did feel better after she had her hair colored and cut the following day. Maureen had accompanied her and insisted they both get a pedicure and a manicure, saying it would boost their spirits. At the end of the session, seeing herself in the mirror with her regular platinum blonde hair color and her nails done in Flame Red, DeeDee felt slightly more like herself.

Back home, she marveled at how much better the place looked since her sisters had whipped through it and cleaned it up.

Maureen glanced at her wristwatch. "We should get on the road. It's almost noon."

"We can drive until midnight and find a place to stay over," Nadine suggested.

"Sounds good."

Before DeeDee knew what was happening, she was piling her suitcase into the trunk of her car. The one thing that was non-negotiable was her taking her own car so she could return to Florida as soon as she was ready. Her sisters didn't fight her on that point. It was decided that Nadine would drive with DeeDee, and Maureen and Angie would drive back in Maureen's car.

The birdcage took up too much room in the back seat of DeeDee's small car, and it didn't fit in the trunk. Finally, Maureen said, "Leave it. I'll call Mom and have her pick up a cage." She pulled out her phone and stepped away to call Louise.

Gently, DeeDee put Peaches into the newly purchased bird carrier, speaking softly to him, reassuring him that everything was going to be all right. He replied with a few chirps. She made sure there was plenty of birdseed and water in the feeders. Maureen was already pulling out of the parking space in front of the condominiums.

Nadine offered to drive, and that allowed DeeDee to cradle the carrier and talk reassuringly to the bird. Before they pulled away, Nadine said, "Did you want to tell any of your neighbors you're leaving? Ask someone to keep an eye on things?"

"I don't really know my neighbors," DeeDee said. "I know them only to see. Not well enough where I'd hand over my keys or ask them to collect my mail." Most were elderly and retired. She had nothing in common with them. "I can let management know when I get to Lavender Bay."

For most of the ride, DeeDee stared out the window, watching the geography change from the flat, sunny landscape of Florida to the equally flat Georgia, then on to the Carolinas—a straight run through a lot of dense trees—and then to Virginia, where hills and mountains started to appear. Several times, she offered to drive, but Nadine said no. By eleven, through text communication, it was agreed they'd pull over for the night, choosing a nondescript motel off of one of the exits.

The following morning, they were all up at six at the motel and on the road, all anxious to get to Lavender Bay.

DeeDee sighed when they passed the large sign on the side of the thruway welcoming them to New York State.

Nadine sat up straighter in the driver's seat. "Come on now, none of that. It'll be fine, you'll see."

DeeDee wanted to believe her but was doubtful.

CHAPTER THREE

By the time they turned onto Heather Lane in Lavender Bay, they were all tired and grumpy. The bird's chirps had decreased as time went on, and DeeDee's main concern was getting him out of the carrier and into a cage. Nadine had tried playing the radio for the bird, but Peaches remained mute. *I knew I should have stayed home*, DeeDee thought sourly.

The house was just as DeeDee remembered it, right down to the color of the paint, which had been the same for as long as she could remember. It had been several years since she'd been home and from her brief glimpse of the town as they drove in, she could see that nothing had changed. She didn't know how she felt about that. Was the familiar comforting, or was the sameness stifling? Tired and achy and crampy from being stuck in the car, she decided it didn't bear thinking about in that particular moment. She'd forgotten how summer here was so different from the stifling heat of June, July, and

August in Florida. She'd never minded it, but this heat was decidedly gentler.

And it had been a long time since she'd thought about the landscape of Lavender Bay: the lake, the hills, and all the vineyards. Grapes and sunflowers were everywhere, unlike the continuously flat landscape of the Sunshine State.

As soon as Nadine pulled into the driveway and parked behind Maureen's car, their mother, all smiles, pushed through the screen door and walked down the front steps, greeting them with hugs as they got out of the car. A small, slender woman, she wore her silver hair in a short pixie.

She pulled DeeDee into her warm embrace, and DeeDee took in the light, familiar scent of her mother's signature perfume, Philosophy's Amazing Grace. It was comforting.

"How's my baby?" Louise asked, pulling back and studying her youngest daughter.

"I'm fine, Mom, thought I'd come home for a visit," DeeDee said with a forced brightness.

"How was the drive up?" Louise asked.

"Uneventful, thank God," Maureen said.

"We're glad to be home," Nadine added.

"Come on in, I've got pastries and coffee on."

"No thanks, Mom. I want to get home," Maureen said, "and take a shower."

"I'll call you later, Mom," Angie said. "Can you drop me off, Maureen?"

Maureen nodded. "I'll drop you both off." She removed DeeDee's suitcase from the back of the car and hugged her youngest sister goodbye. "Glad you're home. I'll see you later."

Nadine and Angie hugged her as well, and her three sisters got into Maureen's car and drove away. DeeDee cradled the box carrying her bird against her chest.

"Come on, let's get my grand-bird inside and into his new cage." Louise reached for DeeDee's suitcase, but instead DeeDee pushed the bird carrier toward her mother.

"I'll take the suitcase, Mom. You can carry Peaches."

Her mother's smile was generous. "I'm honored." Taking it, she said to the box, "Hello, Peaches, I'm Louise, but you can call me Grandma." There was one feeble chirp as a reply.

DeeDee followed her mother into the house. It even smelled the same: of coffee and vanilla. As long as her mother was alive, DeeDee thought, this house would always be "home."

"I've put his cage in the corner in the kitchen," Louise explained. "Google told me not to put it in a drafty place, so I put it near an interior wall."

DeeDee's eyes widened at the large ornate gilded cage. "Oh my, that's gorgeous."

"Gail gave it to me. She said it was taking up space at her shop and you were welcome to it."

"That's sweet," DeeDee said, touched by her aunt's gift. To her bird, she said, "You're moving up in the world, Peaches."

Yawning, she opened the door of the birdcage, noting it was a lot bigger than the one she had at home. Her mother had filled the water dish and there was some birdseed in the feeder. Old newspaper lined the bottom of the cage. Carefully, she opened the top of the carrier. Peaches hopped around inside. Gently, she took hold of him and put him inside the cage.

"There you go, sweetie," she said with a smile. "You've got an upgrade."

The bird perched on one bar and looked at her, but there were no chirps.

DeeDee sighed. She supposed it would take some time to get used to the new environment. *I know how you feel*, she thought. She smiled at him and hoped the long journey had not done irreversible harm.

As if reading her mind, her mother said, "He'll be fine. Don't worry. Come on, let's have some breakfast."

"I'm really not hungry. If it's all right, I'd like to go upstairs and go to bed."

Disappointment clouded Louise's features, but she recovered and said, "Of course! You must be exhausted."

"I am, Mom, really," DeeDee said.

She whispered goodbye to Peaches and promised to be back soon. There was one lone chirp in response.

Her mother made a motion to go upstairs but DeeDee said, "No need to go up, Mom. I can find my room."

"All right, then," Louise said, her voice laced with uncertainty.

With her purse over her shoulder, DeeDee carried her suitcase up the stairs and to her bedroom at the end of the hall on the left. It was the smallest room in the house, but as it overlooked the backyard and she'd been able to decorate it as she'd seen fit, she hadn't minded.

It remained as she'd left it. The pink walls were covered in framed movie posters: *Gone with the Wind*, *Now, Voyager*, *Giant*, *Funny Girl*, and *Casablanca*. Frilly pink curtains her grandmother had made hung at the windows, and the small room was furnished with a dated faux–French provincial bedroom set in white with gold accents. But she looked beyond all of that at the bed, covered in a handmade pink, white, and rose quilt. It was one of the last quilts sewn by Grammie, and DeeDee was glad to see that it was still there. Without bothering to unpack her suitcase, she left it and her purse in the middle of the floor and pulled down the shades. She climbed into bed, settled on her back, and looked around her room, at things once familiar but now strange. Things that had been important to her at one time but now were nothing more than junk. She felt odd being back in her old room. It was like a time capsule of another life, when she'd been young, full of hope, and with stars in her eyes.

She closed her eyes, wondering whether it had been a mistake to come back to Lavender Bay. She wasn't sure she could pretend that everything was fine. It was a role she was unprepared for.

CHAPTER FOUR

A week after DeeDee's arrival in Lavender Bay, her mother lost patience with her.

"Honey, you haven't been out of the house since you arrived home," Louise said, sliding an omelet out of a pan and onto a plate and handing it to DeeDee.

Immediately, DeeDee protested. "Yes I have. I've gone to Maureen's for dinner, and I went to see Nadine's inn, which is beautiful, by the way. And I went over and met Angie's boyfriend and her cat, Mr. Beans."

Her mother pressed her lips together in a moue of disapproval. "Going to see family doesn't count. What about going to the beach or out to lunch or browsing through the shops in town?"

DeeDee shrugged. What was it about her family? Wasn't it enough that she came home to Lavender Bay for a visit? Now they wanted her to have a full itinerary while she was here. She loved her family, but they could be relentless. Just the other night at Maureen's, her sister had pulled her aside and grilled her on how she was doing.

Initially, she hadn't even wanted to visit family but once she got to their homes, she was fine. It was the getting there. And maybe it was the same with shopping and going to the beach. Maybe she just had to get there. But for now, she wanted to stay home; she was worried about Peaches. The bird, usually quite vocal, had gone quiet since their arrival.

Her mother placed two pieces of whole wheat toast into the toaster and continued to talk. DeeDee only half listened.

"It's very easy to get into a rut but hard to get out of it," her mother was saying.

In between bites of omelet, DeeDee murmured sounds of agreement.

Her mother handed her a plate of toast. "I've got apricot jam and grape jelly."

DeeDee shook her head. "No, thanks. This is fine." In her opinion, warm, buttery toast needed nothing to spruce it up.

Louise fixed herself a slice of rye toast and applied a thin layer of butter and grape jelly to it before joining DeeDee at the table. "Anyway," she said, "I'm going over to the meeting tonight for Grace Gibson's 100th birthday. Gail and I are on the planning committee."

"Gosh, she's a hundred?" DeeDee asked, surprised.

Louise smiled. "I know! It's a wonderful thing. And she's done so much for Lavender Bay that we must celebrate it big."

"That's for sure. What do you have planned so far?"

Her mother paused, half a slice of toast frozen in mid-air. "Well, we're only as far as a cake and a hundred candles. We want to do something special. Like a grand gesture."

DeeDee agreed. As she finished the last bite of her omelet, her mother said, "I'd like you to come with me to the meeting."

"Me? Why? I don't even live in Lavender Bay."

Her mother shrugged, finishing her last bite of toast. She chewed thoughtfully, swallowed, and spoke. "So what? You're from here. You know Grace Gibson. And we need ideas."

"Who says I have any ideas?" DeeDee asked. "And I don't really *know* her." Grace Gibson was someone who was part of the fabric of Lavender Bay. She was a passing acquaintance. DeeDee didn't know much about the woman, other than her being the heiress to the Gibson's Grape Jelly fortune. Who knew there was that much money to be made in grape jelly?

"Of course you do. We all do. And I'm sure you'd have plenty of ideas," Louise countered.

There was no point in debating all of this with her mother. DeeDee stood and walked over to the counter, where she poured herself a cup of coffee. "I'll give it a pass."

When she returned to the table, she noticed her mother's expression had soured.

"Mom, I'm thirty-eight," she said firmly. "I won't be ordered around." Being the youngest, she'd had her fair share of that from her parents and her older sisters as she was growing up. Thank God their grandparents had lived with them; they'd been natural allies and served as a buffer.

But Louise wouldn't take no for an answer. "It'll do you good to go out in public."

DeeDee bridled. "I'm fine as I am."

Her mother sighed. "Just because you keep telling yourself that doesn't mean it's true. You can't operate like this. It isn't healthy, hiding in the house."

"I'm not hiding!" DeeDee snapped.

Her mother pressed her lips together.

DeeDee softened her tone. "I'm happy to be home and see everyone, but I need to start thinking of returning to Florida."

Louise's brows furrowed. "What's the rush?"

"I've got things to do," DeeDee replied. It was weak. Her family knew there was nothing in Florida for her to go back to. No job, no boyfriend. Nothing. There were, however, a lot of bad memories. Some worse than others.

"If you're running back to Florida to hide out in your house, that isn't a good idea."

"I'm not—" DeeDee was about to say she wasn't running back to do those things when she realized it would be a lie.

"Stay here for a little while," Louise said easily. "I miss you when you're not here."

"I know, Mom. I miss you too." That was the truth. She had missed her mother. Phone calls and texts weren't the same as being with someone.

"Look, humor me and go with me to this meeting tonight," Louise said softly. "*Please*."

"All right, Mom, I'll go," DeeDee said. It was only a meeting. One hour of her life. Somehow, she'd soldier through. Her mother didn't ask for much.

Pleased, Louise stood, cleared the plates, and said, "Come on, it's too nice to stay indoors. We'll go for a walk."

DeeDee had assumed they'd head to the beach, but her mother walked in the direction of town. DeeDee's hands went clammy and her heartbeat picked up, though not to the point yet where it was uncomfortable. It was a beautiful, sunny day. A gentle breeze blew through the town, keeping everything comfortable. Main Street was busy, and DeeDee noticed that more shops had opened up since she was last home. She was trying to take everything in, looking in at shop windows, and didn't notice right away that they'd landed in front of Prime Vintage, Aunt Gail's antique shop. The shop had two big bow windows that ran the height of the first floor, occupied with various and sundry things. Louise entered first through the narrow, black-framed glass door, and DeeDee followed her in.

Gail spotted them from where she stood at the back of the shop, and bellowed, "Have a seat, I'll be right up."

Louise walked over to where a red Victorian chaise lounge occupied the center of the shop. Hanging off one arm was a sign that read *Not for sale*. The reason being, it was the favorite spot for Gail's dog, Rufus, to stretch out. Rufus was a retired bloodhound from the South. Currently, he lay on his back, snoring loudly, one tawny ear hanging over the side of the chaise.

DeeDee and Louise settled into a pair of embroidered occasional chairs. DeeDee sniffed the air and scowled. "What is that smell?"

Louise laughed. "Rufus farts on a regular basis."

DeeDee threw an accusatory glance at the old dog. "That's not right. Aunt Gail needs to change something in his diet."

Louise covered her mouth with her hand to keep the volume of her laughing down. The dog slept right through it.

Aunt Gail arrived wearing a purple, turquoise, and pink dress that fell to the tops of her silver-sequined sneakers. She hugged DeeDee. "How are you?"

"Good," she lied.

"She's coming to the meeting tonight," Louise informed her sister.

Gail turned another chair around and joined them. "Really? That's great! We need some fresh ideas."

"I make no promises," DeeDee said.

"We'll see." Gail paused. "Did you know that Grace Gibson is the first resident of Lavender Bay to reach one hundred years old?"

"I wondered about that," Louise said.

DeeDee didn't point out that it was only August and Grace wouldn't be turning one hundred until the following April. Anything could happen between now and then for a ninety-nine-year-old.

"Are you getting out of the house?" Aunt Gail asked.

DeeDee sighed. There were no secrets between her mother and her aunt. They told each other *everything*.

"I'm out now, aren't I?" she said blithely.

"There's a pole dancing class starting in town next week. I could sign you up for that," Louise said.

DeeDee turned her head in her mother's direction. "What?"

"Pole dancing. It's supposed to be great exercise."

Gail spoke up. "Your mother and I would do it in a heartbeat if our bodies were a little more flexible."

"And a little younger," Louise added.

"You should have seen us fifty years ago!" Aunt Gail said with a smile.

Louise snorted and Gail added with a laugh, "Maybe it's better for all concerned that you didn't." Soon the two of them were howling.

DeeDee shook her head. Once they settled down, her mother returned to the subject of the pole dancing class. "I know you like to take all sorts of classes, and I thought you could do this one."

It was true that DeeDee took many classes to make herself more available for any role that came up. She'd taken ballet and tap dancing. She took voice lessons for years. She knew how to play the piano and the flute. And she'd even taken fencing and kickboxing.

"What do you think?" Aunt Gail pressed.

"I've already taken pole dancing lessons," DeeDee mumbled. They looked at her with amused expressions on their faces. "I was going up for a bit part as a stripper in a nightclub."

Gail leaned forward, her expression hungry for more information. "Did you get the part?"

DeeDee shook her head. "Sadly, no."

"Maybe that worked out for the best," her mother chimed in. "You might have had to do nude scenes."

Gail grinned.

With emphasis, DeeDee said, "I think it's in the name. Stripper."

Soon all three of them were laughing.

DeeDee shook her head. She would never admit that it felt good to have a laugh.

CHAPTER FIVE

L ouise and DeeDee picked Gail up after dinner for the meeting. DeeDee climbed into the back seat so her aunt could sit up front. On the way over, she'd learned that her sisters weren't attending, and she couldn't help but wonder why they got a free pass. But according to her mother, they'd all had plans, and she would fill them in later.

Gail turned in her seat to ask, "How's Peaches? Is he singing yet?"

DeeDee shook her head. She was worried about her bird.

"You could take him to see that new vet over on Truman. I hear he sees reptiles and birds as well as dogs and cats."

DeeDee nodded. "Thanks, Aunt Gail. I'll keep that in mind."

The meeting was held over at the community center, appropriately named the Grace Gibson Community Center as it was Grace who'd picked up the tab for the brand-new building. It was an attractive contemporary structure with landscaped gardens out front. To DeeDee, it looked as if no expense had been spared. There were multiple function rooms, some large enough to host wedding receptions and some more suitable for smaller, private affairs like birthday parties. She wondered if this was where they'd be hosting Grace's birthday party in the spring. The walls of the large lobby were painted in soft cream shades, and recessed lighting shone down on the sofas and chairs and the green-and-pink floral carpet. Along the walls, vintage black-and-white photographs depicted scenes of Lavender Bay from back in the day. DeeDee was impressed.

"I want to show you something," Louise said, walking over to one of the doors off the lobby. DeeDee assumed it led to another function room but to her surprise, it opened on a small theater. At a glance, it looked to hold seating for about three hundred. Small and intimate.

"Well, this is a surprise," she said.

"I thought I told you they'd built a theater," her mother said.

"It's possible, but I don't remember."

"It's a shame it's only used for school plays."

"Don't they have a theater company here in town?" DeeDee asked.

"No, unfortunately."

"DeeDee, is that you?"

She turned to see Edna Knickerbocker racing toward her. Before she could say hello, the octogenarian pulled DeeDee into an embrace.

"As I live and breathe!" Edna said.

Despite being squeezed, DeeDee managed to get out, "Hello, Mrs. Knickerbocker, it's great to see you."

"I heard you were back in town. Where've you been hiding yourself? I see you're still looking like a movie star. How's Florida? What are you playing in now?"

DeeDee laughed. She had always liked Edna. "Thank you." She was glad now she'd let Maureen treat her to a cut and color. It was important to look your best even when you were feeling your worst. "I'm home for a visit. In between plays."

"Lucky for us. Maybe we can convince you to stay," Edna said, and she elbowed Louise a little harder than she intended. Louise winced and rubbed her side.

"You know," Edna said, "I remember you when you were little, in all the talent shows at the elementary school. You sang and tap-danced your heart out!"

DeeDee smiled. "Thank you."

"I want to introduce you to my neighbor, Hal." Mrs. Knickerbocker turned, arm outstretched to take hold of her companion, but it landed on thin air. Scowling, she said, "Now where did he go? He was right behind me. Honest to goodness, he has a hard time keeping up with me. Well, I better go and see where he's gone before he gets into mischief." As she turned to leave, promising to talk to them later, her sister, Edith Bermingham, whom Edna had been feuding with for decades, approached. Mrs. Knickerbocker narrowed her eyes at her sister. "I see they let anyone in here," she sniffed, and walked away.

Mrs. Bermingham, or Mrs. B as she was known, had arrived in a powdery haze of Chanel No. 5 and wearing a Donna Karan pantsuit. She was as different from her sister as day was from night. Whereas Mrs. Knickerbocker had never married, her sister had gone through three husbands. To the residents of Lavender Bay, it was hard to believe they were sisters. The only giveaway was their sharp, bright, green eyes, their most similar and most arresting feature.

"I wanted to say hello, DeeDee," Mrs. B said, "and welcome back to Lavender Bay."

"Thank you. It's good to be home."

"What are you up to these days?" Mrs. B asked.

"Home for a visit. In between plays," she said automatically. Her sisters had been right; it was enough. People weren't digging into her troubles or parading her poor reviews in front of her.

Mrs. B excused herself, wishing her well, saying she had to go get a seat as far away as possible from her sister.

"Come on, girls, let's call this meeting to order," Gail said, leading the way like she was leading the Charge of the Light Brigade.

The meeting was held in one of the function rooms. Inside there were only five people gathered around the long conference table. Mrs. Knickerbocker and Mrs. B sat at opposite ends.

DeeDee joined her mother at the table. Her aunt took a seat and put on her glasses, which had been hanging from a lanyard around her neck. She pulled a notebook and pencil from her large purse.

"All right," Gail began. "At the informational meeting last month, we all decided that the town is going to celebrate Grace Gibson's one hundredth birthday next April. Other than a large cake with one hundred candles, we haven't come up with any other ideas that would do her justice."

"How about a parade?" asked Mrs. Knickerbocker.

Gail shifted in her chair. "I love a parade as much as the next person, but Lavender Bay has their share of parades every year: Jacques Aubert Day, the Fourth of July, and Christmas."

"What about the town creating a Grace Gibson Day and she gets the keys to the town," suggested Mrs. B.

Gail, pencil in hand, peered over the top of her glasses. "I like that one." She bent her head and scribbled in her notebook. Looking up, she asked, "What else?" and she scanned the faces around the table.

Everyone spoke at once. Ideas were shouted out: crowning her queen of the grape festival—DeeDee didn't know how serious that one was and by the look on Gail's face, it had been summarily dismissed. Someone suggested they write and publish a book about Grace's life and donate the proceeds to the charity of Grace's choice. And although Gail was encouraging, she pointed out that they didn't have a lot of time. Seven, eight months tops. Someone else suggested a party, to which Gail pointed out that of course there was going to be a big party, the specifics of which would be decided at the next meeting, but for now they were concentrating on this aspect: something spectacular. A grand gesture, so to speak. That way, Grace would be under no illusion as to how the town felt about her.

"Fireworks?" Mrs. Knickerbocker suggested.

Gail nodded, flipping back a page in her notebook. "That was brought up at the last meeting. I think that's a runner. We'll have to get a permit from the town to have a fireworks show."

Gail looked over at Gloria Jeraldi from Gloria's Gifts. "What have you got for me, Gloria?"

"How about a contest? People make up a poem or a song about Grace?"

Gail tilted her head back and forth, mulling over the suggestion. "What do we think about that?" she asked the group.

There was a slow murmur of approval.

She wrote the idea down in her notebook.

"What about a gift?" someone asked.

Without looking up from her notebook, Gail replied, "To be determined at a later meeting."

Tentatively, DeeDee raised her hand, but then thought better of it and immediately lowered it, thinking she shouldn't interfere. She wasn't staying long enough to get involved. Unfortunately, her aunt spotted her.

"DeeDee, what have you got for us?"

"Um, well . . ." DeeDee cleared her throat. "What about a play about her life?" Granted, she didn't know much about Grace Gibson, but nearing one hundred, she must have had some interesting experiences.

A murmur of excitement rippled around the table, surprising her. Her mother nudged her and smiled.

Gail's smile was broad. "I like that one."

The meeting went on for another hour, with people raising their hands and volunteering their ideas. Some were interesting. Kay Bright from the historical society wanted to do a photo display of Grace's life in all the shop windows in town. That generated a lot of buzz. Frank Furniss, the man who organized the parallel parking championships every year, suggested getting Grace a kitten or a puppy.

Gail scowled. "As much as I love dogs and cats, I would not assume everyone else does. We'll shelve that idea for now."

Afterward, Kay and Gloria brought in urns of coffee and tea, and Louise brought in a platter of cookies. Now that the main part of the meeting was over, DeeDee was anxious to return to her mother's house, but Louise was knee-deep in conversation with Kay Bright. Half an hour on, there was no sign that it was even starting to break up. This disheartened DeeDee. She was ready to leave. It was like her battery needed to be charged.

She approached her mother, who was now talking to Gloria. Her mother turned and took hold of DeeDee's arm.

"This is my youngest daughter, DeeDee," she said, smiling. "She's an actress."

"Oh my, how wonderful. Have I seen you in any movies?"

DeeDee shook her head. "No, I mainly do theater."

The other woman gushed at how exciting it must be to be an actress.

DeeDee smiled politely and thought, *You have no idea.*

When there was a lull in the conversation and it seemed as if all the pleasantries had been exchanged, DeeDee said to Louise, "Mom, I think I'll walk home."

Her mother's smile disappeared. "Honey, I'll only be a few more minutes."

DeeDee shook her head. "There's no reason for you to leave. Stay. Enjoy yourself."

Louise hesitated. "I don't mind leaving."

DeeDee smiled at the lack of conviction in her mother's voice. "Mom, seriously, stay. I'm heading home. I think I might prefer to walk." This was a lie, but DeeDee was anxious to get out of there.

"Only if you're sure," Louise said.

"I am." DeeDee turned to the other woman. "It was nice meeting you." And before her mother could protest or throw up another roadblock, she headed for the exit.

The night air was warm, and the crickets were loud. She headed away from the community center, taking the long way, and found herself walking in the general direction of the beach.

Streetlights were on, casting the lanes in alternating shadows of light and dark. The air was still. As she approached the beach, she headed to the parking lot side, thinking she might sit for a while on the low concrete wall. Beyond the parking lot area where the lampposts cast shadowy light onto the sand below, the beach was blanketed in darkness. Although she could barely make out the lake in the darkness, she could hear the gentle lapping against the shore. She hopped up onto the concrete wall, swinging her legs over to the beach side, and positioned her bum to get comfortable. She wouldn't stay long, she told herself. But she needed to think, and this was as neutral a place as she was going to find.

She exhaled a deep breath and looked around. Farther down the beach, there was a bonfire, likely with a group of teenagers around it. It didn't seem that long ago that she, too, hung out on the beach with her friends. But it was twenty years ago. She remembered what it was like to be young: to be full of hope and that unrelenting, eager sense of waiting for something, *anything*, to happen.

As she approached forty, she had to take a hard look at her life. Her reaction to one incident, when she'd been in the wrong place at the wrong time, had changed the course of her life. This is what surprised her the most, that something so seemingly random could have such a detrimental effect on her. She swallowed hard. It was worse than being back at square one. Tears pricked the back of her eyes, and she blinked several times to get rid of them.

She didn't know what to do next. She felt inert, afraid to make any decisions in case it was the wrong one. Afraid—no, terrified—to move forward. Afraid of any more random events that might have adverse consequences. This visit home was only another version of hiding. Apparently her suspicion had proved true: the change of scenery had done nothing except transport her troubles from one place to another.

First thing in the morning, she'd let her mother know that she was returning to Florida.

After a while, she pivoted on her bum and slid off the concrete wall, brushed off her bottom, and walked home. Town was just as quiet on the walk back. There was the occasional dog walker who waved, and a group of kids flying by on their bikes under the streetlights.

Her mother's car was in the driveway when she approached the house. She hadn't realized she'd been gone for that long. The front door was wide open, and the sound of the television floated out through the screen door.

When she went inside, her mother, who was sitting on the sofa, turned to her and said into the phone, "Gail, I'll call you back in a few minutes."

"Was that Aunt Gail?" DeeDee asked. What could they possibly have to talk about after just seeing each other at the meeting?

"It was." Louise picked up the remote and muted the television. "We're both watching *Dateline*."

As DeeDee headed to the staircase, Louise said, "Where did you go?"

"I went for a walk down to the beach."

"Good. The fresh air is good. You'll sleep better tonight," her mother said.

DeeDee didn't tell her that she had no problem sleeping. In fact, if anything, she was sleeping too much. She could barely pull herself out of bed.

"Did you want some ice cream?" Louise asked. "I'm going to get myself a bowl."

She shook her head. "No thanks, Mom." She paused at the bottom step. "I'm going to head up to bed."

"Tired?"

DeeDee didn't answer her right away, choosing instead to say, "I'm thinking it might be time for me to head back to Florida."

Louise jumped up from the sofa and walked over to her. "What? Why? You just got here."

If she was going to lie around and do nothing, she wanted to do it in the comfort of her own home. And she was worried about Peaches and hoped that returning to a familiar place might help the bird find his voice again.

"I really should get back home. And back to work," DeeDee explained.

"Why don't you look for a job here?" Louise asked.

"Doing what? There's no theater here," DeeDee said.

"Does it have to be acting?"

DeeDee folded her arms across her chest. "Mother, I'm an actress."

Louise gave her a reassuring smile. "Now come on, honey, don't get your feathers in a ruffle. I didn't mean permanently. Just something temporary to tide you over."

DeeDee was about to snap back but her mother said, "I love having you here, honey. It's so good to see you."

That tempered DeeDee's response. "I appreciate that, but I have to get home. Florida is my home."

Louise nodded and said quietly, "I understand."

DeeDee didn't think she did, but she said goodnight and headed upstairs to begin packing.

CHAPTER SIX

It had been DeeDee's intention to get on the road to Florida by dawn the following morning, to get as much driving done as she could during the daylight hours. She'd text her sisters before she left to avoid any teary goodbyes or any more attempts to strong-arm her into staying. She woke early, as planned, to birds chirping outside the window and the sun rising on the horizon. But then she yawned, stared at her packed suitcase parked by the bedroom door, and rolled over and went back to sleep. When she awoke the second time, she glanced at the clock and saw it was nine thirty. If she was serious about leaving that day, she had to get out of bed.

She showered quickly and headed downstairs in search of breakfast. As she made her way to the kitchen, she was aware of the voices of her mother and Gail. Their tones were hushed, as if they did not want to be overheard. And in the same way a person knows that someone is staring at them, DeeDee knew that she was the topic of their conversation.

As she stepped into the kitchen, the conversation between her aunt and her mother halted abruptly and they looked up at her.

"There she is!" Gail's voice boomed throughout the kitchen.

"Would you like some breakfast?" Louise asked, standing up.

"Morning, Mom. Aunt Gail."

"What would you like?"

"I can get it," DeeDee said. She didn't expect her mother to wait on her, though it was nice.

"I don't mind," Louise said.

Rather than argue, DeeDee deferred to her and said, "Toast is fine."

"Wouldn't you rather have pancakes or French toast or bacon and eggs?"

"No, that's too heavy. A piece of toast will be fine," DeeDee said.

Louise pulled a slice of bread out of the breadbox and dropped it into the toaster, then reached for her phone and began texting furiously as she waited for the toast to pop.

DeeDee pulled up a chair and sat across from her aunt, who cradled a mug half full of coffee.

"Gail, do you want me to make more coffee?" Louise asked.

"No thanks, hon," she said. "Rufus and I have to go to work." She leaned back and peeked beneath the table. "Isn't that right, Rufus?" That was met with a loud, gurgling snore from the bloodhound. DeeDee hadn't been aware of his presence when she entered the room. But she should have known better; her aunt never went anywhere without her dog. She looked over to the birdcage, where Peaches sat quietly on his perch, staring out the window. She hoped he hadn't lost his voice forever. He'd always been a champion warbler. Another reason to get back home as soon as possible.

Her mother carried over one slice of toast on a bread plate and handed it to her.

"Thanks, Mom." She bit into it, enjoying the buttery goodness.

"I'm so glad to have caught you before I went to work," Gail started.

DeeDee looked at her, expectant, and Gail went on.

"Last night at the meeting, I thought your idea of a play about Grace's life was exceptional. That's something really different but also like a tribute as well."

Louise piped in. "Not to mention how original it is. Not many people get a play written about their lives."

"Glad I could help," DeeDee said, her attention wandering. She was calculating how far she would get and to what state if she were to leave in the next half hour.

"Your mother and I think you'd be the perfect person to organize it," Gail said triumphantly.

DeeDee set her half-eaten slice of toast down on the plate. "Me?"

"Of course," Louise said. "You're perfect. Who knows more about plays and acting than you?"

Louise and Gail looked at each other and said in unison, "No one!"

They were so loud that Rufus startled beneath the table with a loud groan before rolling over to his other side and resuming his snoring.

Giggling, they looked beneath the table at the aged dog and Louise said, "Sorry, Rufus."

"That's great that you think I could do something like that," DeeDee said. "But I'm going home."

"There's no one else as qualified to take this on as you," her mother said, ignoring DeeDee's last comment.

DeeDee shook her head, steadfast, not wanting to get roped in. "There must be someone."

"You must know how to write a play, having been in so many," Gail said.

It was true. She'd taken a playwriting workshop two years ago and had a drawer full of unpublished scripts back at her condo. But she wasn't about to admit that; they'd only use it as ammunition.

Before she could answer, the front door opened and Maureen, Nadine, Angie, and their cousin Esther paraded in. In an instant, DeeDee realized that reinforcements had been called in and there was an ambush underway.

"Oh my, what a surprise," DeeDee said, arching an eyebrow and folding her arms across her chest. "What a spontaneous, unplanned arrival of all of you at the same time."

"Isn't it just?" Esther said with a laugh. She bent over and hugged her. "How are you, cuz?"

Angie set a bakery box from her café in the center of the table and opened it up. Inside were a dozen pastry hearts.

There was a lot of scraping of chairs as everyone sat down. "Is there any coffee?" Maureen asked, her gaze traveling to the coffeemaker.

"A little bit left," Louise replied.

Maureen walked over to the counter. "I'll make another pot. Everyone want some?" This was met with a round of yeses.

Louise spoke up. "Gail and I were just saying how we thought DeeDee would be perfect to write and direct a play for Grace Gibson."

Maureen carried a small stack of plates over to the table.

As if they hadn't already known, there was a round of feigned surprise and positive affirmations. DeeDee rolled her eyes.

Nadine and Esther helped themselves to a pastry heart each, and Maureen rejoined them at the table. As soon as she sat, she spoke.

"Mom and Aunt Gail are right. It would be the perfect project for you. It would pull you out of your rut."

DeeDee tilted her head slightly. "Gee, Maureen, why don't you tell me how you really feel?"

"Come on, honey, everything is transparent here," Louise said. "We all know you've been struggling a bit."

A bit? She had fallen into a pit she didn't think she could climb out of. It would take a lot more than a play to pull her out of that. Besides, she should be the last person going anywhere near the stage. And to put on a production about the town's most prominent citizen? She practically shuddered. Too much pressure. They had to see that.

They all spoke at once.

"It'll be like riding a bike," Gail said.

"You can do this," Nadine said. "I have confidence in you."

"It'll be great," Esther enthused. "You'll see."

Maureen took a more practical approach. "What's waiting for you in Florida that you have to rush back?"

That felt sharp. Maybe she had nothing going on right at that moment, but she did have a home in Florida. And maybe something would come up. But even as she was thinking that, she knew she was lying to herself. She felt anger toward Maureen for calling her out.

"Honestly, I feel like I'm being ganged up on," DeeDee said, looking around at all of them.

Angie snorted. "See all the fun you've been missing? This is their jam," she said, referring to her mother and aunt. "They pulled this same thing last year with me."

Louise took mock offense. "And weren't we right?"

Before Angie could answer, Gail said, "Of course we were. Look at Angie now, all loved up with Java Joe."

"Tom," Angie corrected, blushing.

DeeDee's gaze landed on Peaches. "I really should get Peaches home. He's not singing like he used to. Actually, he's not singing at all."

"We'll get him singing lessons," Gail said bravely, waving her arm around. This resulted in a round of laughter and twitters around the table. Even DeeDee's resolve faltered a bit and she smiled.

Giving it one last attempt, she said, "I can't stay, I don't have a job. There's not a plethora of opportunities for actors here."

"Oooh, plethora, I like it," Esther cracked with a grin. "As in, 'There are a plethora of bowling balls at the alley.'"

Everyone groaned and Aunt Gail shook her head and said, "I don't remember ever once dropping you on your head as a baby."

This only caused Esther to laugh harder.

Angie spoke up. "That's easy. I can give you a part-time job in the café."

"And I could use some help at the inn," Nadine added. "It's booked most days and sometimes, I feel like I can't come up for air."

"And I'll pay you to walk Rufus. The vet said he needs more exercise," Gail said.

From the sound of the snoring beneath the table, DeeDee wondered how feasible that would be. Some temporary work—even if it was charity from well-meaning relatives—was appealing.

Finally, she said, "Let me see if I have this right. If I stay and write a play and possibly act in it"—she was still at the stage where she wasn't sure she ever wanted to act again—"My life will magically improve."

"The real magic doesn't happen until you join my bowling team," Esther said with a broad smile.

Maureen looked at Nadine with a sigh of resignation and said, "I've got nothing."

"Esther," Nadine teased, "you might have to let that go."

"Even you have to admit that we're having a lot of fun in the league," Esther pointed out, deliberately looking at Maureen and Nadine, who withheld comment. She turned to DeeDee and said, "You can sign up for the fall and be on our team."

The whole scenario was so ridiculous that even DeeDee had to laugh. Stay in Lavender Bay, write a play, organize it, possibly star in it. And as an added bonus, join her cousin's bowling team. It was so sad it was funny.

But she knew they weren't joking, and they wouldn't take no for an answer. In a way, she knew they were right. What did she have to return to in Florida? No job, terrible reviews, and an ex-boyfriend who'd moved on. She looked around at their eager faces and swallowed hard. They sat there, all of them, like a big roadblock on her path to the confines of her Florida home.

"All right," she said with a little more sharpness than she intended. "I won't leave today. And I'll see what I can do about the play."

That was met with shouts of glee and clapping around the table.

She looked over at her still-silent canary, then interrupted them, holding up her hands. "But I make no promises."

CHAPTER SEVEN

Once she'd made the decision to stay on a bit longer, the first thing DeeDee did was notify the building management at her condo complex that she was staying a little longer than expected in New York. The second thing she did was take Peaches to the local veterinarian her aunt had recommended.

Fur Ever Pet Clinic was over on Thistle Street, right next door to the Dog Days Bar, which DeeDee thought was ironic, and across the street from the town's bowling alley, which she hoped wasn't some sort of sign.

There was only one other person in the waiting room of the pet clinic, a brightly lit space with pale yellow walls and a practical industrial tile floor. DeeDee approached the reception counter and was checking in when something caught her eye. She spotted Debbie Melvin standing in the doorway of one of the examination rooms down the long hallway. Debbie had a thing about windowless rooms and wouldn't go into one. Unseen, the vet was saying something to Debbie, who nodded.

DeeDee took a seat and cradled the bird carrier on her lap.

Next to her sat an older man with a German shepherd on a lead. The dog paced and whined and looked toward the narrow hallway that led to the examination rooms and then back at his owner, whimpering in a plaintive tone. The dog looked briefly at DeeDee and her carrier box but quickly lost interest and started pacing again.

Debbie soon appeared, holding a cat carrier. She was followed by a man around DeeDee's age in navy blue scrubs and sneakers, who DeeDee assumed was the vet.

"Milo?" the vet asked, looking toward the German shepherd.

The elderly man stood, and the dog trotted in the direction of the veterinarian. The whining had stopped, and the three of them disappeared into an exam room.

"DeeDee, what are you doing here?" Debbie asked.

DeeDee stood and hugged Debbie. She'd known her since she was little. Debbie was like another sister to her.

She held up her carrier and said, "My canary stopped singing."

"Oh no," Debbie said sympathetically. She looked down toward the examination rooms. "Brett will get to the bottom of it. He's a great vet."

"That's what Aunt Gail said." DeeDee glanced at the cat carrier. "Is that your cat?" She knew Debbie had a menagerie of pets at home.

Debbie held up the carrier and DeeDee peered inside at a ginger cat who looked as if he'd seen better days. He was missing a leg, and one of his eyes appeared to be permanently closed. Immediately, DeeDee felt sorry for him.

"What happened to him?" she asked.

Concern contorted Debbie's freckled face. "This is Peter. He's been living on the streets for three years. He lost his leg in a car accident and his eye in a fight." She shook her head and sighed. "But he's resilient if he's anything."

"Poor kitty," DeeDee said. "Have you adopted him?"

Debbie shook her head. "No. He's a foster. He's coming home with me for a few weeks or months, depending on how long it takes for him to adjust. And then I have to find him a home."

"What happens if you don't find him a home?" DeeDee asked.

"I don't know," Debbie said. "I'd take him, but I can't take one more animal. My house is already full. There's barely any room for me."

DeeDee didn't think there were a lot of people looking for a three-legged, one-eyed cat.

"Good luck," she murmured.

"Thanks, I'll need it."

They said their goodbyes, and Debbie paid her vet bill and with a final wave to DeeDee, disappeared out the door with Peter.

After Debbie left, DeeDee didn't have to wait long before she was called in. By that time, the man with the German shepherd had left, the dog pulling on the lead toward the door.

"Peaches?" the vet said.

"That's us," DeeDee said. She lifted the carrier and followed the vet down the hall.

He was younger than she'd expected. Somehow, she was expecting an older, dour man. Or woman. Not someone her own age.

The view from behind was not shabby. He was tall and broad-shouldered with blond hair. He reminded her of the jocks back in high school. She hoped he didn't have a shallow personality to match. Immediately she chastised herself for stereotyping; she wouldn't like it if someone thought she were a dumb blonde simply because her hair was the same color as Marilyn Monroe's.

DeeDee followed him into an exam room and set the carrier down on the stainless-steel exam table. The vet walked around to the other side of the table.

"I'm Brett Jovanovic," he said.

"DeeDee Cook," she replied. "And this is my canary, Peaches."

The vet's facial features were chiseled, and DeeDee thought he'd be a photographer's dream. She imagined different black-and-white photos of him for a portfolio.

"What's wrong with Peaches?" he asked.

"He's stopped singing."

With a nod, he opened the carrier and gently reached in and tucked the bird in his hands before carefully lifting him out. "Hello, little friend."

DeeDee's eyes landed on the vet's hands. Big, strong hands, but gentle. She raised an eyebrow.

"Any stress recently?" the vet asked.

"We drove up from Florida recently."

"That certainly could be the cause."

Brett looked him over, examining him. "He appears healthy."

DeeDee waited. It gave her a chance to get a good look at him. He was very handsome, but his demeanor seemed aloof.

"He hasn't been fluffing up his feathers?" Brett asked.

DeeDee shook her head. "No. Not that I've noticed."

"Has he been coughing or sneezing? Do you hear any wheezing?"

"No, nothing like that. He's gone mute on me."

The vet nodded and said, "I'll take an x-ray and we'll do some bloodwork."

"All right." She felt better knowing something was being done for her bird.

"In the meantime, keep him warm, and maybe put a small hand towel in the corner of his cage so he has a safe space."

She hadn't thought of that.

"Even animals need some space," he said with a glimmer of a smile.

DeeDee could certainly understand that.

"I was thinking about driving back to Florida—that's where I live—but I don't want to do any more harm."

"No, of course not," the vet said, not taking his eyes off the bird as he examined him. Once the x-ray and bloodwork were completed, he set Peaches back in his carrier and said, "I'd hold off on returning to Florida if you could."

Brett gave her a sheet of printed-up instructions and told her he would call her when he had the results of the x-ray and the bloodwork. She felt encouraged that they'd get to the bottom of it and soon Peaches would be singing once again.

When she left the vet's office, a thought occurred to her. Had her bird picked up on her own depressed mood? She hoped not. She knew some animals were sensitive to their owner's emotions, but she didn't want to burden Peaches with her problems.

CHAPTER EIGHT

A schedule was worked out where DeeDee would work three days a week at Angie's café, Coffee Girl, and then spend two mornings from seven to twelve helping Nadine at the inn with breakfast, the cleanup, and cleaning the rooms. She was no stranger to this kind of work; she'd waitressed in the beginning of her acting career between gigs until she'd secured more stable employment, and she'd worked at the Holiday Inn in the housekeeping department during college. If that job had done anything, it had made her stay in college, realizing she didn't want to spend the rest of her life cleaning hotel rooms and wrestling flat sheets onto king-sized beds. And now here she was, twenty years later, right back where she'd started. Despite this, she was grateful for the extra money.

Angie had suggested she work five full days the first week to get into the swing of things. She was trained by an energetic young woman named Erica, who seemed to be in constant motion. By the end of the first week, DeeDee felt as if she had a handle on things. It reminded her of what Grammie had once told her: the key to anything was organization.

With all this work, she wondered when she was supposed to write a play, cast it, and start rehearsals. And then there was the worry that she knew absolutely nothing about Grace Gibson's life. But for the moment, she had to push that thought to the back of her mind. There was still plenty of time. It was only September.

Coffee Girl was a busy place. Sometimes, it seemed like the customers never stopped coming in. She was proud of Angie for all she had accomplished. The upside of working at the café was all the delectable desserts. She was setting out a fresh supply of pastry hearts one day, trying to decide between those and the cinnamon rolls with cream cheese frosting as her favorite, when next to her, Erica abruptly said, "Oh no."

DeeDee frowned. "What?"

"Look." Erica nodded toward the entrance. Edith Bermingham had entered and joined the queue at the counter, looking around the café for an open table. But approaching the café from across the street was her sister, Edna Knickerbocker. That was the one rule that had been emphasized over and over: the two sisters were to be kept as far apart as possible and, even better, not in the café at the same time. Despite their advanced years, they sniped at each other and fought like children. Angie had been firm on this. People came here to enjoy their coffee and pastry, not to have ringside seats to a decades-old feud.

"You wonder what started the fight," DeeDee said.

Erica shrugged. A thick strand of her dark hair escaped her ponytail, but she took no notice of it. "It's been going on for so long, they probably don't remember either."

"Sad."

Edna walked through the door, spotted her sister, and scowled.

"They can't be in line next to each other. That won't work at all," Erica whispered.

"Let me help," DeeDee said. She intercepted Mrs. Knickerbocker just as she was about to step in line behind her sister. "Mrs. Knickerbocker!"

A smile formed on Edna's lips. "Hello there, DeeDee. I heard you were planning to stay a little while. And it's great that you're able to help your sister out here. She gave us quite a scare!"

"I know."

"There's a rumor going around that you're going ahead with the play about Grace Gibson's life for her birthday next year," Edna said.

DeeDee opened her mouth to respond, but Edna was still talking. "You know, I used to act now and then when I was younger. I was told I had a knack for it," she said proudly.

"Really?" DeeDee said.

"Don't look so surprised, young lady. I'm a woman of many hidden talents." Edna lifted her chin slightly as if to prove her point. "Anyway, when you go to cast the role of the older Grace, I'd like to be considered."

Surprised, DeeDee said, "I'll keep that in mind."

"When are auditions?" Edna asked.

"I'm not sure yet."

"Chop-chop, don't let it get away from you."

"No, I won't," DeeDee promised.

Edna looked past DeeDee and smiled. "The coast is clear, dear. My sister has gotten her order and taken a table in the back." Then the smile disappeared, and she muttered, "Where she belongs."

DeeDee was about to say something, but Mrs. Knickerbocker said, "Ta-ta. Remember what I said." The elderly woman sidestepped her and joined the line.

Satisfied that the sisters were as far apart as possible, DeeDee grabbed a bus box and began clearing tables, wiping them down with a cloth and disinfectant. As she passed Mrs. B's table, the older woman reached out and touched DeeDee's arm. "DeeDee, can I speak to you for a moment?"

DeeDee stopped and balanced the bus box on her hip. "Sure, what can I do for you, Mrs. B?"

"I'd like to be considered for the role of Grace Gibson when you cast for your play."

"Oh," DeeDee said, her eyes widening. "I'll take that into consideration. At some point, there'll be auditions."

With a knowing smile, Mrs. B. said, "I wouldn't need to audition. I'd be a natural. I used to perform in some dinner theater up in the Adirondacks, where I spent several summers with one of my husbands."

"I'll keep it in mind," DeeDee said.

"That's all I ask," Mrs. B. said sweetly.

Lugging the bus box to the back of the café, DeeDee wanted to roll her eyes. She hadn't even written the script yet and she already had an issue with casting.

When she recounted the problem to her mother later that evening over dinner, Louise said, "The solution is simple. Don't give either one of them the part. It's an unwinnable situation. If you choose one over the other, it'll cause problems with the one not chosen."

"I figured as much."

Because it was warm out, her mother had opted for a light dinner of grilled chicken and salad, and that was fine by DeeDee. Her mother didn't have air conditioning, unlike Gail, who kept her house at "arctic" in the summertime. Louise preferred the windows open and the fresh air. Currently every window in the house was open, but the air was clammy. DeeDee was looking forward to autumn and the change of color of the leaves. And it was just around the corner. It had been years since she'd been home during the fall weather. She missed the four seasons.

"Earth to DeeDee," her mother said, leaning forward and waving her hand in front of her daughter's face.

DeeDee blinked. "I'm sorry. I wasn't paying attention."

"Where'd you go?"

"Nowhere," DeeDee fibbed. "I was thinking about something."

"You do that a lot," her mother said.

"Do what?"

"It's like you're not here. Not present," her mother said, worry clouding her features. "Like you go somewhere else."

"Do I?"

"Yes. Anything you want to tell me?" Louise asked.

"Nope," DeeDee said with an emphatic shake of her head.

Her mother went to say something else but thought better of it and resumed eating her dinner.

DeeDee changed the subject. "I suppose I should get on writing that play, but I don't know anything about Grace Gibson's life." She pierced a piece of grilled chicken along with a little salad and popped it into her mouth.

"I don't know much either," Louise admitted. "She volunteered as a Red Cross worker during World War II, and then of course, ran Gibson's Grape Jelly, becoming one of the first female CEOs in the country at a time when women were encouraged to stay home and raise children."

"Wow. She never married?"

"No, she never did."

"That's curious," DeeDee said.

"I suppose she had her reasons. Maybe she never met anyone. Maybe she was disappointed in love."

"Maybe," DeeDee agreed. She took a sip of water. Thinking out loud, she said, "I wonder if the historical society would have anything on her."

"Why don't you talk to Grace herself?"

"But I don't want to spoil the surprise," DeeDee said.

"Oh, she probably already knows that we're planning something for her 100th birthday. Not too much gets past Grace. And there are a lot of blabbermouths in Lavender Bay."

"What would I say?"

"Be creative. Tell her you're writing an article for *The Lavender Bay Chronicles*."

"I'd hate to lie to her," DeeDee said.

Her mother shrugged. "I'm all for telling the truth, but it's only to keep it a surprise."

NEW BEGINNINGS IN LAVENDER BAY   83

"I suppose." DeeDee took a few more bites of her dinner. "Do you think she'd be willing to talk to me? She doesn't really know me."

"I'm sure she would. Grace has always been generous with her money and her time."

"All right." DeeDee's tone was one of uncertainty. She couldn't simply march up to the top of the hill and start asking all sorts of personal questions about Grace's life.

"Why don't I call Grace and ask her if it would be all right for you to go up and have a chat with her."

"Would you mind?" DeeDee asked, thinking this was something she should do herself but on the other hand, she might need a shove from her mother.

"Not a problem. I'll call her in the morning."

With that sorted, DeeDee looked over to her canary, who remained mute. "Anything from Peaches today?"

"No, honey, I'm sorry. I do try and talk to him during the day."

"Hopefully with time," DeeDee said, but she remained unconvinced. On top of everything else, she could add guilt to her list of unpleasant emotions she was currently feeling.

CHAPTER NINE

At the end of a long week, DeeDee was invited over to Angie and Tom's house for dinner. Angie had said she'd like her to get to know Tom better. And as it was obvious that her sister was in love with this guy, DeeDee accepted.

The vet, Brett Jovanovic, had called her earlier to let her know that all of the bloodwork and the x-ray had been normal. She was advised to keep an eye on Peaches and if there was no improvement, to bring him back. As she made her way to Angie's house, she realized she had mixed feelings about this result. On the one hand, she was relieved that her bird was okay. Physically healthy. But on the other hand, if they'd been able to identify what was wrong, it could have been treated.

Angie had been insistent that DeeDee wasn't to bring anything, but she didn't want to show up empty-handed, so she'd picked up a box of candy and some flowers. Her go-to would have been a bottle of wine, but with

Tom being a recovering alcoholic, she didn't want to be the one to shove him off his wagon.

Angie's house was all lit up as DeeDee pulled up. She recognized Angie's car in the driveway. The pick-up truck behind it must belong to Tom.

She knocked on the side door and stepped inside. "Sorry I'm late," she called out.

Angie appeared, holding a pair of oven mitts in her hand. "Don't worry about it."

DeeDee stepped into the kitchen. "Wow, something smells good."

Tom turned around from the stove and waved. "Tuscan chicken."

"He cooks, too?" DeeDee said.

"I told you he was perfect," Angie said, beaming.

DeeDee handed the flowers and candy to Angie.

"I told you not to bring anything."

DeeDee shrugged.

"I'll take those," Tom said, and Angie handed him the flowers and the candy. He went in search of a vase.

"Come on, meet Tom's brother, Jim," Angie said casually, leading DeeDee into the dining room.

She froze mid-stride. Angie hadn't said anything about Tom's brother being there. She'd been under the impression that it would only be the three of them. For a brief moment, she thought of fleeing, but her feet resumed their forward motion, clearly not listening to her brain.

The man seated at the four-person dining table stood when they entered. He resembled Tom in many ways: T-shirt snug over a well-muscled body, military haircut, and tattoos covering both arms. But whereas Tom had dark hair, his brother was blond.

"Jim, this is my younger sister, DeeDee," Angie said by way of introduction. There was a moment of panic when DeeDee thought her sister might be playing matchmaker. If she weren't the one being set up, it would almost be hilarious given Angie's history and previous thoughts on romance. Obviously, she'd done a one-eighty, and they had Tom to thank for that.

"Jim owns the Ink Stain, the tattoo parlor over on Main," Angie went on. "He's across the street from Aunt Gail's store." She looked at Jim and said, "DeeDee's an actress."

Jim Sloane reached out and shook DeeDee's hand. "Hey there. Nice to meet you."

"Same," DeeDee mumbled. Her heart began to race.

"Sit down. Tom and I will be in in a moment," Angie said, and she disappeared into the next room.

DeeDee sat, unsure of what to say. It felt awkward. She felt as sorry for Jim as she did for herself. What made Angie think this was a good idea? Her heart continued to race, and there was an accompanying tingling along her nerves. Her palms went clammy. She wanted to get out of there.

Across from her, Jim rearranged his silverware and said softly, "Do you get the impression that Tom and Angie are trying to fix us up?"

DeeDee laughed with relief. This brought a smile to his face. "Yes!"

"Well, we won't take the bait, will we," he said.

She was about to shake her head when he said hurriedly, "Unless . . ."

"No, really, no. I'm sure you're very nice, but I'm not looking to date at this point," DeeDee said honestly.

He nodded and leaned forward on his elbows on the table, the silverware forgotten. "Noted. I'm glad we got that out of the way."

"Me too," she said. Her heart rate began to calm down.

"Tom mentioned that you live in Florida," he said.

"I do. I've been down there for years."

"I lived in the Keys for three years, working on charter boats."

They easily slid into conversation about their common experiences living in Florida. He was interesting to talk to.

Angie and Tom carried dinner in, a shallow Le Creuset dish of Tuscan chicken and rice and vegetables.

Tom poured wine for the three of them. He must be okay with other people drinking in front of him, DeeDee thought. Good for him.

He lifted the lid off the casserole dish as Angie poured a glass of club soda for him.

"That looks wonderful," DeeDee said.

"I'm starving," added Jim.

Tom laughed. "You're always hungry, Jimbo."

"True."

The doorbell rang, and there was the sound of the door opening followed by, "Angie, you home?"

They all looked toward the kitchen as Debbie appeared, and DeeDee was almost sure she saw Jim's face brighten. When Debbie saw the four of them seated, she looked sheepish. "I am so sorry. I was heading home, and I saw the lights on . . ."

"Don't be ridiculous," Angie said, jumping up and beckoning her in with a wave.

"Come on, Deb, we've got plenty," Tom said. He stood and went to the kitchen to grab an extra chair. He squeezed the chair between DeeDee and Jim so that it was positioned in front of the window.

Debbie pulled her hat off and her red hair spilled out. Angie took her coat and carried it off into another room. Debbie made her way around the table, and Jim jumped up to pull her chair out for her.

"Thank you," she said, settling in between DeeDee and Jim. She leaned slightly forward and looked into the casserole dish. "Mmm. Chicken, my favorite."

"Where are you coming from?" Angie asked.

"The rescue."

"How's Peter?" DeeDee asked.

"He's all right. He's not very charming. It comes from living rough for so long," Debbie said.

"Peter. Is this your boyfriend?" Jim asked with careful nonchalance.

Debbie snorted and then burst out laughing. "No, he's a rescue cat."

They all laughed, and Jim reddened.

"He's only got three legs and one good eye," DeeDee informed them.

Tom served up the Tuscan chicken and passed the plates around.

"Help yourselves to rice and vegetables," Angie said with a nod.

Debbie looked around the table. "Anyone want a cat? He's going to need to be rehomed."

"No thanks," Tom immediately said. "We've got Mr. Beans."

"What about you, Jim?" Debbie asked. "Would you consider taking in a cat?"

Before he could speak, Tom said, "Don't do it. You know what I've learned about cats? They're most active between three and four in the morning. Racing around the house, knocking things over."

Angie smiled. "Tom, you know you secretly love Mr. Beans."

Tom said nothing, but he grinned.

"What Tom won't tell you," Angie continued, "is that he bought Mr. Beans a bed, a cat playhouse, and toys."

"Uh-oh," Jim teased. "It sounds like you're getting domesticated yourself, Tommy boy."

"Doesn't it?"

"Where is Mr. Beans?" Debbie asked, looking around.

"Most likely sleeping on our bed, resting up for his midnight run later," Tom said.

Angie playfully swatted him. "Leave our kitty alone."

"Where's this rescue?" Jim asked Debbie.

She answered his question and then turned to DeeDee. "How did it go with Peaches?"

"Good. All his tests came back normal," she answered.

"Is this another cat?" Jim asked.

"A canary," DeeDee and Debbie said in unison.

Jim shook his head, laughing, and returned his attention to his dinner.

"Isn't the vet wonderful?" Debbie asked.

DeeDee wouldn't go that far. "He was nice. Knowledgeable for sure, but I thought he was a bit standoffish."

Debbie reared her head back and stared at her. "Really? He's usually so chatty."

DeeDee frowned. "He is? There was no small talk when I was there."

"Huh, that's odd," Debbie said as she cut up her chicken breast.

All in all, it was a pleasant evening. DeeDee was more than happy to be a spectator to their conversations. She felt safe just observing. As soon as dessert was served, eaten, and washed down with a cup of tea, she stood.

"You're not leaving, are you?" Angie asked.

"I'm afraid so," DeeDee said, pushing in her chair.

"Stay," Tom said.

DeeDee shook her head. "I can't. I'm meeting with Grace Gibson in the morning, and I want to be prepared. Need to go over my notes." The notes were already done, but it was a handy excuse. She said goodbye to everyone, and Angie retrieved her coat and walked her to the door.

"Are you all right? You were quiet tonight," Angie said.

"Oh sure, I'm fine," DeeDee said easily. "I had a great time. The food was delicious, and the company was fabulous."

"I'll text you tomorrow," Angie said, opening the side door.

"Okay." DeeDee stepped outside, turned around, and said, "For future reference, please don't try to play matchmaker again."

Angie laughed. "Was it that obvious?"

"Was it that obvious?" DeeDee repeated. "It was like getting hit on the head with a mallet."

"All right then. But what did you think of Jim?"

"He's very nice," DeeDee said. "But I think he only has eyes for Debbie."

Angie's eyes widened. "What?"

"Oh yeah." She smiled at her sister and began to walk away. "Pay a little more attention."

"Will do."

CHAPTER TEN

Grace Gibson lived in a mansion on the highest hill in Lavender Bay, which wasn't very high at all. It was more like a little bump in the landscape. As DeeDee drove through the main gates, which probably cost more than her condo, she took the winding drive as it ascended to the top of the hill. The driveway was wide and long and flanked on both sides by cherry trees. DeeDee imagined the sight must be beautiful with the blossoms in full bloom during the spring. The colorful tree-lined drive opened up to a round clearing in front of the Gibson home. In the middle was a large stone water fountain that gurgled. Surrounding the fountain were rosebushes in various colors, still blooming in the late-September sunshine.

DeeDee parked her car on the other side of the fountain, next to two other vehicles. She suspected the older Cadillac was Grace's, and she wondered if she still drove. As she walked toward the front door, she looked around, taking everything in. She'd never been up here before and most likely, she'd never be back here again.

The house was an imposing three-story structure of white clapboard, with wide windows flanked by black shutters upstairs and down, reminding her of the houses at the Kennedy compound at Hyannis.

The lawns surrounding the house were immaculate and well-manicured. There were flower gardens everywhere. It must be so pleasant to sit outside here, she thought.

A bee buzzed nearby, and in the distance was the sound of a lawn mower. When DeeDee stepped up to the covered porch, she pushed her sunglasses up to the top of her head. The porch was wide and deep, with wide plank flooring in robin's-egg blue, and white wicker furniture with green-and-white striped cushions.

The wooden screen door had recently received a fresh coat of white paint. Through it, she spied the shadowy interior of the house. She rang the bell, and a pleasant chime rang out. Eventually, the petite figure of Grace Gibson appeared.

As Grace laid her hand on the screen door, she said with a laugh, "I don't move as fast as I used to."

"I'm fine," DeeDee said. "It's a beautiful day."

"It sure is." Grace opened the screen door to allow DeeDee into the house. The older woman had a full head of white hair. Nice volume and styled short. A pair of clip-on earrings and a gold signet ring were the only pieces of jewelry she wore.

DeeDee stepped into a large foyer with an oriental rug covering a hardwood floor. In the center was a walnut pedestal table holding a large vase of fresh-cut flowers. The top half of the walls were covered in striped damask wallpaper in pale blue and cream, and the bottom half was painted cream and covered in coving. There was a staircase that led up to the second and third floors. Off each side of the foyer was a reception room. Grace indicated that DeeDee was to follow her to the back of the house. They went through a long hallway that continued in the same wallpaper and paint. She followed her through a butler's pantry and to the back of the house, past rooms with closed doors, a large to-die-for kitchen and finally, out back to a sunroom that overlooked an inground pool and expansive gardens.

As she walked, Grace surfed along the walls with her fingertips, and DeeDee wondered if the elderly woman might benefit from a walker or a cane.

The back room had windows on three sides and had a black-and-white tiled floor with white trim. The windows were unencumbered by blinds or drapes, giving an unobstructed view of the backyard. There was a gentle slope to the land and from this elevated position, one could see Lake Erie. DeeDee thought it must be a spectacular view in the evenings, when the sky was lavender and pink and the sun was setting over the lake.

"It's lovely out here," DeeDee said.

"Thank you. I think so too. This room was added on later. When Dad was elderly, he liked to sit out here, rain or shine, until the first snowflake fell," Grace said, smiling at the memory.

She indicated that DeeDee should take a seat. The white wicker furniture was similar to the set on the front porch, except the cushions here were bright red. They were comfortable and plush in an expensive sort of way. Grace sat on the rocker which, by the general wear of its seat cushion, looked to be "her" chair.

Grace's longtime companion, Ada, appeared in the doorway, wearing a pair of capris, slip-on sneakers, and a short-sleeved shirt. She was tall with dyed dark hair that she wore short. "Would you like me to bring out some lemonade?" she asked.

"That would be lovely, Ada," Grace said.

"How long has Ada been with you?" DeeDee asked.

Grace laughed. "For as long as I can remember!" She appeared thoughtful and said, "I was around eighty. It was only supposed to be temporary." She laughed some more. "And yet here we are, some twenty years later!" She appeared momentarily lost in thought before saying, "I was good friends with her mother."

Ada reappeared with a tray bearing three glasses and a pitcher of lemonade with ice cubes and mint leaves in it. She set the tray down on a glass-topped wicker table, poured lemonade, and handed out the glasses. She took a seat across from DeeDee and sipped her lemonade before setting it down and picking up her readers, sliding them on, and reaching for her sudoku magazine.

"You don't mind if Ada joins us?" Grace asked.

"Of course not," DeeDee said, taking a sip of the lemonade. It was perfect and refreshing. Just the right mix of tart and sweet.

"That way, if I should doze off, she can fill in the blanks."

Ada looked over at Grace and smiled.

"So you're here for my life story because they're going to make a play about me," Grace said.

DeeDee's mouth fell open.

"It's a small town, dear, they couldn't keep a secret to save their lives," Grace said with a laugh. "Of course, wouldn't it be something if I didn't make it to my hundredth birthday? That'd be a hoot!"

Although DeeDee was horrified at the thought, Grace and Ada broke into peals of laughter. There was certainly nothing wrong with the elderly woman's sense of humor.

DeeDee had brought a notepad and pen but was sorry she hadn't brought a tape recorder. Did they even make them anymore?

"That's a beautiful ring," she said with a nod to the ring on the fourth finger of Grace's right hand. It was square and from where DeeDee sat, she managed to read the engraving. GGG.

Grace lifted her hand. "My initials. Grace Gloria Gibson. Mother and Dad gave me that for my eighteenth birthday. That's a funny story, actually. Mother had picked out a large sapphire surrounded by diamonds, but Dad thought it was too fussy and bought this ring as a backup." Grace's laughter sounded like little chirps. "He was right, of course. Dad knew me better than anyone. We were cut from the same cloth." She looked down at the ring with fondness.

"Was your mother upset?" DeeDee asked.

"By that time, she knew I was my own person and wasn't going to have my head turned by couture or jewelry. I was too much like my father. Dad was new money, whereas Mother was old money. It made a difference." Still smiling, her eyes misted over, not with tears but with looking through the veils of the past. "Funny. Dad and I were both as stubborn as a pair of old goats." She paused, drew in a deep breath, and said, "Anyway, that's the story about that. Where did you want to start?"

"Wherever you want." It was important to DeeDee that Grace run the interview. It didn't necessarily have to be in chronological order. She was open to the idea that Grace went wherever the interview took her, and maybe DeeDee could prompt her as needed.

"What was it like growing up in Lavender Bay, as the heiress to Gibson's Grape Jelly?"

Grace looked heavenward and rolled her eyes. "How I hate that word. Heiress."

"Why?" DeeDee prompted, curious. She hadn't expected a reaction such as that.

"Because it singles me out from everyone else. My dad started his business making grape jam with his mother in their kitchen over on Fourth Street when there were only residential homes there. Dad was proud of his background. And so was I. He only happened to create something that people wanted and were willing to pay for."

"But still, you can't deny the fact that you were the wealthiest girl in town," DeeDee said.

"I know," Grace said with a sigh that sounded old. "It separated me from everyone else when all I wanted was to belong. When you're young, you want to belong, you want to be a part of something. And I think people were intimidated by my wealth, or at least my contemporaries were. Or so it seemed. Often, I felt left out."

"Do you still feel that way?"

"Funnily enough, no," she said.

DeeDee was relieved to hear it. It had never occurred to her that you could be excluded *because* of your wealth.

They were quiet for a few moments as DeeDee penned some notes in the notebook she'd brought along.

Gathering her thoughts, she asked, "What would you say was the single most important event in your life? The thing that had the greatest impact?"

When there was no immediate answer, DeeDee looked over at Grace, who was now dozing in her chair, head lolling back. She supposed if you were almost one hundred years old, you might nap more frequently.

Ada looked up from her sudoku magazine. "She does this, dozes off."

"That's all right," DeeDee said. She stood. "Maybe I could come back another time."

Ada also stood and set her magazine and pencil down. "That would be advisable. She could be asleep for five minutes or half an hour."

DeeDee realized it had been wrong of her to assume she could conduct an interview in one afternoon. She hadn't given consideration to the idea that she might have to return more than once. There was nothing to be done about it now.

CHAPTER ELEVEN

Louise was out in the backyard, moving the lawn chairs to the shed in preparation for fall and winter. DeeDee joined her, picking up one of the heavier chairs and carrying it back to the shed.

"How'd it go with Grace yesterday?" Louise asked.

"It went well until she fell asleep."

"That's to be expected. She's got over sixty years on you."

"She has a beautiful home," DeeDee said. "We only touched the surface. We didn't do a deep dive into her life story. It might take longer than I thought."

"You've got plenty of time," Louise said.

"I think it would be easier to record our conversations," DeeDee said.

"Make sure you ask Grace permission first," Louise advised.

DeeDee bristled; she wasn't stupid. She bit back a snarky reply. "I will." She finished helping her mother store all the garden furniture away.

When she was finished, Louise locked up the shed with a padlock and said, "Well, that's another summer in the books."

They went inside, and DeeDee went and checked on Peaches. The bird sat silently on a bottom perch. When she arrived and began to coo at him, he hopped from one perch to another.

In the background, soft elevator music was playing.

"I put that on to encourage him to sing," Louise said.

"Thanks, Mom."

"Don't worry, he'll sing again. Now, would you mind doing me a favor on your way to Grace's today?" Louise headed to the refrigerator in the kitchen and pulled out a casserole dish with a lid.

"Sure," DeeDee said.

"Can you drop this off at Esther's?" Louise lifted the casserole dish.

"Doesn't she work from home?" DeeDee asked. She certainly didn't want to interrupt her cousin. She supposed she could drop it off in the evening.

"She won't mind," Louise said breezily.

"Are you sure?"

"Positive," her mother said with a nod.

"What is it?"

"Golabki. They're her favorite. And whenever I make some, I send her a dish over."

"I love golabki too," DeeDee said.

"Don't worry. It's what's for dinner tonight."

"Great."

Esther lived in a converted cottage over on Beach Street, which was a side street that ran between Oak and Orchard. Esther had lived in the single-story mission-style home since DeeDee was in high school. DeeDee went around to the side door and knocked twice. When no one answered, she shifted the casserole dish over to one hand and opened the door and stepped in.

"Esther?" she called out softly.

There was the scrabble of nails across the floor as Esther's dog came running from the other room. She was a mutt of indistinct parentage. Some brown coloring, some black, and some white. Medium-sized. Medium weight.

"Hello, Pebbles," DeeDee said.

"Come on in, DeeDee," called Esther from another room.

She set the casserole dish on the counter in the kitchen, which was a little bigger than a galley kitchen. There was a table for two against the far wall, beneath a sunflower clock.

DeeDee headed into the small dining room off the kitchen, where her cousin sat in front of her laptop, wearing a headset and talking to someone. Immediately, DeeDee took a step back into the kitchen, not wanting to disturb her cousin while she worked. But Esther waved her back in.

"Hold that thought, Greg, I need a bathroom break," Esther said, and she muted and turned off the video portion of her Zoom meeting.

"I didn't know you were working."

"No problem. Work meeting." Esther rolled her eyes. "I hate when he does that."

Esther stood from her chair, and it was then that DeeDee saw what she was wearing. On top she wore business casual: a fitted white blouse, a delicate gold chain with a small diamond, and a smart blazer. Her short hair, dark with blonde highlights, was carefully styled, and she wore understated makeup. From the waist down, she sported a pair of purple pajama bottoms with pink hearts all over them.

DeeDee lifted an eyebrow. "Nice fashion choice."

"If I could extract myself from this call, I'd have the matching top on by now." She shook her head. "I hate it when I have to put my bra on. I like the girls to have their freedom." She walked to the kitchen. "I've got coffee."

"No, I'm not staying," DeeDee said. "I'm only here to drop off a dish of golabki from my mother."

Esther stopped in her tracks and looked at DeeDee. "Really." She looked up to the ceiling and said, "Thank you, Aunt Lou, you're a beast!"

"There's plenty there for you and your boyfriend."

Esther frowned. "I wouldn't share these with him."

DeeDee didn't know if she was serious or not.

"Are you sure you won't have a coffee?" Esther asked, pouring a cup for herself.

DeeDee shook her head. "You're only on a bathroom break."

"They're fine. Typical work meeting: one person finds different ways to say the same thing over and over again and of course, there's the one who asks the stupid questions. Always. Every time."

It was hard to take her cousin seriously as she leaned against her kitchen counter in a mix of work gear on top and pj's on the bottom.

"Mom told me you've decided to write the play," Esther said.

"Yes. I'm on my way to Grace Gibson's house as we speak."

"Good. You know, I was in the theater club over at McKinley High from freshman to junior years," Esther said casually.

Surprised, DeeDee said, "I did not know that."

Esther nodded and stirred creamer into her coffee. "Yep. It was a lot of fun."

"Why didn't you stick with it?"

Esther laughed. "I was asked to leave by the director halfway through junior year."

"No way. Why? What did you do?"

"I kept trying to do his job. I thought I could do it better than him."

"Grammie used to call you a bossy-boots."

"Wow, I haven't heard that in a long time." Esther smiled. "Anyway, he was right and so was I."

"That's too bad, especially since you must have enjoyed it."

"It all worked out for the best. Because when I got kicked out of that club, I joined the bowling team." Her expression was one of glee.

DeeDee groaned. "That's my cue to leave."

Esther was still laughing as DeeDee closed the door behind her.

Ada answered the door when DeeDee arrived, and they chatted amiably as Ada led the way to the back of the house.

"Hello, Grace," DeeDee said, stepping into the back room.

"DeeDee, it's good to see you. I told Ada I'm going to make the effort to stay awake longer today."

DeeDee laughed. "It's all right. Look, would you mind if I recorded our conversation?"

"Not at all," Grace said.

DeeDee parked herself in the same chair she sat in the day before.

"Where do you want me to start?" Grace asked.

After thinking about that for a moment, DeeDee said, "Why don't you start at the beginning?"

Grace nodded.

DeeDee laid her phone on the table between them and pressed the record button.

PART TWO

GRACE

CHAPTER TWELVE

1930

Ten-year-old Grace Gibson stood behind the heavy red velvet drapes of the school stage. She loved being backstage. There were interesting things back here. An old piano whose missing keys looked like a gap-toothed smile. A large wardrobe that housed costumes from previous productions. How Grace wanted to rifle through that.

She peeked around the corner, noting that the auditorium was full. Immediately, she spotted her father and mother in the first row. Her father wore his three-piece suit with the expensive pocket watch, and her beautiful mother was dressed elegantly as always in a cloche hat and a sable coat. As much as she wanted to wave to her parents, she stayed out of sight.

Again, she adjusted her blue mantle. She had the prize part in that year's Christmas pageant at Benjamin Franklin Elementary School. It was the last act of the night: The Nativity. And she'd been cast as Mary. She'd longed for the part. Hoped for it. With her lines memorized, she was ready for her time in the spotlight.

Behind her, her fourth-grade teacher, Mrs. Henkleworth, stood with Mrs. Frost, whose daughter was in Grace's class. Mrs. Frost was a wiry woman with thin brown hair and a sharp nose. Her daughter, Carrie, looked nothing like her mother, being fair-haired and pretty. She'd been cast as an angel in the play.

Both women were practically huddled together, whispering. Grace's ears perked up at the low tones and as unobtrusively as possible, she took a few steps back to try and hear what they were saying. She'd learned long ago that if the adults didn't want you to know what they were saying, they either closed the door to the rooms they were in or they dropped their voices to whispers. But Grace had learned how to get around those barriers. How was she ever to find anything out if she didn't eavesdrop?

Mrs. Henkleworth was a woman as old as Grace's father, with short, waved hair and a sturdy figure.

"Again, I am so sorry, Mrs. Frost," the teacher was saying.

Grace wondered what her teacher had to be sorry about. She couldn't imagine Mrs. Henkleworth apologizing for anything.

"It's only that Carrie was better suited to the part," Mrs. Frost said.

"I agree, especially with her blonde hair and blue eyes."

Grace frowned.

Mrs. Henkleworth continued speaking. "I had no choice but to give the part to Grace, especially after her father made a generous donation for the play. We were able to get real costumes for everyone and all the Christmas decorations."

Grace's eyes widened.

Mrs. Frost made a *tsk-tsk* noise. "That will do no favors for Grace when she grows up. Everything handed to her on a silver platter."

"I agree, but Mr. Gibson is so generous with his money," Mrs. Henkleworth added. "Especially during these difficult times. If it wasn't for him, all the shepherds would be walking around wearing dish towels on their heads."

"A little *too* generous," Mrs. Frost sniffed. With a sigh, she added, "I better prepare Carrie for the reality that she will always lose out to Grace Gibson because of her father's influence."

Grace froze to the spot. She'd mistakenly assumed that she'd been chosen for the part of Mary because she was *perfect*. She had never given a thought to it being because of her father's money and influence. It was a distressing realization; maybe she hadn't been so perfect for the part after all. Maybe it should have gone to Carrie.

Suddenly, Mrs. Henkleworth sprang forward, startling Grace. "Children! Children, line up. The last act is about to start. Hush!" She placed her hands on some of the children's shoulders to herd them into place. Mrs. Frost retreated backstage.

"Grace, come on now, child, pay attention," Mrs. Henkleworth said. The teacher's perfume was so strong Grace's eyes watered.

Grace hesitated. How could she play a part that was given to her because of her father? She hadn't earned it on her own merit. For a moment, she thought of backing out. But then she remembered that her father always told her to finish what she started, no matter how it turned out. To see things through.

There was momentary confusion as the curtains closed and the choir came running off the stage after singing a few Christmas carols accompanied by the music teacher, Mrs. Parker, on the piano.

One of the girls from the upper grades rushed by Grace, bumping her shoulder so that Grace half turned.

The older girl scowled, but when she saw that it was Grace, her features softened and she said, "Sorry, Grace, I didn't see you there."

"Don't mention it," Grace said automatically. Did she get special treatment because of who her father was? Was she singled out?

"Grace!" Mrs. Henkleworth was on the stage, getting everyone in their place. But Grace was still backstage.

Someone gave her a gentle push and she was propelled forward onto the stage, stumbling.

"Grace!" Mrs. Henkleworth's expression was one of concern.

"Sorry," Grace mumbled. She took her place next to Charles Beck, who was playing Joseph to her Mary. In the manger was one of her dolls she'd brought from home. She'd even swaddled it in a receiving blanket before she left the house, showing it off to her parents. But now, the excitement she'd felt toward the Nativity play had evaporated in a matter of minutes, leaving behind a strange flatness.

Mrs. Henkleworth ran off stage as the heavy red curtains opened, and the spotlights blinded Grace. She felt as if she were in some kind of fog. For the rest of the play, she went through the motions, the previous eagerness absent, anxious to get off the stage and go home. Not once did she look for her parents in the front row or acknowledge them in any way.

Afterward, when their act was over, she raced off the stage before the curtains had fully closed. They were rushed by the reappearance of the choir, who were about to sing their finale.

"What happened Grace? Did you have stage fright?" Mrs. Henkleworth asked once she was safely backstage. Grace could only shrug.

Halfway through the choir's singing, they were joined by the rest of the school, Grace included, to sing "Jingle Bells." Grace wasn't feeling it. Her lips moved along to the words, but no sound came out.

On the ride home, her parents went over all the things they enjoyed about the Christmas pageant. Grace listened mutely in the back seat. They tried to engage with her, but Grace refused and by the time they reached the long, winding drive of their estate, both her father and mother had gone quiet.

Her father pulled the car right up to the front door. It was brisk and slushy outside. Mrs. Gibson pulled her sable coat closer to her, almost hugging it, and ran into the house, shivering, followed by Grace and her father. George Gibson left the car out front, as the chauffeur would take the car around to the back and park it in one of the bays of the garage.

Grace removed her coat and hung it in the cloakroom off the front hall. Once, she'd thrown it on one of the chairs for the staff to put away, but her father had marched her back and admonished her to be responsible for herself.

The three of them gathered in her mother's parlor, and her mother pulled the bell pull that hung on the wall next to the fireplace.

When Irene appeared, Aleida Gibson said, "We'll have tea and maybe some hot chocolate for Grace, and a couple of biscuits."

George went over to the wet bar, poured himself a brandy, and sat down near his wife. Staff had prepared the fire before their arrival, and it blazed in the hearth, making the room warm and cozy.

Irene soon returned with a tray bearing a teapot and a cup and saucer in delicate fine bone china for Aleida and a mug of hot chocolate for Grace. Her mother handed Grace her mug, and Grace took the seat across from her on the opposite sofa. Her father sat next to her mother. He loosened his tie, leaned back against the deep sofa, crossed his legs, and sipped his brandy. He set the brandy glass on the coffee table and pulled out a cigar from the box on the table, clipped the end of it, and used the table lighter to light it.

Grace cradled the mug with both hands and sipped, slurping the hot chocolate. Irene always put a good bit of milk in it so it wouldn't be too hot to drink.

"What's wrong, pet?" her mother asked, drinking delicately from her teacup. "Did something happen at the play?"

Grace didn't answer right away.

"Grace, your mother asked you a question," George said, regarding his only child.

She looked across the coffee table at her parents. "Was I chosen to play Mary because you gave Mrs. Henkleworth a lot of money?"

George burst out laughing, but Aleida shifted uncomfortably on her side of the sofa.

"Whatever gave you that idea?" her father asked, wearing an amused expression.

She decided to go for honesty. "I overheard the teacher talking with Mrs. Frost. They said Carrie would have made a better Mary, but you'd given so much money for costumes and decorations that they *had* to give the part to me."

"Yes, I did give them a substantial donation. But I make donations to a lot of things here in town. I believe in supporting this community and those in it."

"Is that why I got the part?" Grace asked again.

Her father leaned forward, uncrossing his legs. "I didn't ask them to give you the part, but they may have given it to you as a gesture of gratitude."

"Why? Because we're rich?" she asked. She knew they lived differently than other people in Lavender Bay. She'd been in other girls' homes, and they were small compared to the one she lived in. She'd never been in another house as grand as her own.

Her mother scrunched up her nose. "Grace, please don't use the word 'rich.' It's in poor taste and it sounds vulgar."

George looked at his much younger wife and laughed, teasing her. "But darling, we are rich."

Aleida regarded him with an "Oh, George" look and said, "I know that, but we don't have to broadcast it."

Grace rolled her eyes. Sometimes they forgot she was there when they were talking to one another. She cleared her throat and they both looked over at her. "I don't like getting something I don't deserve."

"Who says you don't deserve it?" George said, an uncustomary darkness passing behind his eyes.

"Darling," Aleida started. "There are perks to being . . ." she faltered, and her husband looked over his shoulder at her and winked.

"There are perks to being rich," he said.

"Oh, George, you are so droll."

They didn't seem to understand that Grace didn't want the perks of being rich. She didn't want to be singled out from the rest of her classmates. She wanted to blend in. Be like them. Be one of them.

She stood and set her mug on the tray and excused herself.

"But you haven't finished your hot chocolate," her mother said.

"Grace, you love chocolate," her father added.

She attempted a smile. "I'm tired. I think I'll go to bed." There was a book waiting upstairs for her, and she wanted to sink into it and be left alone. She said good night, kissing each of her parents on the cheek.

As she walked out of the room, the smell of spruce was strong. She looked at the large Christmas tree taking up much of the front window and that part of the room with its sixteen-foot ceilings. As she closed the door softly behind her, she wondered if her classmates ordered such grand trees with delivery service from the southern tier. Somehow, she doubted it.

CHAPTER THIRTEEN

1942-1943

G race Gibson and a fellow volunteer sat at a small table at the entrance to the pavilion, selling tickets for the dance. In the other room, the band had struck up, and Grace tapped her foot in time with the music. She would have preferred to be in the other room, dancing with the GIs who were home on leave. But that would come later.

She had graduated from college the month before with a degree in art history, but she wasn't sure what she was going to do with it yet. The war had thrown everything into turmoil. Aleida had suggested she join her in her charity work.

Grace couldn't think of anything more boring. Not that charity work wasn't important, but she didn't want to hang out with her mother and her contemporaries at the Ladies Auxiliary—or as Grace called them behind her mother's back, the Lunch Ladies. It seemed as if her mother was always going out to lunch, day in and day out, all under the guise of charity. Grace was looking for something a little more exciting than that.

She turned to the girl she was working with. "Sally, if you want to go into the dance hall, I can manage."

"No thanks," Sally said. "I'll stay here. You go inside."

"Are you sure?"

"Yes. The dance has already started. It'll only be stragglers coming in now."

Grace didn't need to be told twice. She jumped up from the table and went into the main room of the pavilion. The room was warm, and the smell was a mix of women's perfume, soap, laundry detergent, and male sweat. The dance floor was crowded as couples jitterbugged all over it. As much as she'd love to be out there, she noticed that a crowd had swarmed the refreshment table. Maybe they could use some help.

She slipped behind the table and joined the two harried-looking volunteers serving up hot dogs and bottles of Coke.

"Need a hand?" she asked.

"Yes!" came the reply.

To the uniformed man in front of her, Grace asked, "What can I get you, soldier?"

"Hot dog, mustard and relish, and two Cokes," he said, holding up two fingers. Grace was reminded of

Winston Churchill's victory gesture, and it brought a smile to her face.

"Sure thing." She grabbed a hot dog from behind her and two Cokes and pointed to a second table next to the one she stood at. "There's condiments over there."

With the Cokes and hot dog in his hands, he said, "Thanks," and walked off.

Her gaze followed him. There was something very attractive about a man in uniform, she thought.

The rush for food and drinks soon abated, and Grace found herself standing there, hands clasped behind her, watching the dancing. Her gaze roved around the room and landed at a table on the far side of the pavilion, where a lone soldier sat, staring at his lighter on the table in front of him. He seemed oblivious to the music and the people around him. Grace was intrigued. And concerned.

She looked at the other two girls, both of whom were relaxing with a bottle of Coke. "You girls all right for a minute?"

"Sure thing."

"I won't be long."

"Take as much time as you need."

Grace made her way to the soldier at the table. He didn't even look up as she approached. He looked as if he were thousands of miles away.

"May I join you?" she asked.

Startled, he looked up. "Um, sure. Okay." He hopped up to pull a chair out for her.

"Thank you," she said.

When he sat next to her, she extended her hand and said, "Grace. My name is Grace." She didn't mention her last name, not wanting him to make the connection to who she was. Sometimes, it was a burden. A weight that she didn't want to carry.

"John," he said, shaking her hand. His grip was firm.

"How long is your furlough?" she asked, settling into her chair.

"Fifteen days. I leave the day after tomorrow." He pulled out a gold cigarette case from the breast pocket of his uniform, opened it, and offered it to her.

Grace shook her head. "No thank you."

His looks were indistinctive; if you were to draw a composite of the typical white American male, John would be it. Open face, wide forehead, brown eyes and brown hair. His hair had a cowlick right at the crown that looked untameable. Strong hands, which were currently trying to light his cigarette but couldn't because they were shaking. Grace reached over, smiling, and took the lighter from his hand.

"May I?" she asked.

He nodded. "If I can't manage my lighter, what makes them think I can manage my rifle?" he cracked, but there was no humor in his eyes or his voice.

She flipped open the lighter and rolled the spark wheel with her thumb. It took three attempts until a flame appeared. John leaned forward, cupping his hand around it to light his cigarette. Grace snapped the lighter shut and slid it across the table to him. He leaned back and took a long, hard drag on his cigarette like his life depended on it.

The air around him was heavy. She'd only just met him, but she was concerned about him.

"Would you like to dance?" she asked.

Immediately, he shook his head. "No thank you. I was never one for dancing." He looked around at all the jitterbugging couples. The women far outnumbered the men, so some of them were dancing with other women. He turned his gaze back to Grace. "But if you want to, don't let me stop you."

She had wanted to dance a minute ago, but now her feet felt glued to the floor. She didn't want to leave him. "I'm here all the time," she told him. "My feet will thank me for sitting this one out."

John surprised her by laughing, his first real laugh since she'd joined him. It made her smile.

"It's great to see American girls again," John said. "It's a sight for sore eyes."

"Your family must be so glad you're home on leave," she said.

He nodded, picking up his cigarette from the ashtray and taking several puffs. "They are. Mother and Dad are older. They had me later in life. I'm an only child. My father always called me the pleasant surprise." The smile that formed on his face was one of pure affection and appreciation. It gave Grace goose bumps. "But with me being away, they worry, you know."

"Of course," Grace said readily. She couldn't imagine sending a young man you'd raised through scraped knees and teenage acne off to war, gun in hand.

"Since I left, I can see they've aged," he continued. "I mean, they were already old when I left, but now they look ancient." He shook his head.

She thought he looked old as well. It wasn't his appearance so much as his countenance. He was a man who looked as if he'd lived a thousand lifetimes. War weighed heavily.

John sipped from his Coke bottle and winced. "Flat." He stood abruptly and Grace wondered if he was going to leave. "Can I get you something to drink?"

"A Coke would be lovely."

"Coming right up."

He walked toward the refreshment table and briefly, Grace wondered if she should get back there and help out, but she felt compelled to remain there and keep him company. She couldn't explain it and gave it no further thought. John returned carrying two bottles of Coke and set one down in front of Grace.

"Thank you" she said.

"Why don't you tell me about yourself, Grace."

She shrugged and smiled. "There's not much to tell. I've lived in Lavender Bay all my life. I've recently graduated from college."

"You seem kind of young for college."

"I skipped a year in elementary school and graduated early."

With a smile, he said, "You must be smart, then."

"I can hold my own," she said.

"What did you study?" he asked.

"Art history."

"Do you like it?"

"I do, it's interesting," she said. She didn't mention that before 1939, she'd spent her summers traveling to Europe with her mother to places like France and Italy. She couldn't imagine what those cities looked like now. She preferred to remember them as they were. Those trips had caused her to fall in love with art and history. As her mother shopped, Grace had spent her days in museums and art galleries.

"That's the one thing that can't be taken away from you: your education," he said.

"Are you in college?"

He shook his head. "Not anymore. I was in my last year when Pearl was bombed, and I joined up right after. I had only one more semester to go."

"After the war is over, you can go back and finish," Grace said. So many lives had been disrupted. How would things look after the war? Would they pick up where they left off or would they move on? It remained to be seen.

He gave her a smile. It was a smile that was old. Of someone who knew things she had no idea about. All he said was, "Maybe."

"What was your area of study?"

"Science. Chemistry. Leave me in a lab with beakers and a Bunsen burner and I'm in heaven," he said.

Grace laughed.

"You're a pretty girl but when you smile, you're beautiful," he said.

Grace blushed and lowered her head. "Thank you."

"I only speak the truth."

They spoke for over an hour as the band continued to play and the dancing went on around them, until John announced that he should get going. Grace refrained from asking him to stay longer. When he stood from the table, so did she. She needed to get back to work. But she'd felt his need for company and conversation was more important.

"It was nice meeting you, Grace," he said. "Thanks for keeping me company."

"I enjoyed it," she said truthfully. Before he could walk away, she asked, "Will you be here tomorrow night?"

He shook his head. "It'll be my last night of leave. I'll spend it at home with my parents."

"Of course. Are they taking you to the train station in the morning?"

"No, I won't let them. Goodbye is too much for them. I can spare them that."

Grace frowned. "Who's driving you to the station, then?"

"No one. I'll get a cab."

This bothered Grace so much, she blurted, "Give me your address and I'll drive you." You couldn't send a man off to war by himself.

John couldn't hide his surprise. "I can't ask you to do that."

"You didn't ask, I offered," she said firmly.

He hesitated, then patted the pockets of his jacket. "I don't have any paper. Or even a pencil."

"No matter. Not needed. I've got a great memory," she said.

"I get the feeling you won't take no for an answer."

She tried to appear apologetic. "No, I'm afraid not."

"All right then. You've twisted my arm. 320 Bluebell Lane."

She knew the street. She repeated the address several times in her mind. "Very good. What time will I pick you up?"

"Is eight a.m. too early?"

Grace shook her head. "Not at all." They shook hands, and Grace promised to be on time the morning of his departure.

The evening was winding down. The girls she'd left at the refreshment table an hour ago stood there with their hands clasped behind their backs.

"Did that soldier need a shoulder to cry on?" the taller of the two asked softly.

"He was sitting there all evening by himself," said the other.

"He was a nice fella, I think he just needed someone to talk to," Grace explained.

They nodded, understanding.

The band played the final song, and the dimmed lights brightened, signifying the night was over.

"Look, I can do the cleanup," Grace offered. They'd been so gracious about her sitting at that table with John, it was the least she could do. Looking around, she added, "There isn't much."

"We couldn't leave it all to you."

"I insist. Come on," Grace persisted. "You've been on your feet all night. Go on home. It won't take long, and I don't mind."

"Gee, Grace, that's swell of you," the taller one said with a smile. The girls said good night to Grace and exited with the rest of the crowd. Grace began clearing off the table of refreshments. There were only two hot dogs left, and she took them and walked to the back door. Lavender Bay had a couple of stray dogs, and they knew to hang around for scraps.

She opened the door and sure enough, two scraggly dogs she'd named Glenn and Benny, after the band leaders, waited and began whining when she appeared. "Here you go," she said. She tossed each one a rubbery, sweaty leftover hot dog, and they wolfed them down. There were some people who'd be offended that she'd give these hot dogs to strays, especially given the food shortages and rationing. But to Grace's thinking, they needed to be fed too. And who was going to eat leftover hot dogs? Certainly not her.

As the band packed up their equipment, Grace shook out the tablecloths and folded the ones that didn't need to go into the laundry bag. One couple remained on the dance floor, clinging to each other despite the fact that the music had stopped playing and the room was now brightly lit.

"Come on now, it's time to leave," Grace said gently. "We're closing up and we all need to go home."

The couple pulled apart, and a strand of the girl's hair remained on the man's collar, still connecting them.

They both looked around as if they hadn't realized the pavilion had emptied out.

The soldier smiled at Grace. "Sorry about that, miss." He looked at his girl, took her hand, and said, "Come on, Jean, I'll walk you home." And they were gone.

Grace pushed a broom around, sweeping all the debris into a corner before brushing it onto a dustpan.

Soon the stage was empty as the band had hauled all their equipment out the back door to their car. The bandleader, Stuckey, approached Grace.

"You all alone tonight, Grace? No one to help?"

"There wasn't much to do so I told them to go on home."

He nodded. "We're all loaded up. But we'll wait until you're finished to walk you to your car."

"That's not necessary," Grace said.

"It is. Look, we're out back. We're gonna have one more smoke before we leave."

"All right," Grace said. "Give me ten minutes."

She hurried with the rest of the cleanup, turning off lights and righting chairs and tables as she went. She put all the empty Coke bottles into the crates out in the back, then made her way through the pavilion, making sure everything was neat and orderly. At the back door, she turned off the last light and locked the door as she headed out. The band members sat around on upturned crates, smoking cigarettes. One was holding out his hand for one of the stray dogs, but the dog was wary, approaching him hesitantly, ears flattened.

"Come on, poochie," the guy said, cigarette hanging out of his mouth.

The dog took a chance and was rewarded with a gentle rub on the head. "That's a good boy."

Stuckey looked up to Grace. "All set?"

"I am. Thanks for hanging around, fellas, I appreciate it."

"No problem."

Their car wasn't parked far from Grace's. The band piled into their old Ford and Grace got into her newer-model Packard, feeling slightly conspicuous. They waited until she started her engine and pulled out.

At home, Grace went upstairs to bed, turning off lights as she went. The house was quiet; her parents had already gone to bed.

In her room, she peeled off her clothes and hung them carefully in the closet. After she pulled on her nightgown, she stood in front of the vanity mirror and brushed her thick, dark hair. She shut off the overhead light and the lamp on the dressing table, leaving on only the reading light at the side of her bed. She climbed beneath the sheets and stretched out on her back, hoping to feel tired, but she didn't even so much as yawn. She picked up her book off the bedside table, *Evil Under the Sun* by Agatha Christie, and opened up to the page she'd bookmarked. She was a voracious reader and was some-times guilty of staying awake with a book until dawn. But tonight, she couldn't focus. She thought of John. It wasn't that she was attracted to him romantically, because she wasn't. But he had a charisma if that was the word. Or maybe the better word was melancholy. She felt compelled to help him.

And she decided she would do just that.

CHAPTER FOURTEEN

The morning Grace was to drive John to the train station was gray, warm, and drizzly. She'd woken early, afraid she'd miss the alarm, and was dressed and down for breakfast by seven. Her father sat at the head of the cherrywood table, eating his breakfast with a stack of newspapers piled next to his plate.

Her mother was still in bed. She never appeared before ten a.m., preferring to take her breakfast upstairs in her room.

"Well, Grace, this is a pleasant surprise! What are you doing up so early?"

"I've got an errand to run," she said.

Her father leaned forward and grinned. "Sounds mysterious."

"Not at all," she said. She took a plate and walked along the sideboard, helping herself to some toast, grapefruit wedges, and a hard-boiled egg. She joined her father at the table, smoothing out the bottom of her skirt before sitting down.

"Nothing mysterious about it," she said, slicing up the egg on a small plate and sprinkling a bit of salt over it. "I'm giving a friend a ride to the train station."

"Would this friend be of the masculine persuasion?" George Gibson asked, his eyes twinkling.

"Oh, Dad!" Grace said in mock indignation.

"I can only ask, can't I?" He smiled.

"His leave is up and he's returning to war. He had no one to drive him to the train station."

Her father nodded. "Is this a romantic interest, maybe?"

"Boy oh boy, you certainly don't beat around the bush, do you?"

"Nope. I'm a straight shooter."

"To answer your question, no, it isn't romantic. I wanted to do something nice."

"Good for you. You know, Grace, more than anyone, you remind me of my mother."

"Is that right?" She'd never met her paternal grandmother; the woman had died years before Grace was born.

"Yep, she was sensible and kind, just like you, buttercup." He leaned over and pinched her cheek.

"Dad, I'm not six anymore."

"Sadly, no," George said. "Well, time to go to work." He took the last bite of toast and washed it down with the rest of his black coffee. Taking the cream linen napkin from his lap, he folded it neatly and set it on the table. He picked up the pile of newspapers from the table and carried them out beneath his arm.

"See you tonight, Dad," she said.

"Have a good day, Grace."

Grace left shortly after her father, walking out back to the garage. The chauffeur was gone, having driven her father to work as he liked to read the newspapers in the back seat on his way in. All the doors to the bays were open, revealing the fleet of cars owned by George Gibson. Grace grimaced as she looked over them. They were all so spiffy-looking.

She herself had been gifted with a red Packard Roadster and she loved to kick around in that car, but she was looking for something a bit more demure. Her mother's car was no better. If anything, it was worse. A bright yellow convertible Cadillac coupe—she'd stick out like a sore thumb driving around in that. She looked down the line at the touring car and the other roadster, her gaze finally settling on the older-model Chevrolet sedan in an awful shade of brown.

That's perfect, she thought. She only hoped it would start. It was the chauffeur's job to keep all the cars running, but she had no idea when this car was last driven.

Still, it was her best option. She walked inside the garage, the smell of gasoline and motor oil prominent. On the wall near the desk were all the keys to the cars. She read the labels, finally landing on the keys for the Chevrolet. She walked past all the other cars to her car of choice in the last bay.

It started on the first try. She made her way over to Bluebell Lane, getting used to driving a different car. The steering was a little more difficult than she'd imagined it would be, and she had to stretch her leg to reach the pedals. As she turned on Bluebell Lane, she slowed down, peering out the window to read the house numbers, but she spotted John waiting on the porch of his home, dressed in his Army uniform and hat, his green duffel bag at his feet. He stood with an old man with snow white hair Grace presumed to be his father.

When she pulled up at the curb, she threw the car in park and got out, lingering at the side of the car so as not to interrupt the father–son goodbye. John shook hands with his father, nodding as the older man spoke to him. Grace was just out of earshot.

As John stepped off the porch, his father pulled a voluminous white handkerchief from the pocket of his pants and swiped at his nose and dabbed his eyes.

"Hello, Grace," John said in that serious voice of his.

"Good morning, John. All set?" she asked.

"I am."

She walked around to her side of the car and climbed in as John turned and waved to his father. He gave Grace a nod, and she pulled away from the curb and headed down the street. In her rearview mirror, she saw that John's father remained standing on the porch.

"Did your mother not want to say goodbye?" she asked.

John looked out the window. "The goodbyes are hard on Mother. She had breakfast, said goodbye, and went to her room."

"It must be so difficult," Grace sympathized.

"It is. Mother's health isn't the best," he said.

They made small talk as they drove, comparing notes on the books they were reading. John was reading *The Grapes of Wrath*, which Grace had read two years previously. It wasn't far to the train station, and Grace experienced a wave of sadness when it came into view. She parked the car and got out as John climbed out and retrieved his duffel bag.

"Grace, I appreciate the ride, really I do, but it's not necessary for you to come inside."

"But I'd like to see you off," she said. The thought of someone going to war with no one to wave him off was appalling to Grace. "Why, are you afraid I'll cry?" she teased.

"No, I'm afraid I will," he said with a laugh.

"Come on, let's go," she said, walking toward the entrance. "If we stand out here debating, you'll miss your train."

"That wouldn't do," he said.

They walked side by side into the concourse of the small Lavender Bay train station. Grace waited while John went to the window and purchased his ticket. Then, in silence, they walked outside to the platform. Grace was disappointed to see that the train was already there, waiting, steam rolling out from beneath it. The platform was crowded with servicemen in uniform waiting to board. None were alone. Some were with family, others held on to sweethearts. Grace thought about all the photos tucked safely away of girls back home and the letters that would crisscross back and forth across the ocean. It was all so sad.

She pulled a piece of paper from her pocket and pushed it toward him. "John, here's my address. If you'd like to write, I'll write back."

He studied her address and smiled. "I'd like that." Carefully, he folded it up and tucked it into the inside pocket of his coat.

"I don't know your last name," she said.

"McNamara."

John McNamara.

The train whistle blew, loud, sharp, and shrill, and the conductor stepped off the train and blew his whistle.

"Well, that's me," John said, hoisting his duffel bag over his shoulder. "Grace, I can't thank you enough for seeing me off. It means a lot."

Grace shrugged, going for nonchalant. "It was nothing."

"It's everything to me," he said.

He was about to step away when Grace stepped forward and held out her arms to him. "Let me hug you goodbye."

Grinning, he said, "I'd like that." He moved his cap up from his forehead with this thumb.

Easily, Grace wrapped her arms around him and held him tight for a moment, wishing she could transfer whatever strength and courage she had to him. She wouldn't need it here in Lavender Bay. His arms were big and strong, and they held on to each other for a minute.

The train whistle blew again, and they stepped apart.

"Take care of yourself, John," Grace said.

He smiled. "You do the same." He looked at her with sharp, intelligent eyes. "I will write to you, Grace."

"Good." She didn't take her eyes off him as he boarded the train, and she followed his course through the windows, walking parallel to his movements on the train. He took a seat near the windows facing the platform. He spotted her and gave her a wave.

She decided she would wait until the train pulled out so that John would know there was someone on the platform until he left. The final train whistle blew, and she stepped back as the last few passengers bolted to board the train.

With her arms crossed, she watched as the train pulled out, waving goodbye to John, who never stopped looking at her. She stood there on the platform long after the train disappeared from view.

They'd made no promises. No whispers of undying devotion, no mention of counting the days until they saw one another again. To do so would have been insincere on both their parts. There was the implied understanding that their paths might never cross again. But what they had done was show kindness to each other with the expectation of nothing in return. Because sometimes, it was all you had.

CHAPTER FIFTEEN

G race stared out the dining room window as she and her mother ate a lunch of cold salmon and salad. It was pouring outside. The sky was dark, and the weather matched her mood: foul. She hadn't been right since she'd seen John off at the train station a month ago. Not that she missed him, though she did worry about him. She was too sensible to mistake that for any sort of romantic attachment. But she felt utterly without purpose. Aimless.

"It's no good to sulk around the house, Grace," her mother said, picking around her plate. Grace didn't think her mother ever finished a meal.

"I know, Mother."

"What about college-related things? Your sorority?" her mother inquired. There was an undercurrent of disapproval in her voice, still, at Grace's decision—supported by George—to attend the local college rather than the finishing school Aleida would have chosen for her only child.

Grace shook her head. She hadn't been in touch with her sorority sisters since she graduated. She finished her lunch and laid her napkin alongside her plate to signify she was done. She stood and poured more coffee from the urn into the delicate china teacup. "I feel so useless."

"What? What do you mean? You're young. You're supposed to be useless."

Grace ignored her mother's comment. "I wish there was more that I could do for the war."

Her mother sighed, tired of the endless conversations of war and wishing that it was over so things could go back to the way they used to be. "It's not your job."

"It's all of our jobs," Grace pointed out.

"Why not come with me this afternoon to the Ladies Auxiliary. We roll bandages on Saturday afternoons."

She could hardly say no after complaining that she wanted to do something. Rolling bandages did not inspire excitement, but she supposed it was better than doing nothing.

"Good. That's settled then." Her mother glanced at her diamond wristwatch and added, "Let's finish up and we'll head over to the pavilion."

Grace spent so much time at the pavilion that sometimes she felt like she lived there.

"You might want to go upstairs and change," her mother suggested, straightening the cuff of her own tailored blouse. Mrs. Gibson did not approve of her daughter's daily uniform of a baggy sweater, skirt, ankle socks, and saddle shoes.

"I could put on a pair of those new trousers," Grace countered, knowing her mother hated those even more.

Her mother scowled. "Goodness no. A woman in trousers is never acceptable." She looked at Grace, who now stood, and with a sniff, she said, "You'll have to do."

The chauffeur brought Mrs. Gibson's Cadillac around to the front. Before they stepped out of the house, Mrs. Gibson pulled on her driving gloves and hung her pocketbook over her arm. There was the faint scent of Arpège about her, the only fragrance she ever wore.

Grace hated driving in this car. She slumped down in the seat, her hand covering her forehead. It was the only yellow car in Lavender Bay. It was for this reason her mother had chosen the color.

"Grace, don't slouch. Do sit up. You'll ruin your posture," Aleida said.

Having spent many evenings at the pavilion at USO dances, Grace thought the space looked oddly different during the daytime. Maybe because it was brighter. Or perhaps because the place was filled with tables lined up end to end. Or maybe because it was full of women and there was not a man in sight. The walls were lined with all sorts of posters selling war bonds and recruiting for volunteers.

A sturdy woman in her late fifties approached them. "Mrs. Gibson, you are so very welcome." The woman's face was lined but her eyes were clear, and she wore the uniform of the Red Cross: white with a red cross over the left breast. A white headband with a red cross in the center secured a dark scarf over the rest of her head. Her curious gaze landed on Grace.

Mrs. Gibson introduced them. "Mrs. Wickson, this is my daughter, Grace, who's come to help." To Grace, she said, "Mrs. Wickson runs the Red Cross here in Lavender Bay. We'd be lost without her."

Mrs. Wickson beamed at the compliment. "Your father is one of our most generous benefactors, Grace. It's wonderful that you're going to join us. We can always use an extra pair of hands. Why don't I find you a seat? You'll want to sit with girls your own age." Smiling knowingly, she added, "You don't want to get stuck with us old fuddy-duddies."

Politely, Grace said, "I'll sit wherever you need me to, Mrs. Wickson."

"Come along."

Grace parted from her mother, who was tugging off her driving gloves and tucking them securely in her pocketbook. With a smile, her mother stepped away and headed to a table at the front, where a seat had been reserved for her. With a raised eyebrow, Grace watched as her mother donned the Red Cross headdress and took her seat, tucking her pocketbook beneath her chair and acknowledging each of the ladies at her table.

Ahead of Grace, Mrs. Wickson pulled out a chair at a table populated with young women close in age to Grace, along with several in their later twenties and early thirties. This table was a little more boisterous and chattier than the others, and she was grateful that Mrs. Wickson had sat her with this crowd.

Mrs. Wickson instructed her to wash her hands in a basin at the end of the table. After Grace did this, she took a seat. Mrs. Wickson stood over her and said, "As you can see, the volunteers at this station are folding gauze. This is how you do it." She demonstrated, adding the neatly folded gauze to the growing pile on the table.

"No sloppiness either," Mrs. Wickson said kindly. "Remember, they're for our boys."

"Of course." Grace nodded. She looked around. Farther down the table, some of the women were cutting lengths of gauze, using a ruler to measure it precisely before passing it along to the others to fold.

Some of the girls she recognized from her time at McKinley High School. Although she hadn't been friendly with them because they weren't in her year, she knew them to see.

The girl across from her had striking blue eyes and wore her auburn hair in stylish victory rolls. She smiled at Grace and said, "You're Grace Gibson, right?"

"Yes."

"My name's Norma Fox."

"I remember you," Grace said. "You were two years ahead of me at McKinley."

The other woman smiled, pleased to have been remembered. "That's right." She introduced Grace to the rest of the women at the table, all of whom seemed friendly enough.

The conversation flowed, and as much as Grace was happy to help, after an hour, she had to admit to being bored.

"Do you do this every day?" she asked Norma. Her eyes would cross if she had to do this daily.

"Actually, this is my last day. I got a job at Cheever Aviation."

"Oh? Doing what?"

"They make cargo planes for the war. C-46s. I start there next week. There's a push to hire workers. It's mostly women."

"Of course." Grace had read about this, about women going to work in the defense industries. How had she missed this call? Cheever wasn't that far from Lavender Bay.

"They're still hiring if you're interested," Norma told her. "But plan to be there the whole day. Filling out an application, interviews, getting measured for coveralls and steel-toed boots."

"What sort of skills do you need to have?"

Norma snorted. "A pulse and a willingness to work. You have to be over eighteen, though."

Grace checked the box on all those things, but she found it hard to imagine working in a place where they used heavy machinery. In a man's job. Since this war had started, everything had been turned on its head.

"I can't wait. I'll be doing my part, but I get to sleep in my own bed," Norma said with a laugh. "Not like my sister."

Grace looked at her questioningly.

"My older sister, Noreen, is a nurse. She joined the Army and is out in the Pacific." Norma shuddered. "No thanks. If the heat isn't unbearable then it's torrential rain."

"But does she like it?"

Norma nodded. "She's the oldest daughter. She's bossy and likes to tell everyone what to do. She's probably out there giving Hirohito the what-for. She's also a little bit of a martyr, so the posting suits her perfectly." She laughed. "Not for me, though. I want to contribute, but I want to do it from the comfort of my own home."

Grace liked the other girl's frank honesty. She stored all this information at the back of her mind and returned her attention to the task of folding the gauze bandages.

Chapter Sixteen

The following week, Grace could think of nothing else but the aviation plant. It kept her awake at night. This might be the perfect thing for her. Although she'd hoped for a career using her college degree, that would have to be put on hold until after the war. To her, nothing was more important than doing her part for the war effort.

On Wednesday, a beautiful, sunny day, she left right after breakfast and made the hour-long drive to Cheever. Right before the exit ramp, a large Cheever Aviation billboard next to the highway seemed to be speaking directly to her. Beneath the image of three women dressed in coveralls and headscarves were the words *Do your part, apply today.* Then, in smaller letters below, *2 miles from the turnoff.*

Cheever was a much smaller town than Lavender Bay, and the aviation plant wasn't hard to miss. The steel hangers could be seen for miles around. After she went through the security checkpoint, she parked her car and walked through the front entrance, confident and determined. There were a lot of women in the reception area. Making use of any space they could find, they laid their application forms down and filled them in with the pencils that had been provided. Grace asked for an application and was given instructions on what to do next. It took her all of ten minutes to fill it out. Norma had been right; it looked like the only thing required was a pulse. Regardless, she carefully double-checked her form. She didn't want to lose this opportunity because of a careless technicality.

She handed her job application to one of the employees, who looked it over briefly, not focusing on any one thing. From there she was directed to a side room lined with wooden benches. She sat with all the other applicants, waiting for her turn to be called for an interview, form in hand. The room was packed with women, and she was sorry she hadn't brought a book with her to pass the time. It took ninety minutes before her name was called.

Now it was her turn to enter the small office she'd watched women going in and out of all morning long. Two men sat behind a table, and the older one wearing glasses indicated she should sit in the chair across from them. He held his hand out, and she handed him her application.

He introduced himself as George Treadwell, the plant foreman, and the man to his left was introduced as Les Stockton, his assistant. Mr. Treadwell looked like he had a bunch of kids at home and the weight of the world on his shoulders. In other words, he looked harried. Les Stockton, on the other hand, was younger, maybe in his thirties, and too skinny, with facial features that didn't appear to align properly. His eyes were too close together and he had thinning hair. Grace didn't like the look of him.

The interview was fairly straightforward. Mr. Treadwell asked basic questions, and when he found out she was a college graduate, he said, "What are you doing here? This is grunt work, not the most pleasant job."

"I'm laboring under no illusion," Grace replied. "This is important work. Like everyone else here, I want to do my part."

Mr. Treadwell nodded and smiled as if pleased with her answer. She was aware of the other man staring at her, and she refused to make eye contact. She hoped he wouldn't spoil the work environment.

Finally, she was forced to look at him when he said, "You've never worked a proper job before, have you?"

His tone made it sound like an accusation. She leveled her gaze at him. "This would be my first job. But I can assure you that I'm a quick learner." He went to say something, and she interrupted, saying with a slight nod over her shoulder, "I'm sure there are many women here today who have never worked before."

"You're correct," Mr. Treadwell said. Aware that there was still a long line of women waiting to be interviewed after Grace, he said, "Okay, you're hired. Go back out to the main hall and they'll direct you to get measured for your coveralls and to fill out more paperwork." He held out his hand. "Welcome to Cheever Aviation, Grace."

Beaming, Grace shook his hand. "Thank you, sir." She then shook Mr. Stockton's hand, and her smile faltered slightly at the touch of his clammy skin.

She could barely contain her smile as she walked out of the office and headed back to the main hall. She'd gotten a job! And an important one too. All by herself, without her father's influence. She couldn't wait to get started. There was a buzz in the air around the plant. Throngs of women smiled and laughed. She asked for directions to get her uniform and was shown down a corridor off the main hall.

She joined another line of women, and measurements were taken for uniforms and boots. She was told that head coverings were mandatory and if she didn't have a headscarf, one would be provided for her. Once that was done, she was led to the canteen, where the rows of tables held stacks of forms and piles of pencils. As instructed, she sat, took a form and pencil, and began to fill it out. It was more involved than her application form, asking for information on her next of kin and such. The next stop was another office to be assigned a job. Perhaps because her application form stated that she was an art history major, she was assigned to the unit that painted the insignias on the planes. She liked that idea.

She practically floated home. Her father wasn't back from work yet and her mother was entertaining, so she snuck upstairs to her room. It had been a long day, and she was looking forward to stretching out on the bed for a little while and reading.

Her room faced north, so it never got too hot in the summer. Her windows were wide open, and the drapes remained unmoving at the sills. She changed out of her outfit into shorts and a sleeveless blouse. She considered taking her book down to the pool, but she was afraid if her mother spotted her, she'd drag her into her gathering, which had been known to happen in the past.

After plopping on her bed, she picked up her book off the nightstand. She was almost finished with it, and there were two more beneath it waiting to be read. She looked around her room, noting the stark contrast between it and the steel, concrete, and gunmetal gray of the aviation factory. Her own room was decorated in cream and pale shades of blue. Her mother had wanted to decorate it in pink, but Grace had held firm. The bedroom was large with plenty of room for bookshelves, a double bed, a desk and chair, a settee, and a window seat. It was like her own private sitting room. She remembered hearing a girl in school speaking about sharing a bed with a lumpy mattress with her two sisters. Grace could not imagine. It was one of the first instances where she realized she lived differently from most of the people in Lavender Bay.

Seven o'clock rolled around, and Grace snapped her book shut and placed it on the bedside table, knowing she'd finish it later, at bedtime. She dressed for dinner and made her way downstairs.

Her father was home, and he and her mother were already seated, waiting for her.

"Hiya, Dad," Grace said, laying a kiss on her father's forehead.

"Nice of you to join us," Mrs. Gibson said, with a pointed look to the grandfather clock standing in the corner of the room.

"Sorry, Mother," Grace mumbled, taking her seat as Irene brought out the first course, a chilled soup of cucumber and mint.

"Thank you, Irene," Grace said when she set the bowl of soup down in front of her.

"Irene, how's the family?" Mr. Gibson asked.

"They're fine, sir."

"And how's your boy? Any word?"

"He's in Europe somewhere, but he can't tell us where," she replied. There was no missing the pride in her voice.

"Of course not," George said. "We do appreciate his effort."

Irene smiled and retreated from the room.

"How did the luncheon go?" George asked his wife.

"It went well," she replied.

"What club is this?"

"The Ladies Association for the benefit of the hospital."

"Right. Important."

"Dad, how's everything at the plant?" Grace asked.

"We're jammed," he joked, like he said more often than not. His other favorite was *My legs were like jelly*. Aleida suffered these jokes in silence, but Grace enjoyed them; she was glad her father wasn't stuffy.

"How was your day, Grace?" he asked.

Practically bursting with her news, she said brightly, "I got a job!"

Her mother dropped her spoon into her soup bowl. "A job? Whatever for?"

George reserved comment, narrowing his eyes as if considering his only child. Grace looked from the disappointed face of her mother to the curious gaze of her father.

"Where, Grace?" George finally asked.

Grace almost lifted off her seat with pride. "At Cheever Aviation!"

Her father's expression was unreadable, but her mother spoke up. "Cheever Aviation? What is that?"

Grace turned to her mother and said, "They're making cargo planes for the war. It's a defense plant up in Cheever."

Her mother paled considerably and slumped back in her chair. "Doing secretarial work? Grace, you're not destined to do typing and shorthand."

"No, not exactly," Grace said. Aware of her father's gaze on her, she said, "I'll be painting the Army seals and the stars on the planes."

Her mother blinked in disbelief, her mouth slightly open. "F-f-factory work?" She leaned her elbow on the arm of her chair to prop her head up. "Do you do this sort of thing to torture me, Grace? Do you?"

Grace scowled. "Of course not, Mother."

"Our daughter doing factory work. I don't know what to say."

Grace was aware that her father still had not said anything. She turned to look at him. "Dad?"

He sighed and pushed his half-eaten bowl of soup away. "Grace, I understand your desire to do your part for the war effort but because of your standing, how you do that will be different from other people."

Grace frowned at him. "I don't know what you mean. Unless you mean I'm to sit around and do nothing."

"I mean nothing of the sort," he said. "Working at a factory, at a man's job, is not for you."

Her skin prickled. If there was one thing she hated more than being told what to do, it was being told what she couldn't do.

"Your father's right," Aleida said in a rare unified front with her husband.

Grace's head swung back and forth between her parents, her father at the head of the table and her mother at the foot. "But I *want* to do this. This is important work!"

"Everyone's contribution, no matter how big or small, is important," her father said. "Whether running a scrap metal drive or rolling bandages, it's all important." He paused. "I thought you were helping out with the USO dances and the Ladies Auxiliary."

"But I want to do more," Grace said with conviction.

"We all want to do more," her father said. "But we must help within our abilities and our stations in life."

"Dad, I'm surprised at you. You're not one to tout this class position. You came from nothing—"

"Grace!" her mother barked. She so rarely raised her voice that it startled Grace. "Don't ever speak to your father like that again. Please."

Softening her tone and lowering her voice, Grace said, "I can do this job. I know I'd be good at it."

"What about your college degree?" her mother pointed out. "You were the one who wanted to go to college. Now you're abandoning that? Now that you have the degree, you're not going to pursue it?"

"I'm not abandoning it," Grace said tightly. "I'm simply putting it on hold until the war is over."

She looked at her father and in a pleading voice, she said, "Dad, this is important to me."

Her father sighed. His instinct was always to give in to the whims of the two most important women in his life, but at this point, they were diametrically opposed, and someone would end up angry. It was inevitable.

"I have reservations about this, Grace. Many reservations," he said.

Grace jumped up from her chair, her napkin falling on the floor. She stomped her foot. "I'm over eighteen. You can't tell me where I can work or what I can do." She stormed out of the room but not before she heard her mother pleading with her father.

"Please, George, you've given in to her every whim since she was a child. I am asking you, as your wife, to please consider my feelings on the subject. I don't want her to work at that factory. It's no place for our daughter."

Grace didn't stick around to hear her father's reply. She took the stairs two at a time and slammed her bedroom door with such force that the upstairs shook. She crossed her arms over her chest and paced back and forth over the luxurious Persian rug that covered the hardwood floors, something her mother had picked up on her travels. Occasionally, she kicked things: the purple velvet ottoman, the clawed foot of her canopy bed. She left a scuff mark on the painted base of the window seat.

Finally, she settled down and found herself staring out the window. The lights were on in the upstairs apartment over the garage, and she spied the chauffeur, cigarette in his mouth, sitting by a table lamp with a book open in front of him. It was such a lovely scene that it calmed her down.

What she'd said was true. She was over eighteen. She certainly didn't need their permission to go to work in Cheever. They couldn't stop her. She clung to this thought and her anger dissipated. She got comfortable on the window seat and picked up her book and settled in for the night, looking forward to the job she was about to start the following week. What could be more important than building planes for the troops? She couldn't think of anything.

She slept soundly that night.

The following evening as she bounced down the stairs to head out for the USO dance at the pavilion, the phone rang. It had been a good day. There had been no mention of her upcoming job at Cheever Aviation by either of her parents, and she figured they had come around to her way of thinking. Dinner was unlike that of the previous night—no theatrics, and her parents seemed solicitous of her. Relieved, she was looking forward to the dance. She'd washed her hair in the morning, so it had a lovely shine, and she'd applied some red lipstick.

As the phone rang again, she called out, "I'll get it!" She picked up the handset from the rotary phone in the front hall and leaned against the wall, her fingers curling around the telephone cord.

"Hello?"

"May I speak with Grace Gibson?" said a male voice.

"Speaking."

"Grace, this is Les Stockton over at Cheever Aviation."

"Oh, hello, Mr. Stockton," Grace said excitedly.

"Look, I'm sorry, but we'll have to rescind our offer of employment."

"What? Why?"

"Again, we're not offering you a job," he said firmly. "No need to show up next week."

"I don't understand. I was told I'd be painting the insignias on the planes. What's changed?" She clenched her teeth.

There was a long, exasperated sigh from the other end of the line. "Look, it was out of our hands. Talk to your father." And with that, he hung up.

Grace stared at the phone; the dial tone was obnoxiously loud. She slammed the receiver down and marched off in search of her father. Never mind her mother.

She found him in his study, a cozy room with dark green walls and dark wood paneling. A banker's lamp cast a spotlight on the surface of the desk, which was covered in papers. A stand lamp with a frilly shade cast an amber glow over the corner of the room. The bookshelves were crammed with books as well as the evolution of the different jam jars used since the early days of Gibson's Grape Jelly. On one wall was a watercolor print of the current jar in use standing in front of a bunch of purple grapes.

Her father looked up at her and smiled. "Off to the pavilion?"

She ignored his question. "How could you? How could you do that to me?" She didn't know who she was angrier with, her father and his interference, or herself for her eyes that were brimming with tears.

Her father looked sad. "I'm sorry, but I have to agree with your mother on this one. That factory is no place for women."

"Wake up, Dad. The place is now full of women. Someone has to do this work! The men are gone!"

"True, but it doesn't have to be you. You can do other things."

"I want to do more than fold bandages and hand out hot dogs and Cokes at USO dances!" The more she spoke, the further her voice rose. It was as if he wasn't hearing her and the only way to get him to listen, to understand, was to shout. "If I were a son instead of a daughter, I would have had to go off and fight."

Her father did not respond to that. A pall of determination settled over his expression. "I'm sorry, Grace. That's the way it is."

"Arrgh!" She balled her hands into fists at her sides, refraining from the urge to give his desk a good kick.

George Gibson's eyes widened. "Grace—"

She turned on her heel and walked out. Once she was out of sight, she angrily swiped at the tears that fell. Trembling, she walked out the front door and around to the garage. She tried to shake it off. The door to the bay where her car was housed was open, and she hopped in her car, started it up, and pulled out.

As she drove over to the pavilion, she decided she would not have her father interfering with her life. Just because he could pull some strings did not give him the right to run her life.

Soft music floated out of the pavilion as she pulled up and parked, and she made an effort to settle down as she headed inside. The fellas home on leave didn't deserve a surly volunteer. By the time she arrived at her station, she'd squared her shoulders, lifted her chin, and pasted a smile on her face, determined to make someone feel better.

CHAPTER SEVENTEEN

Grace remained cool toward her parents in the weeks following that phone call. She was always polite and courteous, but any inquiries on their part were met with one-word answers. She always ate her breakfast alone and she no longer joined her mother for lunch, choosing instead to eat in the kitchen with Irene, which sent her mother into a tailspin. At dinner, she arrived as the first course was being served and skipped dessert, excusing herself as soon as she could, as soon as her plate was cleared. Her mother chalked it up to a phase and refused to play along but her father tried to engage her. She resisted.

She continued with volunteering at the pavilion and folding bandages for the Red Cross. She even signed up to help sell war bonds and helped out at the scrap metal drives. But it wasn't enough. She wanted to do more. She *needed* to do more.

Her restlessness at feeling helpless was remedied by a letter from John. She'd thought about him from time to time and assumed he'd changed his mind about writing to her. Seeing his letter waiting for her on the hall table filled her with excitement.

It was such a beautiful day she took it outside, to the far end of the lawn where there was a paved stone patio beneath a large oak. Off in the distance, the sun shone brightly over Lake Erie, creating the impression of pieces of broken glass on the surface of the water. Grace parked herself on the low stone wall, crossed her legs, and carefully opened the envelope.

Dear Grace,

I bet you're surprised to hear from me after all this time. To be honest, I'm surprised to be writing to you! I see other guys here are so dependent on letters from home, as am I. It always lifts my spirits to receive mail from home.

Initially, I told myself that I wouldn't write to you. I'm away for a long time and I felt it was too much to ask (and yes, I know you offered) to keep up correspondence. I'm sure you're busy enough.

Grace snorted and muttered, "If you only knew how busy I wasn't!" She continued reading.

I'm somewhere in the Pacific. Of course, I'm unable to tell you where exactly. Suffice it to say it's beautiful. The weather is gorgeous, but there's a downside. Snakes and bugs. The latter are relentless. It almost feels like another front.

I remember you being easy to talk to that night at the USO dance. And I thought you wouldn't mind if I poured out my heart, so to speak. I don't want to burden my parents with this. I keep those letters light to keep them safe. But I feel the need to get things off my chest. During our limited interactions, I got the impression that you've got a sensible head and strong shoulders.

There are things about war that I've come to learn. First, there's the boredom of sitting around, waiting for something to happen. It's almost a relief when the action starts, if only to cure the tedium. Then there's the anxiety of wondering when something is going to happen and how you'll handle it and most of all, if you'll survive it. To live in that day-to-day vigilance takes its toll after a while. I can't help but think about how this war will change me. And I know it will. It already has.

Everyone here dreams of something to keep them going. Some think only of their girls back home. Some think of their mother's cooking. Me? I have no girl back home and although I enjoy eating, I don't think about it again after the meal is done with. What I do miss is the ability to do whatever you want, when you want—within the constraints of obligations and work, of course. What I wouldn't give to go for a stroll on the beach in Lavender Bay and look out at the lake and be amazed at the beauty of it. Or maybe go for a walk simply to think. Too much thinking over here is not in my best interest.

I feel better already pouring my feelings out on paper.

I hope to hear from you and although I know this is a heavy letter, I hope it doesn't scare you off!

Please say a prayer for me.

Yours in friendship,

John

Grace reread his letter several times, a smile forming on her lips. She couldn't help but feel touched that he'd turned to her. She stared out at the lake, still smiling. In her mind, she began to arrange her thoughts as to what her response would be. After a while, she stood and made her way inside to pen her letter. A thought occurred to her that she could make the post office before it closed but then she decided against it, thinking she wanted to take her time with her response and not rush it. She'd post it in the morning once it was perfect.

Later that evening, she headed off to the USO dance in an upbeat mood. She'd written her letter to John, telling him about all the goings-on in Lavender Bay and her disappointment at her father interfering with her work at the aviation plant. She shared her own sense of uselessness in regard to the war and encouraged him to continue to share his feelings with her.

The pavilion wasn't as busy as usual, but there were plenty of servicemen there, dancing with their girls or the volunteers. As she manned the grill for the hot dogs, she tapped her foot to the beat of the music. Sammy and the Jackknives were the featured band that evening. They made regular appearances at the pavilion. They could get the crowd jumping and jiving and jitterbugging.

As she placed hot dogs in buns, she noticed the Red Cross had put up new posters along the walls. When there was a lull at the refreshment table, she walked around the perimeter of the room, studying the new posters, her hands clasped behind her back. The US military was recruiting nurses to join the Army and the Navy nurse corps. The posters depicted proud women wearing military uniforms. *And serving their country*, Grace thought. There was a recruitment poster for the Red Cross motor pool. Another poster showed a man and woman in uniform. Beneath the image was written, *In camp . . . and overseas RED CROSS WORKERS serve our fighting forces.*

But the one she couldn't take her eyes off of was one that reminded her of the Statue of Liberty. It showed a woman dressed in white with a navy cape, holding the Red Cross flag aloft. Along the bottom of the poster was one word, *Join.*

"Hey, Grace, how are you doing?"

Grace turned to see Norma Fox. She broke into a smile at the sight of her. "Hello, Norma! What brings you here?"

"My fella's home on leave and he wanted to go dancing."

Grace laughed. "You've come to the right place."

"The band is very good tonight, isn't it?" Norma said.

"They are," Grace agreed. "How's work at the Cheever plant?"

"It's hard work. But I like it. And the pay is good."

"Glad to hear it. How's your sister Noreen getting on?"

"We had a letter from her the other day." Norma rolled her eyes. "She said she was born to do this."

"Really?" Grace said. This buoyed her. If Norma's sister could go abroad, why couldn't she?

They spoke for a few more seconds before something caught Norma's eye.

"I've got to go! He's waving me over," Norma said. "It was great seeing you, Grace."

"You too."

All evening, Grace served up Cokes and hot dogs and made small talk and laughed with the returning soldiers, and by the end of it, she'd made up her mind. If the Red Cross was looking for volunteers, she would be their girl. First thing in the morning, she was going to ask

Mrs. Wickson about volunteering to go overseas. This decision made her feel better than she had in a long time.

By the following morning, after a good night's sleep, Grace had changed her mind about seeking out Mrs. Wickson. She was too afraid the other woman would tip off her mother. As much as the other woman might be devoted to the Red Cross, she might consider it her duty to the local chapter's main benefactors to let them know what their daughter was up to.

So, she waited until she saw the chauffeur pulling out of the garage to take her father to his office. Assured that her mother was still sleeping, Grace dressed and ate breakfast quickly, washing it down with a cup of black coffee. She went out to the garage and pulled her keys off the board, wanting to leave before the chauffeur returned.

The drive up to Buffalo would take almost two hours. She'd been many times, but had never been the one doing the driving and hadn't really paid attention to the route. She checked to make sure the map was in her glove compartment. Gasoline could be a problem. It was rationed and even though she had a full tank, she wasn't sure if she had enough to get there and back. Rummaging around in the drawers of the small desk in the garage, she found the ration books and took one to have on hand in case of an emergency, stuffing it into her purse.

Before she left Lavender Bay, she posted her letter to John.

Although the day was overcast, it was dry, and she was thankful for that. She had no trouble on the highway but as soon as she got to downtown Buffalo, she got lost, and a drive that should have taken two hours ended up being three. It was almost lunchtime by the time she located the Red Cross offices, but only after stopping pedestrians twice for directions.

786 Delaware Avenue was the home of the local Red Cross. It was a Tudor revival building with leaded glass bay windows. Slowly, she pulled into the sweeping driveway and drove around the back, where she parked before walking back around to the front of the building and pushing through the heavy main door.

The place was abuzz. Men and women walked by, and there was the steady sound of typewriter keys clacking and phones ringing. She hesitated, her mouth dry and her hands damp. She tucked her purse in the crook of her arm and thought of turning around and going home. But then she reminded herself that she'd come this far and if she went home, she'd end up kicking herself.

She approached a reception desk. A middle-aged woman wearing a brown dress the same shade as her hair looked up at Grace and smiled. On her desk were three separate phones.

"Can I help you?" she asked.

"Yes, thank you. I'm looking for information about volunteering."

"Certainly." The other woman stood and said, "Follow me."

The woman's shoes clicked on the hardwood floors. Grace followed her, taking everything in. The walls of the corridor were lined with photographic portraits of serious-looking men. Through one open door, she spied a man in a suit and tie and a secretary taking dictation.

At the end of the corridor was a sign on a door that read *Director of Volunteer Services*.

The receptionist knocked and peeked her head around the door. "Enid? I have a young woman here who would like to volunteer."

All Grace heard was "Send her in."

"Mrs. Bixby will see you now." The woman held the door wide open for Grace to step in.

Grace looked over her shoulder as the door closed behind her. Her heart beat so fast she could feel it in her throat.

"Take a seat, please."

The woman behind the desk was in her mid-forties with auburn hair and a terrible underbite but sharp, intelligent eyes. She wore a navy dress with a white lace collar. It made her look older than her years.

Grace took a seat in the chair across from the desk and looked around. The space had more height than depth, with sixteen-foot ceilings. In front of the sharp-eyed woman were a black typewriter and rotary phone. Behind her was a credenza against a set of windows that looked out onto the parking lot. Grace could see her car from where she sat. She almost wished she were in it.

"Why don't you tell me your name first?" Mrs. Bixby said.

"Grace Gibson."

"Welcome, Grace." She jotted her name down on a steno pad in front of her. She looked up again and said, "So you would like to volunteer?"

"That's correct."

"How old are you, Grace?"

"Twenty-three." Grace braced herself for the blow-back that she was too young, but Mrs. Bixby only nodded. She leaned one elbow on the arm of her leather chair.

"Can you tell me a bit about yourself?"

"Sure," Grace replied. She maintained eye contact, remembering her father's advice to always look the other person straight in the eye. "Last May, I graduated from college with a degree in art history. I have a driver's license. I currently volunteer folding bandages for the

Red Cross, and I volunteer at the USO dances in my hometown."

"And where is that? Your hometown."

"Lavender Bay," Grace said, hoping Mrs. Bixby wouldn't make the connection to the Gibson name.

"I've never been there, but I've heard that it's a lovely little town."

Grace relaxed slightly. "It is."

"And you drove up here?"

"Yes."

"My, you are a determined young woman."

"I know I want to help," Grace said with conviction.

"And you shall!" Mrs. Bixby pulled out a large book and flipped through it. "We have canned good drives, food drives, scrap metal drives."

Grace winced. "Truthfully, I was looking for something a little more involved."

"We are recruiting stateside for the motor pool. You'd need your own car."

Grace shook her head. "I was hoping to go abroad. Like Europe or the Pacific. Where I could be of help."

Mrs. Bixby hesitated. "You don't have a nursing background?"

"No, I'm afraid not."

"You have to be made of pretty tough stuff to go to the war fronts." Worry clouded the other woman's features.

Grace sat a little straighter in her chair. She was not daunted.

"You're so young . . ." Mrs. Bixby's voice trailed off.

"I'm sure about this, Mrs. Bixby."

"We have women who run the clubmobiles. The soldiers call them donut dollies. But you have to be twenty-five."

Grace pressed her lips together, disappointed. There was nothing she could do about her age.

"There are rumors that they might lower the age . . . I'll tell you what." Mrs. Bixby tapped her fountain pen against the desk blotter. "I'll have you fill out an application anyway. And when they do lower the age, I'll contact you."

"Thank you!"

Mrs. Bixby located the paperwork and allowed Grace to fill it out right there. She carefully filled out the application and looked it over twice before sliding it across the desk.

"Like I said, when they lower the age limit, I'll be in touch by mail with instructions on what to do next." Mrs. Bixby stood again and escorted Grace out, her application in her hand. At the front door, she held out her hand and said, "Thank you for thinking of the Red Cross, Grace."

"Thank you!" Grace said, and she shook the woman's hand vigorously.

She drove home without getting lost, smiling all the way. As she drove, watching the countryside and Lake Erie on her right pass her by, she realized she could tell no one of her plans. She'd learned that lesson the hard way. She did not need her father calling Mrs. Bixby and screaming down the phone that he was a benefactor of the Red Cross, pulling the strings before she could even get her introductory letter. Anyway, at that moment, there was really nothing to tell. She wouldn't be twenty-five for another eighteen months. For all she knew, the war might be over by then.

The house was quiet when she arrived home. Her father was at work, and her mother had some philanthropy meeting that day. She ran up the stairs to freshen up for dinner, her head full of thoughts of going abroad to help out.

CHAPTER EIGHTEEN

Within weeks of writing John, Grace received another letter from him.

Dear Grace,

Your letter cheered me up to no end. You're a great gal. You're right when you say it's something to be gotten through. And (hopefully), it won't last forever.

I can certainly understand your disappointment in not being allowed by your parents to work at the aviation plant. Forgive me for playing devil's advocate, but I can also understand your father's interference. Isn't it the job of the parent to keep the child safe? And please don't think I think of you as a child. On the contrary. I'm speaking strictly in terms of the relationship, not age-wise or even intellect-wise. I know it's not what you want to hear, but I believe in honesty above all other things. Because if you haven't got honesty, what have you got? Nothing, I'd say. So don't be too harsh with your parents. Besides, it's ob-

vious that God has other plans for you. And the aviation plant isn't part of that.

I worry about my parents while I'm gone. Mother just got out of the hospital with some stomach ailment. And I'm sure Father was lost without her. We all would be. It's hard to be so far away when your parents are failing. It can be distressing at times.

It amazes me how the war changes people right there on the spot, and how everything here is distilled down to kill or be killed. It's something I wrestle with every day. I keep reminding myself that it is something that needs to be done. I'm hopeful that God will forgive me. Sometimes, I wish I were a Quaker instead of a Catholic. There'd be no blurred lines about killing. They might be onto something.

Looking forward to your next letter.

Yours in friendship,

John

Grace folded up the letter, held it against her heart, and sighed. He wrote great letters. His thoughts were so deep. After she read the letter again, she carefully tucked it back into its envelope and put it in the box under her bed. She'd write to him later that night.

1944

Grace had given up on ever hearing from Mrs. Bixby and the Red Cross about an overseas position. She'd even stopped intercepting the mail at home in case anything did arrive from the Buffalo Red Cross. But she continued to volunteer at home. Although she was busy with doing everything she possibly could, she was dissatisfied.

Three months into the new year, unrelenting rain heralded spring. It seemed as if everything was soaking wet. No umbrella seemed any match for the onslaught. Grace finally caved and bought herself a pair of galoshes to wear over her shoes. They looked ugly but they spared her shoes and kept her feet dry.

She arrived home early one afternoon after calling on John's parents. She'd become a weekly visitor, helping out with little tasks such as ironing or picking up groceries. John had been delighted, and she kept him abreast of their condition. They were anxious for their son to return home.

The house was quiet, no servants were about. Most likely back in the kitchen starting to make preparations for dinner. There was no need for lunch as she'd eaten plenty at John's parents' house. Her father was at work and her mother was out at a meeting at the hospital, on whose board she served. Before heading upstairs, Grace quickly sorted through the pile of mail on the table in the front hall. Her heart nearly burst when she saw the package addressed to her from the Buffalo chapter of the Red Cross. Forgetting the rest of the mail, she took the stairs two at a time to her bedroom, closing and locking the door behind her. She tore open the envelope, her hands shaking.

She scanned the letter, her mouth moving silently as she read the words. She was onto the next word before she'd even finished the previous one. In the end, she had to read it three times before she fully understood the context.

There it was in black and white. The invitation to be a non-medical volunteer overseas. Her hands continued to shake as she reread that sentence over and over again.

Enclosed was more paperwork to fill out. Plus, she would need a physical as well as three references. She bit her lip. How would she do all of that without her parents finding out? *Think, Grace, think*. She stared out the window, mulling it over. They would not take this away from her.

The physical had to be done by the Red Cross physician, which meant another trip back to Buffalo. She arranged to go on a day when her mother would be out all day so she wouldn't be missed, pilfering another ration coupon for gasoline.

She went back to her high school to ask two of her favorite teachers for references. She also asked them for their discretion, using the excuse that if she didn't get

the assignment, it would spare her public embarrass-
ment. They both readily agreed. Her final stop was Mrs.
Wickson, the director of the Lavender Bay Red Cross.

Mrs. Wickson was delighted to see Grace on her
doorstep.

"Come in, come in, Grace," she said, throwing open
her front door. "Can I offer you some tea?"

"That would be lovely," Grace said.

They sat in the front parlor of Mrs. Wickson's home.
It was wallpapered, and the fireplace held a small fire
that gave off cozy heat. Oval-framed photos of ancestors
graced the walls. Mrs. Wickson invited her to sit down
and took the rocker with the embroidered seat cushions
for herself.

Grace bent the truth slightly by explaining her need
for a reference to become a volunteer in Buffalo.

"Why not stay here?" Mrs. Wickson asked.

Grace had prepared for this question. "I have loved
helping out here, Mrs. Wickson. But there are more
opportunities for me to help in Buffalo."

"Of course, it's a bigger office," Mrs. Wickson said.
She didn't seem offended that Grace wanted to go farther afield. As they sipped their tea, she said, "I would
be honored to write a letter of reference."

Grace practically sagged in her chair with relief.
"Thank you. Can I ask one more favor?"

"Of course."

"Can you not say anything to my mother or father? Or anyone, for that matter? I want to surprise my parents."

"How lovely. I'm sure they'll be delighted that you're following in their philanthropic footsteps."

"Oh, it'll be quite a surprise all right," Grace said.

Mrs. Wickson said, "Leave this with me and I'll get it in the mail by tomorrow."

"I really appreciate your help, Mrs. Wickson."

"And I appreciate your effort, Grace."

CHAPTER NINETEEN

By mid-April, an official-looking letter from the national American Red Cross arrived, congratulating Grace on her willingness to volunteer. The letter was purely a formality, welcoming her to the Red Cross family. She was glad she'd intercepted it and hurriedly read it in the front hall before going to her room and hiding it in the box beneath her bed with John's letters.

She was to report first to the American University in Washington for training and then she'd be told where she was going in the world. Included in the letter were instructions and a list of supplies she could bring with her.

The problem was, she had to report for duty in four days' time. She couldn't leave it until the last moment to tell her parents. It was amazing that she'd been able to keep it secret for this long.

The following evening, Grace was gathered with her parents in the front parlor, as was their habit when they were all home. It was her mother's favorite room, decorated in various shades of yellow with heavy floral drapes hanging at the windows. Grace was parked on the yellow sofa, laying out cards for solitaire on the coffee table. Her father sat in one of the red-and-white floral plaid easy chairs, thumbing through the newspaper. Her mother sat at her escritoire behind the sofa, dealing with her correspondence.

Grace couldn't concentrate on the cards in front of her.

She'd miss Lavender Bay. But she was eager to get away, to be a part of something greater than herself. Sometimes she felt as if, being young and female, she was summarily dismissed. Not taken seriously. And she hated that feeling. She had just as much to offer as anyone.

Her father lowered his paper. "Grace, you've been staring at those cards for the last ten minutes."

She frowned. "Have I?"

"Yes, you have."

She blew out a breath. Best to get it over with and deal with the fallout. She half turned so she could include her mother in the conversation. Aleida lifted her gaze, her fountain pen held aloft between her fingers.

"Mother and Dad, I have some news," Grace started, her voice shaky.

She felt the stares of both parents as they waited, expectant.

"I've joined the Red Cross as a non-medical volunteer," she told them.

Her mother laughed, a light, silvery peal that always brought a smile to her father's face. As it did now.

"What do you mean, darling, you're already volunteering with the Red Cross. You're rolling bandages with me," her mother said.

Grace shook her head and repeated, "No, I've joined as a non-medical volunteer."

"You're not making any sense." Her mother's tone was one of exasperation.

Grace was acutely aware of her father's gaze resting upon her. It was wrong of her to expect her parents to divine from that one sentence what she was trying to get across. Or what it entailed.

Without looking at either one of them, choosing instead to stare at the forgotten card game laid out in front of her, she said, "I've joined the volunteers for the Red Cross. I'm to report to the American University in Washington for training, and then I'll be heading overseas."

"Now you're really not making any sense, Grace," her mother said angrily.

George remained mute but folded the paper neatly and set it aside.

"So, it's war you're going off to," he said quietly.

"Yes, Dad."

"And you did not include us when making this decision," he said.

"Of course not. You would either try to talk me out of it or worse, try to use your influence to stop it, like you did with the job at the Cheever plant."

"This is worse!" her mother declared. "Now you won't be in Lavender Bay at all."

Grace refrained from pointing out that it was her mother who'd pressured her father into preventing her from getting that job at Cheever Aviation.

"You don't know what you've gotten yourself into," her father said. His face remained impassive, and she had a hard time reading his emotions. Was he angry? Was he resigned? She couldn't tell.

Either way, she bridled at his comment. "Maybe I'm not worldly, but I'm not cavalier about what's going on. I realize I'm not going off to summer camp."

"I'm glad of that," her father said tightly.

"Oh, George, can't you do something?" her mother pleaded.

"One moment, Aleida," George said kindly to his wife. He looked at Grace again. "I can't believe that Mrs. Wickson orchestrated all of this on a national level."

"She didn't," Grace told him. "I went up to Buffalo myself and joined there."

"To keep Mrs. Wickson out of it," her father said.

"Yes, but I did get her to write me a reference letter," Grace admitted.

He leaned forward, his arms dangling over his knees, and sighed. "Grace, you are so impetuous I don't know what to do with you."

"That's easy, George, make some phone calls and put a stop to this nonsense at once," Aleida said sharply.

"That's what I think I will do, first thing in the morning," George said, in a tone that indicated the subject was closed.

Grace saw red. She was determined to have the last word. And her way. "Dad, if you do this, if you interfere *again*, I'll leave."

"Leave? What are you talking about? Goodness, Grace, sometimes you speak in riddles," her mother complained.

Without taking her eyes off her father, Grace elaborated. "Meaning, I'll leave. Run away. Whatever you want to call it. I have some savings, and this country is pretty big. I could go anywhere."

Behind her, her mother whimpered. Her father raised his eyebrows.

"I'm determined to do this, Dad," Grace continued, "and if you get in my way, I'll make sure you never see me again."

"What kind of talk is this?" her mother demanded. "I wouldn't have dared to speak like this to my mother or father. This generation of yours is really something else."

Over her shoulder, Grace snapped, "This generation of mine is off doing God-awful things to preserve your way of life."

She turned and met her father's steely gaze. "I'm doing this, whether you like it or not."

Finally, her father said, "All right, Grace."

Her mother's protests fell on deaf ears. Grace stood and said good night and left her parents alone. Although she felt as if she'd achieved some kind of victory, it had left her hollowed out.

CHAPTER TWENTY

Grace's father insisted on accompanying her to the train station the morning of her departure. She was relieved that he wasn't so angry that he'd let her go off by herself. Her mother had said her goodbyes the previous night, stating she'd be in no condition in the morning for a teary goodbye, and definitely not in public.

The days leading up to her departure had been tense. She had the sense that she'd somehow disappointed her father, which was a rare feeling. That feeling was par for the course with her mother but not with her father. Although her father had been indulgent with her as she was growing up, he also had laid down certain expectations in return. And somehow, Grace felt that she'd let him down.

She'd said her goodbyes to all the house staff, who hugged her and wished her well, some promising to pray for her. She'd even stopped at the McNamara house.

John's parents were upset at her leaving, Mr. McNamara saying that now they'd have two people to worry about. Her intention had never been to upset them or anyone. But she knew for certain that going through life trying to please people all the time was the fastest way to unhappiness.

On the morning of her departure, her stomach was in such knots that she didn't have much of an appetite for breakfast. She skipped her usual meal and opted for a cup of black tea and one piece of dry toast. It was all she could manage to get down.

Her father abandoned his habit of reading the newspapers that were laid out in front of him. Instead, he made small talk, informing Grace of news at the factory or of workers she knew personally. She half listened. When his conversation veered to the weather, she knew it was time to leave. Glancing at her wristwatch, she said, "I think we should go, Dad."

"Of course," he said, abandoning his breakfast and standing from the table.

Without another word, they walked to the front hall, where Grace's suitcase stood by the front door. The grandfather clock in the corner ticked away, the only sound. Upstairs, a door closed.

Her mother appeared on the landing, making her way downstairs in her matching silk nightgown and robe. Even devoid of makeup, her mother was a beautiful woman. The dark hair, the blue eyes, and the porcelain skin were only beginning to show the effects of age. George looked up at his wife, smiling.

"Mother!" Grace said, unable to hide her surprise. As her mother approached, she saw that her eyes were red from crying. "I didn't think you were coming down."

"I could hardly let you leave this morning without saying goodbye," her mother explained.

Grace nodded, surprised but oddly touched.

Her father cleared his throat. "We should get going, Grace, you don't want to miss your train."

"All right, Dad." She turned to her mother and said, "I'll write as soon as I—"

Her mother surprised her by throwing her arms around her and pulling her into a tight embrace.

Surprised, Grace squeaked out, "Oh."

Sniffling, her mother said, "Do take care of yourself, Grace. Be careful." When they pulled apart, her mother pulled a flower-embroidered handkerchief from the pocket of her robe and dabbed at her eyes and nose. "I thought I was lucky because I had no son to send off to war."

Choked up, Grace could only nod. With a smile, her mother kissed her on her forehead, reminding Grace of when she was a child and the affection had been more frequent. She had to get out of there before she lost her resolve.

She coughed and said, "All right, let's go."

Her father picked up her suitcase and followed her outside to the front of the house, where the chauffeur waited with the car. Grace did not look back. Did not want to see the figure of her mother in her nightgown and robe standing there. She lifted her head, keeping her gaze forward-facing as she left the only home she'd ever known.

They reached the train station to find passengers already boarding. Grace felt a momentary sense of panic, as if she needed more time to say goodbye. She looked around quickly.

"Say the word, Grace. I'll make one phone call and make all of this go away," her father said, breaking through her distraction.

She smiled at him. That would be so easy to do. To let him fix it, like he'd done so many times in the past. But she had to do this. It was important. She'd never be able to live with herself if she didn't see it through. And she also knew she'd lose her father's respect for shirking her commitment. It might have been an impulsive decision on her part, but she reminded herself that she wanted to help.

The whistle blew, signaling the boarding call.

"This is it," she said, pulling in a deep breath.

"So it is, Grace," he said quietly. He turned away, squinting, looking off in the distance. It was then that she realized that his eyes were full of tears.

Oh, Dad.

He turned back to her and cleared his throat, pulling out his handkerchief and wiping his nose. "If you need anything, money or anything, make sure you call me, and I'll wire it immediately."

She smiled. "Okay, Dad."

The conductor blew his whistle again for a second time and called out, "All aboard!"

"I better go," she said.

"Of course," he said. His eyes welled up. "It wasn't that long ago you were a little girl with a ridiculously big bow in your hair and a lollipop in your hand."

"I couldn't stay little forever," she said with a soft smile.

"More's the pity."

She watched people clamoring to get onto the train. "Goodbye, Dad." She threw her arms around her father and kissed his cheek. He kissed her forehead and said, "As much as I'd prefer you to stay at home with us, I respect your decision."

"Thanks, Dad, that means a lot to me."

Her father nodded, chin quivering, unable to speak.

Grace picked up her suitcase and stepped up onto the train, climbing the stairs and stopping to wave at her father, who remained on the platform. She found a seat by the window and twisted her body to wave at him. She kept waving as the train pulled out, slowly at first, then chugging along and gaining speed. Even after her father disappeared from view, Grace continued to look back at her hometown of Lavender Bay, not knowing when she'd return.

CHAPTER TWENTY-ONE

Grace would only be at the American University for a few weeks before she'd be sent to Camp Pickett with the other trainees for a couple of weeks for a better understanding of what her role would be.

Her plan had been to write a letter to her parents every day, but that soon became unrealistic with her schedule of training all day and collapsing in bed at night. There was so much training that she wondered if the war would be over before she even left the country. What little free time she had, she spent sightseeing with other girls around the capital. There was a frenetic buzz in the city, and she was unsure if this was how it always was or if it was war-induced. She suspected the latter. It was an exciting time to be there.

Finally, she found herself with the other trainees on a troop train to the West Coast. She sat with another girl in their Red Cross uniforms, which they were required to wear at all times in public. The train was packed with uniformed soldiers and at times, they were loud and rowdy. Grace found them endearing. She didn't blame them for blowing off steam. At night, some played cards, cigarettes tucked behind their ears, crumpled dollar bills thrown into the pool.

Her seatmate, a girl named Dorothy, fell asleep with her head against Grace's shoulder. Grace didn't want to sleep; she wanted to take everything in and not miss anything. As the train rumbled across the country, going through sleepy one-horse towns, she realized how truly big, physically, America was in size. It seemed to go on forever and ever.

The Red Cross was stringent in their requirements for their volunteers. Their purpose in going overseas was to provide recreation to the American soldiers, to take their mind off the war—Grace wondered if that were even possible—and most of all, to listen. Each girl had to be an exceptional conversationalist, not afraid to engage. You couldn't sit there like a bump on a log. The GIs deserved better than that.

Grace's assignment was in the Philippines. They'd been allowed to name three places they wanted to go, and the Philippines had been her second choice, after Europe but ahead of Australia.

Once they arrived in California, there would be a berth on a troop transport ship to Manila, where she'd be assigned an island. She had no idea what to expect.

Now that things were happening, all doubt and uncertainty had been swept away, replaced by excitement.

The night before her departure to Manila, she called her parents collect. She was three hours behind, timewise, but she managed to catch them both home in the evening. They were delighted to hear from her. She let them know that she wasn't sure when she'd be near a telephone again to phone them. That she'd write when she could but most of all, not to worry when they didn't hear from her.

They didn't talk long as Grace was aware of the line behind her of other volunteers waiting to use the phone. She wasn't the only one with a concerned family.

The crossing of the Pacific took seventeen days. Other girls complained of the boredom on the crossing, and some vomited into buckets as they crossed the rough waters, including her roommate, which left their cabin smelling sour. Grace was neither bored nor sick. She'd brought a couple of books to read and a few times a day, weather permitting, she went for long, brisk walks around the deck. They were sharing the ship with troops, but the Red Cross workers kept to themselves. There was easy chat and conversation if you happened to run into someone, and Grace knew of one or two girls who'd taken "entertaining the troops" to a whole new level. Apparently, those bad apples had not been weeded out in the initial interviews. Grace supposed it was like that in every walk of life.

She had assumed that the weather would be similar to a summer in Lavender Bay. She had not been prepared for the wet heat of the tropics. It was so foreign, so unlike her hometown that sometimes she could only stare, trying to take it all in. She'd break out in a sweat simply standing there, rivulets rolling down the middle of her back, and no amount of deodorant or talcum powder could help her underarm situation. Whenever she felt irritated or annoyed, she reminded herself that this wasn't a cotillion, that these were war conditions and she'd better make the best of it. She found herself constantly giving herself a kick in the backside to toughen up.

The Philippines were made up of a lot of islands and she'd been assigned to a remote one, landing there to find a small island with a large Army base. This was it. Finally. She'd been assigned along with one other girl, who was five foot eleven to Grace's five two. Her name was Bernadette Powers, but she insisted Grace call her Bernie. She was tall and lanky with sharp brown eyes, a long nose, clear skin, and dark brown hair that curled just below her ears and which she wore swept back on each side with tortoiseshell combs. Within five minutes of meeting her, Grace liked her. Originally from Kansas, the daughter of farmers, Bernie had a degree in agricultural science and a no-nonsense air about her. She talked about everything and anything. Bernie was twenty-seven and had a boyfriend who was currently fighting in Europe.

"I thought I might as well go off and do something since he's gone," Bernie explained, "And so here I am. He was furious when he found out I'd volunteered." It was the only time Bernie's smile wavered. "But I told him I know my own mind and if he was going to start bossing me around, I would call it quits."

Grace was enthralled with her.

"Do you have a sweetheart back home?" Bernie asked.

Grace shook her head. "No one special."

"Where you from?"

"Lavender Bay, New York."

"Lavender Bay? Never heard of it. What's going on there, lavender farms?"

"Actually, no," Grace said. "Lake Erie and lots of grapes."

"Grapes, did you say?"

"Yes."

"Well, I like grapes just as much as the next guy."

And that's how it was with Bernie. The conversation was easy and it flowed.

They had landed mid-morning under a cloudless blue sky and a blazing sun. The Red Cross club on their island was not up and running yet, and the two of them stood there, sweating, suitcases at their feet, dust covering their shoes, waiting for further direction from their Red Cross director. Grace was glad she'd brought down an old, battered suitcase of her father's from the attic instead of her newer, more expensive one. Her goal was to blend in, not stand out. It was a large compound and there were tents everywhere. Grace recognized the medical tents as they were white and had a big red cross on the sides and the top. She could hear the raucous laughter of men and glimpsed a few crossing the site, dressed in the now-familiar Army green.

A man in a Red Cross uniform approached them, his stride quick, and in his journey over to them, he pushed his glasses up on his nose three times.

"Grace Gibson and Bernadette Powers?" He looked at Bernie first then Grace.

Grace extended her hand. "I'm Grace Gibson."

Bernie shook his hand vigorously. "Call me Bernie."

"I'm your director. Ralph De Smet. You need anything, you come to me. You need supplies, you come to me. Any problems or issues, you come to me. You're not to bother the commanders here. I'm your boss."

"Got it, you're the boss," Bernie repeated, her hands on her hips.

"You've been told there's no going home. You're committed. So, if your mother or father gets sick back home, tough luck," he said.

Bernie nodded. "Got it. No crybabies or whiners."

He looked from one to the other and, satisfied, said, "Come on, I'll show you to your quarters."

"That would be great," Bernie said. "The heat here is like a Kansas summer. Whew!"

They picked up their suitcases and followed him.

"What's that building over there?" Grace asked, pointing to a white clapboard structure.

"That's the officers' club," Ralph answered. "You're to stay clear of there, understood? As Red Cross volunteers, you're here to boost the morale of the soldiers, not fraternize with the officers." Grace nodded in agreement.

"Got it," Bernie said. "No fraternizing with the officers."

Their accommodation was separate from the troops' quarters. They were housed next to the other females on site, namely the Army nurses, in a small hut with a flimsy bamboo door. The roof was layered with palm fronds. There was one window with a pair of uneven plain wooden shutters.

Ralph opened the door and said over his shoulder, "There's a latch on the inside. Make sure it's secure at night."

"Would men come into our hut?" Grace asked, worried.

He shook his head. "Not the men, but the monkeys might. And some of the larger predators."

Grace shuddered and Bernie said nothing, just arched an eyebrow.

Inside were four Army cots lined up against the far wall, with a small table between the middle two. In the corner was a single beat-up looking bureau. The floor was covered in sand.

"Make sure you use those mosquito nets on the cots," Ralph advised. "Or you'll be eaten alive."

"That's a cheery thought. Well, it isn't the Ritz, but it'll do," Bernie announced. Looking at the cots, she asked, "Are we expecting more volunteers?"

"Yes," Ralph said.

To which Bernie replied, "The more the merrier, that's what I always say."

"Set your suitcases down and follow me. I'll show you where the latrines are."

As they walked away, Ralph said, "The showers are segregated by gender for obvious reasons."

"Obviously," Bernie repeated.

The latrines consisted of two outhouse toilets behind hastily constructed wooden boards. The "shower" was a different story altogether. It was an open area surrounded by a tall wooden fence that allowed for privacy. Grace had never showered outdoors before.

"Um, I hate to ask, but where are the faucets?" Bernie said.

Grace looked around. She was right. There were no faucets or showerheads.

"Like you said," Ralph responded, "this isn't the Ritz. We're roughing it out here. You'll bring your helmet to the water pass in the morning, fill it up, and you'll use that to shower."

"Can I get two helmets' worth?" Bernie asked. "Because I'm so tall. More surface area to cover."

Grace clamped her lips together to stifle a laugh.

"No, one helmet," Ralph said tightly.

"Righty-o."

"All right, you saw the club on the way in?" he asked, and without waiting for a reply, he said, "Return to your hut and meet me there in thirty minutes."

Grace and Bernie nodded and headed back to their accommodation, such as it was.

They left the door open, and Grace stood in the middle of the small room, unsure of what to do next.

"Which bed do you want?" Bernie asked. "It doesn't matter to me."

"Me neither," Grace replied. The four cots were identical. "I can take that one." She pointed to the one away from the window.

"That's great." Bernie picked up her suitcase and tossed it on another cot, unlocking the two snaps with a click and opening it. Grace did the same.

"Grace, would you mind if I took the top drawers?" Bernie asked. "I'd have to come down from the heights to open these bottom ones."

"Of course not," Grace said. Once Bernie put her sparse belongings into the top drawer, Grace did the same with the bottom drawers. Like Bernie, she hadn't brought much. Only her Red Cross uniforms and her unmentionables.

"You know, I'm almost sorry I didn't pick Europe," Bernie said. "Somehow, I feel the accommodations might be better."

But Grace was glad that Bernie Powers was in the Philippines with her.

It took them less than ten minutes to unpack, put their belongings away, and slide their empty suitcases underneath their cots.

"Well, no sense in hanging around here. Might as well make our way to the club and get started," Bernie suggested. "What do you say?"

Grace nodded. "Let's go."

They stood outside the designated building and stared at it for a moment. Like everything else, it appeared to have been thrown together hastily. A hand-painted sign hung high across the wall: *The Red Cross Club.*

Ralph was prompt. He showed them the kitchen, where they were supposed to make snacks. Crates of Coca-Cola lined one wall.

Bernie looked around. "What about ice?"

Ralph looked at her and sighed.

Bernie nodded. "Got it. No ice. Warm Cokes for everyone."

Ralph told them there were thousands of soldiers stationed on that particular island.

"But there's only two of us, so I guess dancing is out," Bernie said with a sigh. "That's a shame. I'm a mean jitterbugger."

"On to other business," Ralph said. "We'll be getting another volunteer within the week. She's coming in on the next troop ship."

"Just one?" Bernie quizzed.

"Is there a problem?"

"No. It's just that three isn't a good number."

"Only one," Ralph said, leveling his gaze at her.

"We'll make it work."

"I appreciate that, Powers," Ralph said sarcastically.

"No problem, sir," Bernie said seriously. "Call me Bernie."

Bernie planted her hands on her hips, which Grace would soon learn was her signature pose. If she'd had long sleeves, they'd probably be rolled up. "Talk about 'from the ground up.' Ha! I guess we better get to work."

They spent the morning sweeping debris and sand out of the space designated for them. Being from a lakeside town, Grace was used to sand, and she knew they'd need to sweep every day, that it would always end up back inside, either blown in or dragged in on the bottom of people's shoes. To Grace, the club was nothing more than a glorified hut. Their director managed to procure some tables, chairs, and equipment, and several GIs volunteered to bring things over.

Grace stepped outside and was startled to see a crowd had gathered. There had to be about fifty GIs standing there, most of them bare-chested and tanned with dog tags hanging around their necks.

She craned her neck through the door and said, "We've got company, Bernie."

Bernie came out and stood next to Grace. She'd expected the crowd to approach them, but they remained where they were, staring at the two women.

"Howdy," Bernie said with a wave of her hand. "I'm Bernie Powers from Kansas and this is Grace Gibson from New York."

Some nodded, but most said nothing.

"As I understand it, this is the first Red Cross club on this island. Is that correct?" she continued.

Some nodded.

"We're here to provide recreation."

This resulted in a snicker rolling through the crowd. Bernie rolled her eyes. "*Not* that kind of recreation."

Some twitters of laughter.

Bernie whispered to Grace, "We've got our work cut out for us here." She turned to face the men and said, "Let's establish some ground rules."

There was some huffing, and a few crossed their arms over their chests.

"First, try not to talk all at once. I can't get a word in edgewise with all the talking."

There was laughter and their stances visibly relaxed.

"That's better. Now tell me something about yourself," Bernie instructed. Even Grace looked at her in awe. The tall woman from Kansas was a natural.

A boy from Oklahoma with white-blond hair said to Bernie, "I've never seen a woman as tall as you."

"Then this is your lucky day!" Bernie replied good-naturedly.

"You girls look like Mutt and Jeff," said one soldier, pointing out their height difference.

Bernie put her hands on her hips and said smartly, "You don't say. I hadn't noticed that Grace was so much taller than me. Thanks for pointing that out."

This brought out a ripple of spontaneous laughter. Grace could see that Bernie was going to be a big hit with the guys. She was like an older sister who could easily handle them.

Looking around, she said, "Who's up for a game of poker?"

Many stepped forward and Bernie said, "It looks like we have enough for a tournament. Come on in and make yourselves at home. Grace, put on the phonograph. Let's have some music!"

CHAPTER TWENTY-TWO

The promised third volunteer did not arrive the following week or the week after that. Despite this, Grace and Bernie got on with things. They got the club up and running, and the men seemed to enjoy the books, magazines, board games and cards provided by the Red Cross. Some of the guys managed to make a large enough table for Ping-Pong, and somehow, Ralph managed to secure some balls and paddles. It wasn't long before they started holding regular tournaments, and much to the delight of the soldiers, Grace became quite adept. There was always an album playing on the phonograph, giving the place a festive air.

There were a few guys in particular who were always eager to help out, like Ziggy Stormont, a dock worker from Philadelphia. Like all the other GIs, he was tanned from all the sun exposure, and his blond hair had been bleached almost white by the sun. He had dark eyes and

was always willing to help if they had to move something heavy.

Then there was Tim Cholanewski, or Timid Tim, as
everyone called him, from Chicago. He had the height
and sturdiness of a linebacker, but when he wasn't
with Ziggy, he usually had his head buried in a book.
He quickly went through all the titles at the club and
while they waited for Ralph to get more, Grace lent
him the three she'd brought with her from home.

Grace couldn't figure out if it they hung around
because they were nice, because they were looking for
something to do, or because they simply wanted to
be near some American girls. She and Bernie were
careful not to send out any misleading signals, but
they always made an effort to look nice, doing their
hair as best as they could given the heat and humidity,
and never leaving their hut without applying some
lipstick.

She soon learned that Bernie loved a good practical
joke. One of her favorites was to direct newly arrived
GIs to sit on a particular chair, on which she'd placed
a whoopee cushion. As soon as the soldier sat on it
and the sound of farting filled the room, Bernie would
shake her head and say, "Those rations are something
else, aren't they?"

One day, Bernie and Grace were standing outside, and
Bernie looked up at a tree as Ziggy and Timid Tim

approached the clubhouse, using her hand to shield her eyes.

Ziggy followed her line of sight. "What's going on?"

"I'm trying to figure out what kind of bird that is," Bernie said. "I've never seen anything like it."

"Where?" Ziggy asked. Both he and Timid Tim looked up toward the top of the coconut tree.

"I don't see anything," Ziggy said.

"Here, try these." Bernie handed him a pair of binoculars. Behind his back, she winked at Grace, who wondered what she was up to.

Ziggy adjusted the binoculars and scanned the top of the tree with them. "I still don't see anything."

"Let me have them," Timid Tim said.

Ziggy handed the binoculars to him and stood there, hands on his hips, looking up at the tree. Timid Tim looked through the binoculars and said, "Are you sure your eyes weren't playing tricks on you, Bernie?"

He turned to hand the binoculars back to her, and his eyes were ringed with black where the eyepiece had been pressed against his face.

"What the heck?" Ziggy said when he spotted Timid Tim's eyes. He spun around and faced Bernie, who was bent over laughing. His own eyes were also ringed with black.

Grace covered her mouth to stop herself from laughing, but she couldn't.

They were up early every morning, and they worked all day until dark, keeping the club open for whoever wanted to stop by. It was decided that Grace would write out a calendar of events for each week and post it on the outside wall as Bernie had declared that her own handwriting was illegible, a complaint from her boyfriend and her parents back home.

Grace was dedicated to her letter writing. She wrote to her parents regularly, receiving responses from both her mother and her father. Her mother wrote beautiful letters, telling her which flowers were in bloom and where the trees were in their growth cycle. Grace hadn't known her mother even cared about such things. She also relayed all the latest Lavender Bay gossip and what was happening at the country club. Her father talked about all the goings-on at the plant, musing about possibly changing the design of the label after the war. He signed every letter *Love, Dad*.

One day a few weeks in, a letter arrived from John.

Dear Grace,

I was shocked to hear that you had joined the Red Cross and were coming overseas. We're practically in the same neighborhood, although I doubt we'll ever meet. You've said in your letters how impotent you felt, that you wanted to do more. And here you are.

I wish you weren't here, to be honest. I'll worry about you. But I understand you must do what you need to do. Still, I will continue to think of you in Lavender Bay, far removed from all of this mess, and not out here near the fighting. In fact, I can't even imagine it. If you don't mind, I'll remember you as I last saw you: at the train station, or sitting across from me at the pavilion.

My parents will certainly miss you. They've grown quite fond of you. I can't tell you how much I appreciate all you've done for them. It gave me great comfort to know someone was looking after them.

Please mind yourself, Grace, and be careful.
Yours in friendship and affection,
John

Grace raised her eyebrows and smiled that he'd added the word *affection* to his sign-off. She looked forward to his letters more than anything. She liked that he was a deep thinker, and she knew he wrestled with his conscience at times. Funny how when she'd met him, she'd no romantic notions about him. But now her thoughts drifted in that direction. They were certainly on the same wavelength. And although he was Catholic and she was Episcopalian, she wouldn't let religion stand in her way. After all, weren't they both Christian?

Grace hadn't been on the island for a month when a large crate arrived for her. She immediately recognized the return address as coming from her father's factory. She groaned.

"What do we have here?" Bernie asked as the two of them pried off the top of the crate. Packed carefully were hundreds of jam jars. Gibson's Grape Jelly. Grace reddened. She knew her father meant well, but she wished he hadn't done this. No one here on the island knew of her privileged status in life and she wanted it kept that way. She liked being one of them. It was a novel experience for her.

"Grape jelly," Bernie said, turning a jar around in her hands. "This will be a real treat for the fellas." She examined the jar, narrowing her eyes. "Now this is interesting, it's Gibson's Grape Jelly from Lavender Bay." She looked pointedly at Grace and with a smirk said, "What a coincidence."

Grace opened her mouth and closed it quickly.

Bernie lowered her voice. "Is there anything you want to tell me?"

"It's my father's company," Grace finally admitted. She might as well pack her bags and go home.

"Holy smokes, kid, you never said!"

"I didn't want to be treated differently," Grace explained.

"You mean like an heiress?" Bernie asked.

"Exactly."

"You fooled me," Bernie said.

"You won't tell anyone, will you? I'd like to keep this between us," Grace implored her.

Bernie made the motion of zipping her lip and tossing away the key. "Mum's the word. Your secret is safe with me."

"Thank you, Bernie," Grace said. She wanted things to go on as they were.

"Come on, let's bring these to Chef," Bernie said. "As for me, I love a good peanut butter and jelly sandwich."

Bernie removed the lid of the crate, where the return address was stamped in black. She handed it to Grace. "Go put this in our hut. Hide the evidence."

"Okay, thanks." Grace eyed the crate, which would be too heavy to carry. "How are we going to get that to the mess?"

"We're not. I'll round up some fellas to carry it over for us."

"Thanks, Bernie, you're a gem."

"Hey, if I'd known you were an heiress, I would have buttered you up more," she teased.

The truth was, Bernie couldn't have been any nicer to her. It was just Bernie's way.

Grace tore apart the top of the crate and piled it with the rest of the debris waiting to be burned. Bernie managed to find two guys to carry the crate to the mess, handing each one their own personal jar of Gibson's Grape Jelly, which they stuffed into their pockets.

Later that afternoon, Ziggy and Timid Tim approached Grace and Bernie as they set up tables for the daily poker game. Bernie was a fan of cards and gambling and had lamented more than once the lack of horse racing, as she loved betting on the ponies.

"What can we do for you, fellas?" Bernie asked, pulling a couple of chairs up to the table.

Ziggy held up a jar of grape jelly.

Grace's shoulders sagged. The gig was up.

The private looked at Grace. "We've put two and two together and come up with four."

Before Grace could answer, Bernie said, "Is that so? In some parts of the world, two plus two is really two plus three and that equals five."

If she wasn't so nervous, Grace would have burst out laughing.

"Grace, are you related to this?" Ziggy asked, holding the jar aloft.

"Don't be ridiculous," Bernie said. "Does she look like she's related to a jam jar?"

He ignored her. "You're Grace Gibson from Lavender Bay, New York, and this is Gibson's Grape Jelly from the same town."

"Gibson is a very common name in Lavender Bay. It's their version of Smith," Bernie said.

Ziggy and Timid Tim looked at Grace.

With a sigh, she said, "It's all right, Bernie. Yes, I'm the daughter of the founder."

"I knew it!" said Ziggy. He turned to Timid Tim. "You owe me five dollars."

"What are you doing here, Grace?" Timid Tim asked.

Grace shrugged. "The same as you. I wanted to help out."

"We *have* to be here. You don't," Ziggy said.

"But I want to be here."

He shook his head, but he was smiling. "We've got to get back."

As they walked away, Ziggy looked over his shoulder and with a smile, he said to Grace, "Tell your dad I said thanks for the jelly!"

"I will."

When they were out of earshot, Bernie said, "I knew they'd be okay with it."

Grace hoped so.

It wasn't long before the guys gave Grace the nickname of "Grace Jelly," which she took in the good humor with which it was intended.

Finally, the long-promised third volunteer arrived, to which Bernie joked, "Great. Now I can put my feet up."

Charlotte Arnold was taller than Grace but not as tall as Bernie. She was twenty-five, and her hair was the color of wheat and looked like silk. Her eyes were the palest blue. To say she was striking was an understatement. She'd graduated from college with a degree in education.

Bernie and Grace showed Charlotte around the place, pointing out the various buildings, like the barracks, the mess hall, the storage facilities, and more importantly, the latrines and the showers, and Bernie filled her in on the allowance of one helmet of water every morning to wash up.

"I bet there are decent bathrooms in there," Charlotte said as the girls pointed out the officer's club.

"Don't even think about it," Bernie replied. "That's off-limits to us."

Charlotte frowned. "Why?"

"Because that's the way it is. We're here for the enlisted men," Bernie reminded her.

"We'll see," Charlotte sniffed.

Bernie's eyes widened. "We'll see nothing. Or you'll be on a transport ship so fast your head will spin."

The newly arrived volunteer responded with a careless toss of her head. "Maybe."

"Anyway," Grace cut in, "this is what we do here at the club." She listed all the activities.

"What about dancing?" Charlotte asked.

Bernie shook her head. "Impossible. There's only three of us and there are thousands of them. It would take us the rest of the war to dance with them all."

Grace burst out laughing but Charlotte did not. When Charlotte wasn't looking, Bernie raised her eyebrows.

Charlotte chose the cot on the other side of Grace. They gave her one of the drawers in the bureau, and Bernie declared that the fourth drawer would have to be shared by all.

There was no denying that Charlotte had some good ideas for the Red Cross club. Grace and Bernie readily agreed to her suggestion that they do a talent show, a song and dance revue. She managed to snag a couple of soldiers for the male parts; all were happy to comply to be near Charlotte. She had star power, Grace thought.

One evening, Grace returned to their hut early. She'd had a long day, having been scared by a snake that fell out of a tree in front of her. It had left her shaken for the rest of the day, hypervigilant of her surroundings. Bernie opened the door to find Grace sitting on her cot with her back against the wall, shoes off and legs stretched out in front of her. She was rereading John's letters. She looked up at Bernie as she entered. Her friend looked rattled.

"What's wrong?" Grace asked.

Hooking a thumb over her shoulder, Bernie said, "Charlotte. Just caught her and a private in a clinch beneath a coconut tree."

"Oh."

Fraternizing with the troops was frowned upon. But it happened. Grace supposed it couldn't be helped. With the intensity of the war all around them, it wouldn't be hard to fall in love.

"I saw that GI from Baton Rouge pestering you earlier," Bernie said.

"He is a little relentless, but I can handle him," Grace said confidently.

"Be careful."

"I will. I'm here to do a job, not look for romance. Maybe it was inevitable with Charlotte." The fellas had christened Charlotte "Legs," and she loved her new nickname.

"It will lead to nothing but heartache," Bernie said wisely.

"Do you ever get the impression she's here to look for a husband?"

"Every day." Bernie sighed. "I knew three would be a bad number."

"We'll keep an eye on her," Grace said. "We'll set the example."

Bernie gave her a skeptical look. "We're already setting the example. These guys are love-starved. Even I look like Miss America to them. It could easily go to your head that you're desirable but let me tell you, one week back in Kansas and you're back to being invisible."

"Does Ralph know how she behaves?" Grace asked. She didn't want Charlotte undermining their efforts there with her romantic flings. Ralph was always going on about the rules and regulations and what they could and could not do. It was as if he had the Red Cross policies stamped on his soul. On the other hand, whatever they requested, he went out of his way to get for them. They didn't ask how he came across Ping-Pong paddles and balls and other things, but he took his job seriously when it came to providing recreation for the troops.

CHAPTER TWENTY-THREE

Grace stood outside under the eaves of the club-house, leaning against the wooden rail, drinking warm Coke and talking to Ziggy and Timid Tim and some other fellas. She wore her usual Red Cross uniform with ankle socks and sensible shoes, which had become dull from all the exposure to the sand, and her legs had tanned to a lovely shade of caramel. With the small group of soldiers gathered around her, she felt like she was holding court. She must remember to ask Ralph if he could get her a new tube of lipstick. Her current one was at the end, and she had to use her pinky finger that morning to dab some on.

"What you gals are doing is swell," said Robert "Buster" Baines. "It means a lot to us to see someone from back home."

"We're happy to help," Grace said truthfully.

"Aw, Buster, are you going sweet on Grace Jelly?" Tony Colangelo asked.

Buster took it in his stride. "Of course not. Grace knows I've got a girl back home."

"Tell me about her," Grace encouraged.

"Yeah, Buster, tell us about her," teased Ziggy, his voice unnaturally high. Next to him, Tony clasped his hands beneath his chin and batted his eyelashes. Tim started laughing.

"Aw, shut up, guys," Buster said. To Grace, he said, "Would you like to see a picture of her?"

Grace nodded. "I would."

Buster drew out his wallet from his back pocket, opened it, and pulled out a small photo of his girl, handing it to Grace.

The photo showed a girl a little bit younger than Grace, with dark hair, bright eyes, and a clear complexion. "She's lovely," Grace said truthfully, handing the photo back to Buster.

"That's Sarah," he said. Carefully, he tucked the photo back into his wallet and returned it to his back pocket. "She works at the bank back home. She's a great letter writer. Keeps me going, you know?"

Grace nodded. "That's wonderful." She looked to the other three. "What about the rest of you? Anyone waiting for you back home?"

"Do my mother and father count?" Timid Tim asked. "Or my dog, Sam?"

"Of course!"

"I'm free and easy," Ziggy said proudly, adding, "No ball and chain for me."

"You just haven't found the right one yet," Buster said wisely.

"They made me, they broke the mold," Ziggy said.

"What about you, Tony?" Grace asked.

Tony was about to answer when they heard the low buzz of approaching planes. All four of them looked up to the cerulean sky. Grace used her hand to shield her eyes from the bright sun.

As the squadron of planes came into view, Tony frowned and asked, "Are those ours?"

"Dunno," Buster replied.

As the planes came closer, they saw the big red sun painted on their sides.

"Shit," Ziggy said. "Those damn Japs."

Timid Tim and Tony launched off the step they were sitting on.

They all waited, frozen, until their inertia was broken by the sound of the alarm going off throughout the base. Without so much as a goodbye, the four guys took off, and more men streamed out of the club and took off in the general direction of the base.

Bernie brought up the rear, standing in the doorway, hands on her hips. "What's going on?"

"Japanese planes. I'm not sure if they're bombers or reconnaissance," Grace told her.

"Terrific."

"Will they bomb us?" Grace asked, swallowing hard.

"Being the enemy, I'd say chances are high."

"But they're not supposed to bomb the tents with the red cross on the roofs, right?" Grace asked.

"Somehow, I don't think they'd give a hoot about a red cross on a roof," Bernie said.

The planes passed over without incident, but the rest of the day was subdued, and the club was quiet. There were a few GIs in and out, but no one was in the mood for games.

It was as if they were all waiting around for something to happen. Almost willing it to happen so it would be over with.

Despite the looming anxiety, Grace fell asleep that night as soon as her head hit the pillow, only to be awakened soon after by a strong whistling sound followed by a thud and then the unmistakable sound of an explosion.

Bernie woke with such a fright she rolled off her cot. From the floor, she asked, "Was that what I think it was?"

Charlotte sat bolt upright. "What was that?"

The alarm sounded throughout the base, a high-pitched, keening wail that made Grace want to cover her ears.

"Bomb." She scrambled to her feet and raced to the door. This was followed by a second explosion. She opened the door and looked out. Aircraft formed a silhouette against the moonlit sky, bombers dropping their loads. Bombs fell, looking light as feathers as they headed toward their targets. Bernie and Charlotte flanked her in the doorway as they all peered out.

The base was a beehive of activity, though in darkness so as not to draw any attention. They could hear the shouts of the troops and the rhythmic *clackety-clack* of the anti-aircraft guns.

"Come on, let's get dressed," Bernie suggested. "We'll go to the hospital and see if they need any help."

"What could we do? We're not nurses," Charlotte wailed.

Bernie pulled on her uniform. "I know that. But there might be something we could do. What's the alternative? Stay here and wait for a bomb to drop on our heads?"

Grace agreed with Bernie, and followed suit, getting dressed quickly and running a brush through her hair.

Charlotte hesitated but began to dress.

They left the flashlight behind, knowing they couldn't draw attention to themselves. Quickly, they ran to the hospital tent. The bomber planes drowned out the usual sounds of the jungle around them, sounds they'd gotten used to. But Grace could hear the screeches and shrieks of the monkeys as they raced to find cover. *Poor things*. She followed the tall, lumbering form of Bernie ahead of her in the darkness. Her friend charged forward, determined to get to the hospital tent in one piece. Grace kept her eyes out for any snakes falling out of trees or slithering across their path. She could handle the monkeys, who were mischievous and curious, but she'd never get used to the snakes.

The hospital tent, usually quiet at night, was a hive of activity. One stretcher after another was brought in. Grace looked around, her mouth hanging open. She didn't know where to look first. Next to her, Charlotte had gone white. In her usual manner, Bernie charged forward, approaching one of the nurses. "What can we do?"

The nurse didn't even look at Bernie as a stretcher passed by being carried by two GIs. The patient appeared unconscious. The nurse took one look at him and told the two GIs, "Group one, over there." She turned to Bernie. "What is it?"

"Can we help?" Bernie persisted.

"I don't know. Make yourself useful," the nurse said, and disappeared.

Bernie looked at Grace and shrugged. "Make ourselves useful."

The floor was covered with litters of wounded soldiers.

"Can someone hold this?" yelled a nurse, holding up a glass bottle of intravenous fluid.

"That's me," Bernie said, and she went off to take the bottle from the nurse's hand.

"Thanks, Bernie," said the nurse. "Just hold it up until we can find a stand." Her voice was grave. "They're all being used right now."

"Don't worry, I can hold it all night if you need me to."

"You're a gem, Bernie." And she was gone.

Grace was frozen to the spot, looking in all directions and trying to make sense of what she was seeing as one stretcher after another was carried in, holding a bloodied soldier. It was endless. And although she wanted to help, she didn't know where to start. She swallowed hard.

Bombs continued to whistle through the air. There were several close calls, causing the ground beneath the hospital tent to shake and the lights powered by the generators to flicker on and off. Grace almost lost her footing. She made her way carefully through the stretchers of wounded soldiers, placing a reassuring hand on every shoulder she passed but unable to speak. How could she tell them everything was going to be all right when she wasn't sure that it would be?

"Grace Jelly," someone called out.

She turned her head and saw Buster on a stretcher on the floor. Both his hands were covered in blood-soaked gauze. She stared for a moment. Quickly, she approached him and said, "Buster, what happened?" She realized as soon as the question was out of her mouth that it was a stupid one. A bomb, of course.

"Wrong place at the wrong time." He attempted a smile but winced in pain instead.

Grace knelt on the floor beside him. She looked at his bandaged hands, trying to process what she was seeing. There were his wrists . . . but that's where they seemed to end. With a Herculean effort, she forced herself to look away from the bandaged, bloody mess and laid her hand gently on his shoulder. "What can I do?"

"Nothing. I'm waiting my turn to be seen by the doc." He gasped in pain. Her gaze swept around the room, and she recognized many GIs who frequented the Red Cross club. She swallowed hard and tried to keep from trembling.

"Grace Jelly, do you have a cigarette?" he asked.

"I don't, but I'll get you one," she said. She made to stand up.

Buster shook his head. "Don't go, Grace. Stay."

"All right."

"It's nice to see a friendly face."

Grace nodded.

"What am I going to do without my hands?"

She had no answer for that. She didn't know what to say to him. Before she could formulate a response, two GIs came and took Buster away.

"Good luck, Buster," she called out after him.

On the other side of the tent, Bernie continued to hold the glass bottle that dripped into the arm of a soldier. She shifted from time to time and put her hand to her back. But she never complained.

Charlotte ran from one medical person to another, delivering supplies. She appeared to be on automatic, her gaze blank, and Grace wondered if she'd even remember it.

"Miss, miss," said a voice behind her.

On the stretcher was a soldier who looked about sixteen years old. His torso was wrapped in bandages. "Can I get some water?" he asked.

"Let me see what I can do," Grace said.

She intercepted a nurse and asked for some water.

"Who's it for?" the nurse asked, pausing only briefly.

Grace pointed to the soldier.

The nurse shook her head. "I'm sorry but no. That whole group are going into surgery. Eventually. You can't give them anything. See the sign on the back of the tent? NPO?"

Grace nodded.

"It means nothing by mouth. For all of them."

Grace looked at the numbers—the rows and rows of stretchers holding wounded soldiers—and blinked rapidly, her mouth going dry. The nurse was gone, and Grace made her way through all the stretchers as if in a daze, trying to offer words of comfort, sometimes holding a hand and giving a reassuring word.

By first light, the bombing had stopped, and they were left to tend to the wounded and clean up. Mouths parched and eyes burning from exhaustion, the three Red Cross volunteers continued to help out wherever they could. They did whatever was asked of them. They ran errands, collecting supplies and running them from one tent to another. They cleaned up, picking up bloody bandages and uniforms that had been cut off and tossed to the floor to be burned outside. Three soldiers who were waiting for surgery had died while Grace knelt beside them, helpless.

They kept going, not once complaining, trying to help.

At the end of it, by noon, when things had settled down, they stood there, looking at the dead shrouded in black body bags in one of the tents.

Grace thought she was out of place. What could she really do in times like this? She wasn't trained for this. This was so much more than playing cards or serving Cokes or asking soldiers about their girls back home. She felt helpless and useless. She mentioned this to

Bernie and by her reaction, it seemed her friend did not feel the same way.

"We do whatever we can to alleviate the suffering," Bernie said fiercely. "That's all. Every little bit helps."

Grace nodded in agreement.

Ralph arrived. He'd been up all night like everyone else, helping to carry in the injured. His eyes were blood-shot, with dark circles underneath. "Girls, go back to bed. The club will be closed until later this afternoon. Go get some rest."

They didn't have to be told twice.

CHAPTER TWENTY-FOUR

Buster had to have both of his hands amputated. Grace forced herself to visit him every day. It was difficult, and she had to brace herself every time. She constantly reminded herself that it was much harder for him than it was for her.

Buster lay on his back, staring at the ceiling of the tent. Both his arms were bandaged at the wrist.

"I'm going back to the States as soon as they can get me on a transport ship," he told her.

"There's probably more they can do for you over there," Grace said.

"I doubt they can get me a new pair of hands," he said bitterly.

"No," Grace said, her voice trailing off. She didn't know what to say.

"I haven't told Sarah yet."

"Would you like to write a letter—" she caught herself. "Would you like me to write a letter to Sarah for you? You can dictate to me what you want to say."

"I think I would. She needs to be told. I don't want her to be shocked when I get home. Plus, it'll give her a chance to break up with me."

"Don't say that, Buster," Grace cried. "If she's as wonderful as you've said she is, this won't change how she feels about you. Yes, you'll have challenges—"

He cut her off. "Challenges? I can't even unzip my pants to take a leak."

Grace did not blush. She'd grown used to the way the soldiers talked. Her mother probably would have fainted, but Grace had discovered she was made of sturdier stuff. If swearing and cursing helped them blow off steam, then so be it. Besides, after the bombing the other night, Grace felt like swearing too.

"Let me get some paper and a pen and I'll be right back."

"Yeah, sure, Grace Jelly."

She returned quickly and sat down next to Buster's bed. "I'm ready."

"Wait a minute. I need to gather my thoughts. Start with 'Dear Sarah.'"

Grace wrote that at the top of the paper. Beneath it, in parentheses, she identified herself and explained she was a Red Cross volunteer and that Buster was unable to write.

"How do I tell her I've lost both my hands?" he cried out, his face contorted in anguish.

Grace leaned closer. "You just tell her. Just like that."

He nodded, tears slipping out of the sides of his eyes. She jumped up and grabbed a tissue from his bedside and dabbed at his eyes. He looked up at her. "Thanks."

"No problem." She sat and said, "Okay, I've got 'Dear Sarah.'"

"That's a start," he said with a sigh. He looked over at Grace. "I should just tell her?"

She nodded.

"Okay. Dear Sarah. I'm sorry to tell you this but I was wounded in a bombing here. I've lost both my hands." He choked on the last sentence, and it came out as a sob. Grace rubbed his shoulder.

"I'm okay. Let's do this," he said.

The letter ended up being quite short. He told her about what had happened, about his injuries, and he ended the letter by saying he'd understand if she wanted to call things off. Grace had hesitated, but Buster looked over at her and said, "Go on and write that now, Grace."

She finished the letter just as Ziggy, Timid Tim, and Tony arrived. They nodded hello to Grace.

"Is he behaving himself?" Ziggy asked.

"He's trying," she replied.

"He better be, because we can smack him around a bit," Tony cracked. This resulted in a hint of a smile from Buster.

"I'll leave you all to it," Grace said.

"Mail that letter for me, Grace Jelly, before I change my mind," Buster said.

"Sure thing."

As she departed, he called out. "And thanks."

She stopped and turned. "Any time, Buster."

Within a few days, Buster was transported to a hospital stateside for further rehab. Grace never heard about him again after that, and she often wondered what became of him. Did he get the girl in the end? Or had he been left alone? It was one of the many unanswered questions of her life.

For the next couple of weeks, Bernie and Grace rotated between helping out at the hospital and keeping the club going. Charlotte had excused herself from going to the hospital, stating she'd seen enough blood and gore to last her a lifetime. But Grace and Bernie took turns spending time with the wounded troops, playing cards or board games with those that weren't too severely injured. And it soon became widely known that with Bernie's unreadable handwriting, if someone needed a letter written home, Grace was the person to ask.

Despite all the busyness, the nightmares had started for Grace. She had constant dreams of soldiers, and even her father, approaching her with missing limbs or with their heads covered in bloody bandages.

CHAPTER TWENTY-FIVE

"I've got an idea," Bernie said, pacing the floor of their hut.

Grace sat on her cot, filing her nails, and yawned. She'd woken up in the middle of the night after dreaming again of her father waiting for her on the train platform and lifting up his hand to wave, but it was nothing more than a bloody stump.

Next to her, on her own cot, Charlotte leafed through a magazine, her hair set in pin curls.

"Let's hear it, Kansas," Grace said, calling Bernie by the nickname she had received from a new soldier on the island.

Bernie looked from Grace to Charlotte. "Now, girls, hear me out on this one. Stretch your imagination."

They waited, expectant.

"Let's do our own version of *Snow White*," Bernie said. Her eyes were bright.

Charlotte kneeled on her cot and clapped. "I can play Snow White! I'm perfect for the part."

Bernie pointed in her direction and said, "Hold on to that thought."

Grace narrowed her eyes at Bernie, knowing she was up to something and wondering what it was.

"I was thinking of turning it on its head," Bernie said.

"What do you mean?" Grace asked.

"I'll play Snow White, and you two can play the dwarves."

Grace didn't say anything, but she grinned. Charlotte sat back on her heels and scowled. "That won't work at all. You're not the Snow White type."

Bernie rolled her eyes. "I *know* that. Think about it. I'm the last person anyone expects to play a fair maiden, a damsel in distress, the fairy-tale princess. I mean, look at me!" She held out her arms, palms out, as if to emphasize her point. "That's what would make it so funny."

Unable to help it, Grace burst out laughing.

Bernie locked eyes on her. "See what I mean? You pictured me playing a fair maiden, and it's so ridiculous it's funny."

Grace nodded. "It's a great idea."

Charlotte crossed her arms. "Why would you want people laughing at you?"

"They wouldn't be laughing *at* me. They'd be laughing *with* me. Don't you see?"

"I really don't, Bernie," Charlotte said with a sniff. "I think I should play Snow White."

"With all things being equal, yes, you'd make a perfect Snow White. But we want to give the fellas a good laugh, especially after all they've been through. We want to do something that will lift their spirits."

"I'm with you, Bernie, I think it's a great idea," Grace said. Besides, she could use a few laughs herself.

"Of course you'd agree with her," Charlotte snapped. "You'd never say no to her."

"That's because I agree with everything she says."

Bernie put her hands on her hips. "Didn't she just say no to me last week when I asked her to rub my feet?" At the time, it had been a joke, but Grace had said no all the same.

"No offense, but I don't touch other people's feet," Grace said with an affected gravitas.

"None taken, kiddo."

With Grace's help, Bernie began writing the play in earnest.

"Do you know what you're doing?" Grace asked. Behind her, on her cot, Charlotte snorted.

Bernie ignored Charlotte and said, "I haven't a clue, but you know what? There's not a lot to do in Kansas and I used to go to the cinema all the time. I've got the general idea."

"So you're flying by the seat of your pants," Grace said.

"Pretty much."

When they explained the concept to Ralph, his initial reaction was to look at Bernie and scowl. "You're Snow White?"

"You got it. It's going to be a hoot!" Bernie assured him.

"Let's hope so. I'll see what I can rummage for props."

"That would be great. And paint. Grace will need some paint because she's going to make all the set decorations, isn't that right?"

"It sure is," Grace said.

"It sounds like you've got everything under control. If anything, a good laugh is needed," Ralph said.

"That's the idea," Bernie told him.

Some of the guys had built an impromptu stage, and Grace and Charlotte managed to sew stage curtains out of old fatigues and burlap sacks. During the final rehearsal, Bernie stood in the sand and looked at the stage, and said with a grin, "It all looks great!"

The night of the performance was muggy, and tiki torches lit up the area. Long wooden benches—hastily constructed—were set in the sand in front of the stage.

Grace directed Ziggy and Timid Tim in the placement of the torches and the benches.

Over her shoulder, Bernie quipped about the torches, "Not too close together, we don't want to burn the place down."

Charlotte was behind the curtains making sure the set decorations were in the order they were supposed to go. Tony directed soldiers toward the seating, and they all filed in.

Bernie peeked out from behind the curtain. "Oh goody, we've got a full house!"

"I hope they're not disappointed," Charlotte muttered behind her.

"These guys? Not on your life!"

As soon as Bernie pranced out there dressed as Snow White, followed by Grace and Charlotte as Dopey and Grumpy, there was applause and a burst of laughter.

At the end, when Snow White lay perfectly still on the table after being cast under the witch's spell, Grace and Charlotte were kneeling by her bier and were supposed to be sad, but Grace couldn't keep a straight face. Bernie's feet, hanging over the edge of the short table, were shod in a pair of size fourteen Army boots, and in her mouth was a large apple. She looked like a cross between a pig ready to be roasted and a clown with over-sized shoes. Grace couldn't stop laughing, and neither could the guys.

Every so often, Bernie opened one eye and winked at the audience, which resulted in more laughter. When the prince, played by an enlisted man from Milwaukee who was only five foot three, leaned over to kiss her, Bernie jumped up, startling him and everyone else as she leapt into his arms. He staggered back, his knees buckling, and they collapsed into a heap on the stage.

"Oops, sorry about that, Prince Charming, I got carried away," Bernie said. She and the soldier stood up on the stage and took a bow, and the audience jumped to their feet, shrieking and howling.

It was such a roaring success that the fellas demanded it be played for a few more nights.

Chapter Twenty-Six

"Don't do it, Charlotte," Bernie warned. "It's a bad idea."

Charlotte rolled her eyes and pulled a dress over her head. "Would you relax? Maybe you're jealous." Her eyes shone.

Bernie didn't take the bait. "No, I'm not. But I am worried about you."

"Spare me your concern," Charlotte said, adjusting the dress. She shifted her gaze away from Bernie and asked Grace, "What do you think, Grace? Of the dress, I mean."

"It's beautiful," Grace said truthfully. "But I agree with Bernie, I think you're making a big mistake."

Charlotte rolled her eyes again. "Not you too. Let it go."

A first lieutenant had asked Charlotte to accompany him to the officer's club that evening. All sorts of alarm bells had gone off for Grace and Bernie, but Charlotte could not be reasoned with. He'd even gifted her an evening dress, to which Bernie had quipped, "Where's the boutique on this island that sells evening gowns? I must have missed that."

The class division between the officers and the enlisted men was pronounced. The officers had their club, and the enlisted men had the Red Cross club. To Grace, it served as a stark reminder of the division back home and how she felt as if she didn't really belong. But perhaps here in wartime, you needed the division to get the job done. She wasn't sure how she felt about this.

Once Charlotte was dressed in the smart red gown the lieutenant had gifted her, she marched off to the officer's club, her hair in an updo and wearing bright red lipstick.

It was late when she came back to the tent. Lights were already out, and Grace and Bernie were sound asleep. Grace stirred, hearing Charlotte arrive, but rolled over and went back to sleep, not even asking her how it went.

The following day at the club, Grace was looking for a Ping-Pong ball, as there was a doubles' tournament planned. It was Grace and Ziggy against Charlotte and Tony. Meanwhile, Bernie sat at a table with four GIs, playing poker.

"How about strip poker, Bernie?" one of them suggested.

Bernie arranged the cards in her hand and said, "Keep your shirt on, soldier." She did a double take at his bare chest. "Or maybe put a shirt on."

"Bernie, have you seen the Ping-Pong balls?" Grace asked.

Bernie looked over her shoulder. "Did that darn monkey take them again?"

"Not again," Grace said.

One of the island's resident monkeys, a long-tailed macaque they'd named Joey, had become enamored with the items in the club, so much so that they had to bolt the doors and windows shut when they left for the night. But he still managed to get in and steal things occasionally.

"I'll see if I can find him," Grace said. She went into the kitchen and grabbed a banana. If he had a Ping-Pong ball, there'd be no getting it off him without a trade. Sometimes even that didn't work.

With the banana in her hand, she stepped outside in search of Joey the mischievous monkey.

Ziggy passed her on his way to the club.

"Hey, Grace Jelly, I thought we had a tournament," he called out after her.

"We do. But I can't find a ball. I think Joey has taken them."

"Again? Want some help?" he asked.

"Nah, I've got it. I'll be back soon," she said with a smile and a wave.

She walked through the palm trees and was hit on the forehead with a Ping-Pong ball. She heard the screech of Joey, which she took for laughter. But before she could retrieve the ball, the monkey landed in front of her and grabbed it.

Smiling, she waved the banana in front of him. "How about a banana, Joey? What do you think about that?"

It took a few minutes and some gentle coaxing, but eventually, he accepted the trade. With the ball secure in her hand, Grace ran back to the club.

Before she entered, she heard raucous laughter. She smiled to herself. Nine times out of ten, it was due to something Bernie had said. Ziggy and Tony waited at the Ping-Pong table. There was no sign of Charlotte. Ziggy held up his hand to Grace, who tossed the ball toward him. He picked up a paddle and began paddling the ball against the table.

"I'm ready," she said.

"We need a fourth player," Ziggy said.

At that moment, Charlotte entered the room. She looked tired, but she'd brushed her hair, put on her uniform, and applied some lipstick, albeit a more subdued shade than the bright red she'd worn last night.

Everything went quiet in the club. Grace frowned and looked around. All activity came to a standstill. No one looked at Charlotte. They didn't even acknowledge her. Usually, Ziggy would tease her and say, "Marry me, Legs, and try to make an honest man out of me." But he acted as if she were invisible. Even Timid Tim averted his gaze.

"Hello, fellas," Charlotte said enthusiastically.

Not one GI present in the club returned her greeting or even acknowledged her with a simple nod.

Bernie cleared her throat and broke the spell. "Charlotte, why don't you start the phonograph again. We could use some music."

"All right, Bernie," Charlotte said quietly, walking over to the corner where the phonograph stood on a makeshift table. She selected an album and laid the needle down on it, but even its upbeat tempo did not lift the pall.

"Come on, Charlotte, we're ready to play," Grace called out.

Ziggy laid his paddle on the table. "Not in the mood for Ping-Pong today, Grace. Maybe tomorrow." Tony did the same, and Grace was left standing there, holding a paddle in her hand.

"Okay, tomorrow then," she said to no one in particular.

Ziggy and Tony pulled chairs over and sat behind Bernie, who continued to play poker with the group of GIs.

Meanwhile, Charlotte stood in the corner, arms folded tightly across her chest, head down.

Ziggy kept looking at Bernie's cards and offering pointers. Finally, she laid her hand face down on the table and half turned in her chair. "If I want advice, Ziggy, I'll ask for it."

Grinning, he said, "I thought you might need some help."

"Need some help?" Bernie said in a tone of mock offense. "I'll remind you that you still owe me one dollar and thirty cents from all the times I've beat you at cards."

"Aw, come on, Bernie."

"Come on nothing. Now sit back and mind your own business." Bernie picked up her cards and asked the amused GIs at her table, "Now, where were we?"

A GI entered the club and Grace, paddle in hand, said, "Care for a game of Ping-Pong?"

"Sure, sis," he said, going around to the other end of the table and picking up the paddle. By the end of her two years on that island in the Philippines, Grace was truly sorry she didn't have a brother. She would have liked one.

The highlight of many of Grace's days in Southeast Asia was the arrival of letters from friends and family.

Her parents, bless their hearts, wrote regularly. It was a tenuous connection and a reminder that she had a life somewhere else. Sometimes, it felt so insular on the island it seemed like all she had. But then a letter would arrive and she'd be pulled back, a gentle reminder that not only did she have a life separate and distinct from being a volunteer, but that it was still there waiting for her to return to when the war was over. John touched on the subject of this very thing in his most recent letter.

Dear Grace,

I hope this missive finds you well. All's well here.

Your stage production of Snow White sounds wonderful. And hilarious. I wish I could have been there. Bernie sounds like a great gal. It's no surprise that the two of you have hit it off. I'm sure the troops really appreciate all you and Bernie and Charlotte are doing for them. We have a Red Cross club here as well. The girls are wonderful. It's like having a piece of home here with us. The best parts of home.

You probably wonder why I never mention the war or where I am or what it is that I'm doing. Aside from the obvious, the censors, I don't want to think about it when I pick up my pen to write to you and my parents and some of my friends. I only want to think of normal things: my mother's turkey-and-stuffing dinner, my father's pen-

chant for political trivia, and a certain pretty girl who once gave me a lift to the train station.

In my downtime, I like to think of what I'll do after the war. Will I go back to college? I only had one semester left. Or will I do something else? Sometimes I wonder if I've lost interest in the degree I've been studying for. Do you find that with your art history degree? Are you still interested in that? Or has war changed you so much that you're looking toward a different future?

What about your father's company? Is there any room for you? I know you have no brothers, and you're an educated young woman with a sensible head on her shoulders. Is there room for you at the family business? If you can volunteer for the war effort and live in these conditions, I believe you could do anything. I think once Grace Gibson sets her mind to doing something, there's no stopping her.

Some fellas here don't like to think of what they'll do after the war. There's a sentiment that to try and envision a future after the war jinxes you. I don't believe that. Thinking about a future that doesn't involve picking up my rifle, wondering where the enemy is, and rations, keeps me going.

Here's to our futures, Grace! God willing.

Yours in friendship and affection,

John

CHAPTER TWENTY-SEVEN

There was a banging on their hut door, startling the three of them out of their sleep. Grace and Charlotte immediately sat up on their cots.

"Wake up, girls! The war is over in Europe!" someone yelled.

Grace and Charlotte jumped off their cots and screamed and jumped up and down. Finally! The war was over in Europe. It gave hope that the Pacific might follow suit.

Bernie did not move.

Grace frowned. "Bernie! Did you hear the news? The war is over in Europe!"

Beneath her blanket, Bernie mumbled something incoherent.

Concerned, Grace went over to her friend, lifted the mosquito net, and touched her shoulder. When Bernie half turned, Grace noticed her face was as red as a beet, and she laid the back of her hand against Bernie's forehead. "Bernie, you're burning up!"

"I've got a headache that feels like there's a man inside my head hammering on my skull."

Fear coursed through Grace. She'd never seen Bernie like this. Her friend was all action verbs. She was one who didn't sit still. Grace wasn't even sure she could. "I'll get the medic," she said, trying to remain calm, not wanting to alarm her friend.

Bernie's forehead creased. "Don't bother anyone. They're too busy. I'll be fine."

But Grace had seen this before. As beautiful as the tropics were even during war, they could be deadly. Malaria was just as much of a threat as a bullet or a bomb. It had been an eye-opener for her.

"What should I do?" Charlotte asked, her expression mirroring Grace's, full of concern.

"Get some cool cloths and put them on her forehead and beneath her arms. I'm going for the medic," Grace said, and she was out of the hut before Bernie could protest.

"Where's the fire, Grace Jelly?" a GI called after her when she raced by. But Grace didn't stop to answer, her singular focus on getting help for Bernie.

Ziggy spotted her and called out, "What's wrong, Grace?"

"It's Bernie!"

Ziggy ran off in the other direction, toward their hut.

When Grace returned to their hut with the medic, Charlotte was wiping Bernie's brow with a cool cloth. Ziggy had brought a helmet full of cold water so Charlotte could wring out the cloth compresses. There were other GIs in the hut, watching and asking what they could do.

The medic pushed his way through and knelt by Bernie's cot. He looked over at the GIs crowded against the wall of the hut. "Give us some room, fellas, and step outside."

They did as he asked, and Ziggy left with them. The medic did a quick examination of Bernie and slid a glass thermometer under her tongue. While he waited, he took her pulse, and then removed the thermometer and held it up, turning it to read it.

"You're going to the infirmary," he said.

Bernie didn't protest. She looked around but her eyes were glazed, and she frowned. "Who are all these people in the room?"

Grace and Charlotte looked at each other.

"It's just us, Bernie," Grace explained. "Charlotte and me."

"But who are the rest of them?"

"Her fever is so high she's hallucinating," the medic explained. He opened the door to the hut and instructed

NEW BEGINNINGS IN LAVENDER BAY   257

the first GI he saw to get a litter and return on the double.

"Do you think it's malaria?" Grace asked, fearful for her friend. Although they took malaria tablets that turned their skin yellow, sometimes you still ended up with the disease. The bugs and mosquitos were something else, so big they needed saddles, as Bernie was apt to say.

"Most likely. But you know how it is. Malaria, dengue fever . . . it could be anything," the medic explained.

There was a knock, and Ziggy appeared in the hut, carrying in a stretcher with two other GIs.

"Come on, Kansas, let's get you to the infirmary," Ziggy said. Carefully, they transferred Bernie from her cot to the stretcher, their expressions grim.

Grace wanted to go with her friend, wanted to take care of her, but she had a job to do. And she couldn't leave Charlotte to do it by herself. The two of them walked to the club, not saying anything, too afraid to say out loud anything that might possibly jinx Bernie.

Grace went through the motions of the day. When the GIs arrived and started asking after Bernie, she didn't waver, didn't so much as tremble. She gave one hundred percent, reminding herself of the reason she was there. She played Ping-Pong. Charlotte kept the phonograph going. And together they served refreshments all day long.

Whenever there was a lull, Grace ran to the infirmary to see Bernie, finding her friend in a desperate state. She was hallucinating, and this did nothing to reassure Grace. If someone like Bernie, who was so sturdy and the absolute picture of health, could be reduced to this, what chance did she have? Or anyone else?

The club wasn't the same without her. The atmosphere was different, and the place felt flat. Bernie was missed. There was no doubt about that. Even the GIs who hung around the club were somber. Bernie was someone worth missing. Grace whispered prayers all day long. She realized she had no better friend than Bernie Powers. At one point, Ziggy and Timid Tim and Tony sat down and insisted she learn how to play poker. Grace didn't want to; that was Bernie's game. But she knew they were trying to distract her from Bernie's dire situation, and she couldn't refuse them.

Grace played a lot of cards, but she had trouble concentrating on the rules of poker. Ziggy good-naturedly advised her several times, patient and kind.

No one knew more about loss and heartache than these guys, she thought. She straightened in her chair, determined to make more of an effort. To be present.

Meanwhile, Charlotte kept the phonograph going, her lipstick applied, and the Cokes coming. Her smile never wavered. Once when Grace looked over at her, she spotted her talking to one of the guys. That was a relief.

If one would acknowledge her and talk to her, maybe the others would follow suit.

Bernie remained in the infirmary. Her diagnosis: malaria. Whether damage had been done to her organs remained to be seen. Her convalescence was lengthy, and when she was somewhat better and able to sit up in bed, some of the GIs would visit her and play poker at her bedside. But she tired easily, which was so unlike her. The doctors decided that once she was well enough to travel, she would be sent back to the States.

Grace packed up Bernie's meager belongings and carried her suitcase over to the infirmary, setting it next to Bernie's bed.

Her friend had lost a lot of weight and appeared gaunt.

For her own selfish reasons, Grace did not want Bernie to leave and admitted as much. "I don't know if I can do this without you," she said.

"Nonsense," Bernie said weakly. "You can do this. You don't need me."

"I do," Grace said. She felt the hot sting of tears behind her eyes and her throat began to constrict.

"No, Grace, you're going to be fine," Bernie encouraged. "You know exactly what to do."

Grace was doubtful.

Bernie reached out, took Grace's hand, and gently squeezed it. "You're going to be fine."

"Am I?" She couldn't imagine doing this without Bernie. Didn't know if she wanted to. For the first time in her life, she had a best friend.

"Ziggy tells me you're becoming an ace poker player."

Grace had to laugh. "I'll never be as good as you."

"You'll be better than me," Bernie declared.

"I'm worried about you," Grace said.

"No, don't worry about me," Bernie said quietly. "But if you see that sucker of a mosquito that bit me, squash him for me, will you?"

Grace laughed. "You can count on it."

Dear Grace,

I'm sorry to hear about Bernie. From your letters and your vivid descriptions, I feel like I know her personally. She is someone I would have liked to meet. It's amazing how the circumstance of war throws people together who bond and yet would otherwise never have met.

I can understand your heartache about letting Bernie go. The bonds forged during war are unbreakable. But I agree with Bernie, you'll handle your situation with your usual grace and aplomb, which is why your name is perfect for you.

I often think back to that night we met at the USO dance at the pavilion and how my life is so much richer for knowing you.

As we all wait patiently for the war in the Pacific to end, it's not lost on me how we must eventually say goodbye to those we bonded with. To those we've entrusted our lives to. It begs the question: if we ever see them again, would it serve as a painful reminder of a violent time, or would the fact that friendship was soldered in terrible times be enough to hold it all together.

As you can see, I think too much. It gets me into trouble

. . .

Yours in friendship and affection,
John

Grace loved that about him. That he thought too much. He was a great listener and had given sound advice. Sometimes, she wondered if she was falling in love with him. On paper, he was perfect. While he thought about his future after the war, she was beginning to give serious thought to her future with *him*.

Grace and Charlotte hastily put together a going-away party for Bernie. Grace told Ziggy about it, who nodded and said he'd spread the word. Bernie wouldn't want much fuss, but Grace didn't care. She was going to give her friend a great send-off.

Timid Tim had gotten a hold of some paint. "Don't ask," he'd said. Grace painted broad brushstrokes on a sheet that was doubling as a sign.

Best of Luck, Bernie! She and Charlotte stood on chairs and nailed the sheet to the wall. They spent the rest of the day making snacks and making sure there were plenty of bottles of Coke.

Ralph stopped in to see if they needed anything. He stood in the middle of the room and looked around, hands on his hips, which caused Grace's throat to tighten as it was so reminiscent of Bernie.

Bernie arrived early the following morning. She would be rowed out that day to the transport ship that would take her to the West Coast, and then she'd be transferred to a hospital for further evaluation and treatment.

Grace, Charlotte, Ziggy, Timid Tim, and Tony waited on the small porch of the club. Bernie walked slowly and as she climbed the step, she stumbled and lost her footing. Grace and Ziggy were immediately at her side.

"Who moved that step?" Bernie joked.

"It's all right, Kansas, we've got you," Ziggy said.

When she stepped inside the club and saw the sign and the tables, she turned to Grace. "What have you done?"

Grace was all smiles. "Just a little something. To say goodbye." Her voice choked on the last word.

"I appreciate it."

"How about one last game of poker for the road, fellas?" Bernie said.

They jumped at it.

When the game was done and the Cokes had been drunk and the snacks eaten, Bernie announced, "Fellas, that's my cue. Time to go."

They all followed her outside, where her packed suitcase was set near the bottom step.

"Well, I guess this is it," Bernie said, drawing in a deep breath. She looked at the crowd of GIs who'd gathered to say goodbye. "Take care of yourselves." She looked around at each one of them. "And most of all, keep your head down!"

This resulted in a round of laughter. The crowd formed into a line and one by one, each soldier walked up to shake Bernie's hand. By the time the last GI wished her well, both she and Grace were crying unabashedly.

Ziggy and Timid Tim escorted her to the boat, Ziggy carrying her suitcase for her. Before she disappeared, she stopped, looked over her shoulder, made eye contact with Grace, and smiled and waved.

It was never the same after Bernie left.

Chapter Twenty-Eight

1946

The sky was gray as the train rolled into Lavender Bay, and the fields on the way in had been covered in snow. Grace craned her neck to see her hometown. She'd managed to secure a winter coat from the Red Cross upon landing in New York, but despite its woolly warmth, she shivered. It had been more than two years since she'd left. She wondered what post-war Lavender Bay would look like. More than that, she wondered what she'd look like. The train screeched to a halt and within minutes, the door swung open.

Grace stood and collected her small, battered suitcase. There wasn't much in it as she'd been required to wear the Red Cross uniform at all times. She wore it now, in fact, out of habit rather than necessity, as she'd been discharged from the Red Cross and was no longer required to follow its rules. After two years in the Pacific Theater, the uniform was looking worse for wear. It owed her nothing.

She waited patiently, gripping the handle of her suitcase as passengers filed out of the carriage. As she reached the steps, she took hold of the rail and stepped down onto the busy platform, which was packed with returning soldiers.

She pushed her way through the crowd, looking for her father, her breath coming in wispy clouds in front of her. She'd forgotten how the damp chill of winter seeped into your bones.

"Grace!" She heard the stentorian voice of her father, and a smile broke out on her face. The first one of the day. Her father was here. All would be well.

Her eyebrows lifted when she spotted her mother alongside her father. The only time her mother ever came to the station was to get on a train or off it. They looked well. Her father sported his usual three-piece suit and tie, the chain of his pocket watch extending from one vest pocket to another, an oddly comforting sight. Her mother was decked out in fur, with a small hat trimmed with elegant black netting perched on her perfectly coiffed hair.

Grace didn't need a mirror to know what she looked like. She saw it in the faces of her parents and the way their smiles faltered before quickly recovering. Her father pulled her into a hug. "Grace, it's wonderful to have you back home." When they parted, his eyes were full of tears.

"It's good to be home," she said.

Aleida Gibson was not one to show emotion in public. She considered it vulgar and crass. But now her voice quivered, and she choked on her words. "Darling, welcome home." She surprised Grace by wrapping her arms around her. Grace became ensconced in mink and her mother's perfume, more luxury than she had seen in years.

Aleida studied her daughter, a frown distorting her features. "My goodness, Grace, your skin is gold. What happened?"

"It's from the malaria tablets we had to take over there," Grace explained.

Their chauffeur, who waited discreetly off to the side, stepped forward at a subtle nod from Grace's father and picked up her suitcase. It seemed small in his gloved hand. He tipped his cap and said, "Welcome home, Miss Grace."

"Thank you," she said.

Her parents flanked her, their arms looped through hers, and they proceeded to the exit. The crowd, recognizing them, parted. As they passed, her parents smiled and nodded to people they knew, but they did not stop, heading off the platform and out of the station, to the parking lot out front.

The three of them sat in the back seat as the chauffeur drove them home, Grace sandwiched between her parents. It was only then that she began to warm up.

"You must be so happy to be home," her father said.

Honestly, she wasn't sure how she felt. Every day for the past two years, she'd had important work to do. The habit had become ingrained in her. Then one day, she woke up and it was no longer needed. It was odd.

The car entered through the large gates and wound its way up the long, winding driveway. Grace was able to catch only glimpses of the house until they got past the trees, and then there it was, standing sentinel, quiet and imposing.

Had it always been so grand? she wondered. Or did it seem so because she'd been living in a hut for the last two years?

The car came to a stop near the front entrance. The chauffeur jumped out, opened the rear door, and offered the ladies his hand to help them out. Grace giggled.

"Grace, darling, whatever is so funny?" her mother asked as they climbed the steps to the house.

"I was thinking about the island. Never once did anyone help me in or out of a jeep."

Her mother paled considerably. "Fortunately, all that nasty business is behind us now."

Grace frowned. That *nasty business*, as her mother had called it, had been a major world war. She shut up and followed her mother dutifully inside. She'd planned to go straight to her room, but her mother and father insisted she join them in the parlor for tea and cakes.

Irene brought in one tray after another. She greeted Grace with a smile and a hug. Grace knew from her mother's letters that Irene's son had been invalided home. But he'd survived, and that was the main thing.

Grace's mouth watered at the sight of all the food: crustless sandwiches, smoked salmon and caviar, and petit fours and chocolate bonbons. But first, she wanted a proper cup of tea. Aleida delicately lifted the teapot and poured the amber-colored liquid into fine bone china cups. She passed a cup to Grace first and then to George.

"You'll probably be glad to be rid of that uniform and get back into your own clothes," Aleida said. She studied her daughter. "That uniform is too big. You've gone too thin, Grace. It doesn't suit you. That uniform is hanging on you. I can't believe the Red Cross couldn't provide you with something properly fitted."

Grace didn't bother to explain that it had fit perfectly when she left two years ago.

"She'll put the weight back on once she's been home for a while," her father said. "I suppose the food wasn't very good. It's hard to make it palatable when you're cooking for large groups."

Grace only nodded, sipping from her cup. It tasted wonderful. She hadn't remembered tea tasting this good. What passed for tea over on the island was awful.

"We must go shopping soon to update your wardrobe," Aleida said.

"There'll be plenty of time for that," George said. "Maybe a trip to New York City."

"That would be lovely," Aleida said.

Grace shook her head. "I can find whatever I need here in Lavender Bay." Her tone indicated that it was a subject she did not care to pursue. She was aware of her parents exchanging a look as she helped herself to some smoked salmon.

After a second cup of tea, her father stood and said, "I must head back to the office. I'll see you both at dinner." He bent down and kissed his wife on her cheek. He walked over to Grace and did the same. "What are your plans for the day?"

"I'll probably unpack my suitcase." It wouldn't take more than three minutes to do, and this struck her as funny. She broke into giggles, almost choking on a crustless sandwich.

Her father's smile was indulgent.

"Grace, whatever is so funny?" her mother asked for the second time that day.

Grace caught her breath, drawing in a deep lungful of air, and shook her head. "Nothing, really."

"All right, I'll leave you to it," her father said, and he departed.

Grace ate another sandwich. The food tasted so good. But her stomach soon revolted, and as her mother was mid-sentence about what was going on in town, Grace jumped to her feet. "Excuse me, Mother, I don't feel well."

She rushed from the room, one hand clamped over her mouth and the other over her sore stomach. She dashed to one of the bathrooms and promptly vomited into the toilet, then leaned against the wall, perspiration on her brow. She'd eaten too much; she'd been warned about that, but the food had been too tempting. A cramp gripped her stomach, and she leaned over the toilet bowl again.

When she was sure there was no more to come, she washed her hands and splashed cool water on her face, gripping the edge of the sink and staring at the water swirling around the drain. Finally, she straightened and made her way upstairs.

Grace's room appeared juvenile to her. It felt as if it belonged to someone else, as if she were a guest. Her battered suitcase looked incongruous against everything else in the room. All that had once been familiar and comfortable now looked strange, and she was filled with a sense of unease.

To distract herself, she unpacked, hanging her uniforms in the back of her closet. She removed the pile of John's letters from the suitcase and placed them in the box under her bed. She put her toothbrush and hairbrush and deodorant in her bathroom, looking longingly at the tub. She hadn't had a proper bath since she left. She dropped her things on the small table next to the sink and walked over to the tub, putting the drain stopper in place. She turned on the faucets, the water sluicing over her hand, adjusting the taps until she was satisfied with the temperature.

She disrobed, letting her clothes fall to the floor in a pile. Once the tub was three-quarters full, she sat down in the hot water and leaned back, emitting a sigh.

Pure bliss.

She slid beneath the water to saturate her hair and gave it a good shampoo, the first proper one in years. When her hair was rinsed, she turned the faucet on and added more hot water. Leaning back once again, she closed her eyes.

She woke to find the water had gone cold, and she shivered, goose bumps pebbling her skin. Quickly she pulled the chain on the drain stopper, and the water began to swirl out of the tub. She stood and climbed out, pulling a large bath towel from the pile in the closet and wrapping herself in it. She towel-dried her hair and gave it a good brush-out. She made a mental note to make a hair appointment later that week.

For the rest of the day, Grace went through the motions, trying to get things to not look so strange. To make them fit. To make them make sense. The well-thumbed books she'd taken with her, she stacked in her bookshelf. Someday, she would pull them down and read them again. But not now. She perused the titles on her shelves like she was meeting up with old friends. She pulled one down and curled up with it on the window seat, staring out at the snow-covered landscape before getting lost in the pages of the book.

Later, she dressed for dinner and joined her parents in the dining room.

"Grace, you look so much better now that you're out of that ghastly uniform," her mother declared.

"I feel better," Grace admitted. She felt better physically, especially after the bath and the hair wash. She took her old seat on one side of the table, and her parents took their customary places at the head and the foot. As the staff served the meal, Grace was mindful not to overindulge, and she left half of her soup untouched.

"Aren't you hungry?" Aleida asked as Grace set her soup spoon down.

Grace shook her head. "I think my stomach must have shrunk as I'm not as hungry as I used to be."

"That's the war," her father said. "Give yourself time to get your appetite back. Coax it along a little bit at a time. No sense in getting sick, that would spoil everything."

Neither Grace nor her mother mentioned that very thing happening earlier in the day after he'd left.

Although the food was delicious, standing rib for dinner, Grace ended up pushing her food around on her plate, careful to eat only a few bites. Dessert—a rich custard—she skipped entirely.

"People are eager to see you, Grace, now that you're back," her mother said.

"But we thought maybe tonight, you'd like a quiet night at home with us," her father finished.

"Thank you, I appreciate that."

"Maybe we could go to lunch tomorrow at the country club," her mother suggested.

Grace knew her mother meant well, but she didn't want to be paraded around town. Not yet. Possibly not ever. "Not tomorrow, Mother. Another time."

Aleida did not protest, simply nodded in acquiescence.

They spent a quiet night in the parlor, the fire blazing in the hearth, the heat reminding Grace of the weather in the Philippines.

Later that night, she climbed into bed, glad to be back in a real bed instead of her thin Army cot. But in the end, she tossed and turned, unable to get comfortable until finally, she gave up, pulled her down comforter and pillow off the bed, and made a makeshift pallet on the floor. Within minutes, she was asleep.

CHAPTER TWENTY-NINE

G race's first outing was to the hairdresser a week after her arrival home. Her hair was in dire need of a proper cut and style. She and Bernie had taken turns cutting each other's hair on the island, but it turned out that neither of them were any real threat to the hairdressers of America.

Deciding a walk was called for, she parked her car at the far end of Main Street and walked in the January sunshine to the beauty parlor. Although she knew every nook and cranny of her hometown, she felt like a foreigner here amongst people and places that should have been familiar. She shrugged her shoulders a couple of times in an attempt to shake off the fog of unease that threatened to settle in around her.

The salon was busy. Women were lined up under hairdryers, magazines in their laps. There was a strong smell of ammonia and shampoo. Grace approached the girl at the reception desk, someone she didn't recognize.

"Grace Gibson. I have an appointment," she said.

"Yes. Take a seat and Mabel will be right with you. I'll take your coat," said the girl. She had short, pretty auburn hair and wore bright lipstick. She looked fresh out of high school, and Grace felt old enough to be her mother.

She slipped off her winter coat and handed it and her gloves to the girl, who disappeared with them into the back room.

Grace was leafing through the magazines on the stand when someone called out her name.

"Grace? Grace Gibson, it is you!"

Grace turned to see Lenore Hadley, who owned the boarding house over on Pearl Street. She'd always liked Lenore. She was a quiet, soft-spoken woman who had a kind word for everyone.

Lenore laid her hand on Grace's arm. "I'd heard that you were back. I'm sure your mother and father are delighted to have you home safe."

"They are."

"I imagine it takes some time to readjust," she said wisely.

"I'm getting there," Grace admitted.

"Give yourself time. Before long, you'll feel as if you'd never left."

Grace doubted that but was hopeful. The other woman's kindness and understanding had hit a nerve, and she felt the sting of tears at the back of her eyes. But she steeled herself against them. *I am not going to break down in the hair salon!* she told herself.

She changed the subject by asking after Lenore's son, Johnny, and the other woman went off blissfully about her boy, now twelve, and all the mischief he was getting into.

"Grace Gibson?" Both women looked toward a woman about Grace's age. She wore her platinum blonde hair in a ponytail with a curly bang. "I'm Mabel."

"It was good seeing you, Grace, welcome home," Lenore said.

"Take care, Lenore."

Grace relaxed into the pleasure of someone else washing her hair and massaging her scalp. The hairdresser chatted endlessly while she worked, reminding Grace of a chirping bird.

Mabel led Grace to a chair and asked what style she would like. As Grace explained, Mabel combed Grace's wet hair, which fell just past her shoulders.

"Who cut your hair the last time?" Mabel asked, looking at Grace in the mirror. "It's all uneven."

Grace couldn't help laughing. "My roommate. We used to cut each other's hair. I was a Red Cross volunteer overseas."

"Ohhh," Mabel said, drawing it out. "Where were you stationed?"

"The Philippines."

"Are you just home?"

"I am."

"My brother loved the coffee and donuts the club-mobiles served in Europe."

"I'm happy to hear that," Grace said. It was nice to be appreciated.

"I've got three kids under the age of five at home and let me tell you, that's a breeze compared to going to a war zone." As if to add emphasis, Mabel shuddered.

"It wasn't that bad," Grace said, determined to focus on the best of it. Because there were some good parts.

"You're probably glad to be back."

"I am," Grace said, wondering if she was telling a lie. She was unsure how she felt. The routine of the last two years had been so entrenching it felt at times as if she'd been ripped from it and misplaced.

"Good, now, let's fix your hair. And tell your room-mate not to quit her day job," Mabel teased.

Grace laughed, deciding she already liked her new hairdresser.

An hour later, she left the salon, loving the feel of her new hairstyle. It was modern and much shorter. She was pleased with it.

She stood on the sidewalk, searching through her purse for her car keys. She had promised to meet her mother for lunch at the country club. She was aware of people stepping around her but ignored them as she dug through her purse. She laid her hands on her keys and fished them out, then turned south, toward the area where she'd parked her car.

"Grace! Grace!" someone called out behind her.

She turned and spotted Norma Fox and another woman approaching her. Grace threw her hand up in a wave. When Norma reached her, she flung her arms around her.

"Welcome home!" Norma said.

"Thank you," Grace said, genuinely happy to see a familiar face. The familial resemblance was so strong between Norma and the woman beside her, Grace guessed her to be Norma's older sister, Noreen.

"Noreen, this was the girl I was telling you about, who became a Red Cross volunteer," Norma said.

"Norma said you were in the Philippines," Noreen said.

"That's right, and you were in the Pacific as well."

Noreen nodded. "I was there for three years. I don't think I'll ever forget it."

"Me neither," Grace agreed.

"We should get together and compare notes," Noreen suggested.

"I'd like that," Grace said with a nod.

They parted ways, and when summer rolled around, Grace often accompanied the two sisters to the beach.

CHAPTER THIRTY

There were two things that helped Grace readjust to civilian life. The first was time. Each day, things like her routine and the space in which she now existed became more familiar as the memory of the club and the island receded into the recent past. She kept in touch with Bernie, erupting in laughter when Bernie's first letter arrived and she saw that her friend's claims of having illegible handwriting were true. So she took to calling Bernie on the telephone every Sunday night. Bernie at first scolded her for the long-distance phone calls, but then Grace, tongue in cheek, reminded her that she was an heiress and could afford it. This resulted in a cackle coming down the line from Kansas.

The second thing was the impending homecoming of John McNamara, which he told her about in their continued correspondence. He'd be coming home in the spring, and Grace couldn't wait to see him. She'd been on two dates since being back in Lavender Bay, but all she could think about was John. She'd come to the conclusion that she was in love with him. That he was the one for her.

She offered to pick him up from the train station, but he declined, saying arrangements had been made and offering no further explanation. Although her inclination was to show up on his doorstep immediately, she refrained, exercising patience, a virtue she hadn't possessed before the war. She appreciated that he needed time to acclimate and be with his mother and father. She knew how close he was to both of them, and she also knew from her frequent visits to his parents that his father's health was deteriorating, which would break John's heart.

She refrained from contacting him. Women didn't just ring men up on the phone. But John was only home for four days before he called her, asking her to go for a walk on the beach, and her hope was renewed. An afternoon date was just like him, and there was no more romantic place than the beach.

As she opened the door to John on Saturday afternoon, she realized she hadn't seen him in *years*. But this was forgotten as soon as she glimpsed his smiling face. He was wearing his Army uniform, as many of the returning servicemen continued to do. Like her, he'd lost weight, but the cowlick was still present at the back of his head, and the sight of it filled her with joy.

As much as she wanted to lunge at him and hug him, she held back, unsure. Before she went wild and started making declarations of love, she wanted to see if she felt the same way in his presence. You could read a lot into a letter, and one couldn't base a relationship on a couple of years of correspondence. You had to spend time with that person.

He stepped into the grand hall and looked around. "Well, this is certainly something."

"It's home," was all she said.

"Let me get a good look at you, Grace," he said. He took her hands in his and stepped back and looked her over. "You're still as pretty as ever."

She blushed. "You look the same too."

He laughed. "Is that good or bad?"

"It's wonderful," she gushed.

They dropped hands and she said, "I hope it's all right, but Mother and Dad would like to meet you."

"Of course, I was hoping to meet them."

He followed her to the parlor, and she was aware of him looking around as they walked. She supposed to a stranger, it might be a lot to take in. She bit her lip. She hoped it wouldn't change his view of her. After a brief visit with her parents, they left for the beach, Grace declining their offer of refreshments.

John drove over to Pearl Street and parked his car, and they cut between two large houses, one a Queen Anne and the other a Victorian, to get to the beach. The bright sun in the pale blue sky gave off no heat. There was a chilly breeze, and Grace was glad she'd worn a heavy coat.

"Aren't you cold in only your uniform?" she asked John.

He shook his head. "Nope. Actually, it's a pleasant change from that tropical heat."

"Yes, it is," Grace agreed.

He looked around. "And look, not a mosquito in sight."

"I don't miss them. Or the snakes. But some of the monkeys were cute," she admitted.

They walked along the shore, as near to the water as they could without getting their shoes wet. It seemed chillier near the water's edge. Grace looped her arm through his.

"How does it feel to be home?" she asked.

"Great. I'm so happy I made it," he said. "By the grace of God."

"Your mother and father must be delighted that you're home," she said.

"They are. I prayed that they'd still be here when I returned, and God answered my prayers."

She was a little surprised at how openly he spoke about God. She'd been brought up to think that any discussion of religion was gauche, but John made it seem like it was a natural conversation.

Tentatively, she asked, "You have a very strong belief, don't you?"

"I do. My faith is what got me through the war," he admitted.

"Not my letters?" she teased.

He grinned. "They certainly helped. But I couldn't have made it without my faith. A belief in something greater than myself."

When she didn't say anything, he asked, "Do you not believe in God, Grace?"

She was quick to reassure him. "Of course I do. We go to church every Sunday." She was embarrassed to admit that she'd never given it much thought. During difficult times, she certainly resorted to prayer, but she wasn't sure what he'd say if she admitted that days would go by before she even thought of God. She had the feeling John never experienced that.

"Does it bother you that I'm Catholic?" he asked.

"Not at all!" she said with more vigor than she intended.

He laughed. "All right then."

"I'm not Catholic though."

"I know," he said. He made no further comment, and she wondered if that would be an issue. Would he expect her to convert?

He adroitly changed the subject before Grace could question him further. He looked out at the lake. "It's so good to be home and see this view again. I feel very lucky," he said.

She tucked her arm closer into his and smiled up at him. "I know exactly how you feel."

Looking down at her, he said, "You do, don't you?"

She nodded and they carried on walking.

John spoke again. "I'm so grateful to have survived the war in one piece that it makes me excited about the future."

She wondered if there was any room for her in that future.

"I see wonderful things for both of us," he continued.

Now she was thoroughly confused. Did he mean together or separately? As he'd only been home for a few days, she exercised restraint and didn't try to nail him down on a possible relationship. Though she felt she could talk to him about anything, it didn't seem like the right time to bring this subject up. The Lord was certainly testing her patience.

They continued to see each other a few times a week until summer. What concerned Grace was that although they enjoyed each other's company, they hadn't progressed beyond a chaste kiss on the cheek every time they met. And she wanted to kiss him very much. It seemed to her that he wanted that too, but he never proceeded. It left her confused and if she was honest, a little bruised.

As June rolled into July, John became distant. And although her efforts to cheer him up or make him laugh usually succeeded, he'd inevitably fall back into a quiet mood. As he'd so aptly put it in many of his letters, he appeared to be wrestling with something internally.

One afternoon, they sat outside by the pool at Grace's house, sipping lemonade and watching the afternoon fade in front of them. They'd gone for a swim earlier, after lunch, and had changed back into their summer clothes. Grace was on the chaise lounge with her legs stretched out in front of her, crossed at the ankle. John had opted to sit at the table, taking shelter beneath the umbrella.

"It's really beautiful out here," he said, looking around.

"It's nice to sit out here and look at the lake."

"It is." He went quiet again, staring into his glass of lemonade.

"Are you all right, John?" she asked.

"What?" he asked, looking over at her.

"Are you all right?" she repeated. "Lately, you seem distracted."

He didn't answer right away; instead, he lifted his gaze and stared out at the lake. She waited patiently. One thing she'd learned about John in the time she'd spent with him was that he arrived at things in his own time.

"You know what I like about you, Grace?" he said. Suddenly he became very serious.

"Everything?" she teased, trying to lighten the mood, lifting up her sunglasses to look at him.

He grinned. "Aside from that."

"No, John, I don't know what it is you like about me," she said. He wasn't profuse with the compliments. But when he offered them, they were sincere and quite grand.

"You're so easy to talk to. I feel I can tell you anything," he said.

"I feel the same way about you," she said truthfully.

He regarded her with a warm smile.

"But come on, spit it out, what's troubling you?" she pressed.

He took a sip of his lemonade and set it on the table. She didn't know if he was actually thirsty or if he was stalling.

"I'm struggling with a decision I have to make," he said.

She couldn't imagine what that could be. Her heart thudded against her chest.

"I'm going away for a little bit," he finally said.

All sorts of thoughts filled her mind. Unpleasant thoughts. That he had tuberculosis and was going to a sanatorium—although this seemed unlikely as he showed no signs of illness. Or that he was struggling with things he'd witnessed during the war and was going away to forget. They'd talked about this from time to time, the things they'd witnessed. The only people she could talk to about it were him and Bernie. They understood.

"I'm going on a spiritual retreat," he said.

"A what?" she asked. She hadn't seen that coming and had no idea what it entailed. Or what it meant.

"I'm thinking of becoming a priest."

A bomb could have fallen from the sky and it wouldn't have shocked her more. She was glad she was wearing her sunglasses so he couldn't see the mix of surprise and anguish in her eyes.

"Grace?" he prompted.

"I don't know what to say."

His gaze remained firmly fixed on her.

Finally, she said, "A Catholic priest?"

He laughed. "Well, I am Catholic."

Catholic priests were not allowed to marry. Her throat tightened, and there was the familiar sting in her eyes of impending tears. Quickly, she went into action mode, trying to get to the bottom of things and figure it out. It was either that or burst out crying.

"How long have you felt like this?" she asked.

"It was always at the back of my mind, you know, growing up."

No, she didn't know, but she nodded.

"My parents are devout Catholics," he said.

This, Grace did know. On one visit, Mrs. McNamara had pressed rosary beads and a brown scapular into her hands. They were currently in the top drawer of her nightstand. She couldn't bring herself to throw them out.

"It was my faith that got me through the war," John told her. It wasn't the first time he'd said it. "I don't know when it started—maybe late '42 or early '43. I began to think seriously that I might want to be a priest."

Grace was at a loss for words. "Do you think that feeling might be in response to serving?"

What was the old saying? *There are no atheists in fox-holes.*

"I'm sure that triggered it," he agreed. "Initially, I thought it might be a reaction to what I'd witnessed and done. If I were to become a priest and serve God and man, I could make reparation for all the killing I'd done in the war."

Grace flinched. It seemed reasonable. She was pretty sure a lot of bargaining went on between soldiers and their God.

"But the feeling hasn't gone away," John said. "If anything, it's become stronger." He leaned forward and ran his hand through his hair. The cowlick at the back of his head remained undisturbed. "It's beginning to feel like a calling. I've prayed on it to no avail."

She frowned. She couldn't look at him. "Then what's the problem? What's stopping you?" At least she had an explanation for all those chaste kisses on her cheek the last few months.

"I'm torn."

Now she looked over at him. "Torn about what?"

He met her gaze and said, "Would you remove those sunglasses, Grace?"

Surprised, she removed them quickly and said, "I'm sorry."

"I have strong feelings for you, Grace."

It was a sentence of seven words. But those words floated out there, circling them, rippling out over the manicured lawns and flowerbeds, their meaning and attending complication growing heavy in the air.

Grace didn't know what to say. This was what she'd wanted. What she'd *prayed* for.

"Please say something, Grace," he said quietly, clearly affected by his dilemma.

"I'm in love with you, John, and I want to spend the rest of my life with you," she said blindly.

He nodded, his features softening. His eyes brightened but his chin quivered.

"If I'm honest with myself, I'm in love with you as well." He leaned back and placed his hands on his freckled knees. "But the calling to become a priest is very strong."

Grace looked down at her hands. She read into that sentence that his calling was greater than his love for her. Disappointment filled her. How could she compete with God?

"So, you're going away on a spiritual retreat," she said.

He nodded. "There's a place outside of Boston. My spiritual director suggested it. I'll go and fast and pray on my decision."

She folded her arms across her chest. "I feel like I have no say in this matter. If we love each other, we should be together."

"It's not that simple. I don't expect you to understand."

"Because I'm not Catholic?"

"To be blunt, yes," John said.

Grace bristled and shifted on the chaise. "I think we could have a wonderful marriage."

"I do too," he said softly. "But I'm being pulled in another direction."

She drew in a deep breath and exhaled. She did not know what to say, how to convince him that they were right for one another. It occurred to her that if she had to convince him of the possibility of a beautiful future together, then perhaps she'd already lost him.

When the silence between them lengthened, he stood and said, "I better get going."

Grace nodded, swung her legs off the chaise, and stood. "When are you leaving for Boston?"

"Friday."

"That soon?"

"Yes, I'm taking the train."

As they walked around to the front of the house, he said, "I should say goodbye to your mother."

Grace shook her head. "She's probably napping," she lied.

When they reached John's car, they stood for a moment.

"Will you write?" she asked, searching his face.

He shook his head. "No, Grace, I won't. I don't want any distractions."

So now she was a distraction. It stung. But she didn't snap back.

"I'll see you when I get back." He stepped toward her and placed a kiss on her cheek.

Grace couldn't help it that she flung her arms around his neck and kissed him fiercely on the lips. She was pleased when he responded in kind, pulling her into an embrace, his hands sliding along her back.

But just as quickly, he stepped back, disengaging her arms from around his neck. He coughed and said, "Goodbye, Grace."

And he left her standing there in the driveway as he drove away. Only when he was out of sight did she touch her fingers to her lips.

CHAPTER THIRTY-ONE

John had been gone for a week, and Grace refused to mope around the house, even if her future and her happiness seemed to be under threat. She threw herself into charity work, accompanying her mother to all her committees. But despite all this busyness, Grace was not only bored, she was inert. As if she were simply going with the flow.

She sat at the breakfast table one morning, eating two slices of toast with grape jelly. She thought of all the crates of grape jelly her father had sent to her when she was overseas and how everyone enjoyed it. Nothing beat a slice of toast with grape jelly. As she often did, she found herself wondering what had happened to all the people she'd met during the war, especially Ziggy, Tony, and Timid Tim, and even Charlotte. More than once, she thought of Buster and hoped he was getting on all right.

"You're up early, Grace," her father said as he entered the room, startling her. With a chuckle, he said, "I didn't mean to frighten you. You're lost in thought."

"I couldn't sleep and thought I might as well get up," Grace explained, finishing her toast. She poured herself a second cup of tea.

"The nights are uncomfortably hot," George said. "We'll only have a few more weeks of this." He sat in his seat, and a plate of bacon and eggs was set down in front of him. He pulled his reading glasses from his breast pocket and thumbed through the stack of newspapers to the right of his plate, scanning the headlines before returning his attention to his breakfast. He pulled the linen napkin off the table and draped it over his lap. With a smile, he said, "Let's be glad we don't live in the South."

"Or the Philippines," Grace said. "The heat there was something else."

"Or that," her father agreed. "What are your plans for the day?"

"The same as yesterday," she replied flatly. "Lunch, a committee or two. Brainstorming about the next fundraiser. And then the same tomorrow and the day after that."

George's expression morphed from his usual good-naturedness to concern. "You sound unhappy." He was worried about her, especially since she'd confided in him about what was going on with John. He could sense her heartbreaking disappointment.

Grace had been toying with an idea, and she figured it might be as good a time as any to bring it up. Particularly since they were alone, and her mother wasn't there to run interference.

"I'd like to come to work at the factory," she said. She looked her father right in the eye. Now was not the time for being demure.

George frowned and sipped some orange juice from his glass. "In what capacity? As a secretary?"

Grace shook her head. "I'm looking for something to do for the rest of my life. Other than lunches and committees."

"Your mother does a lot of important charity work."

"It was not intended as a criticism of Mother."

"I know you're not happy . . ." he said, his voice trailing off. "But what about your college degree?"

"I want to do more with my life," she said. How did she explain that she and her outlook had changed? How could anyone, at the age of eighteen, know what they wanted to do with the rest of their life when they hadn't even *lived*? "I will always love art and history but my goals have changed. I realized that Lavender Bay and my family are very important to me."

Her father smiled. "I'm glad to hear that."

"I want to learn how to run the business." For emphasis, she added, "The *family* business."

A bark of laughter escaped her father, which not only startled her but annoyed her to no end.

Her father, sensing her irritation, said, "I'm sorry, Grace, I didn't mean to laugh. But you've taken me by surprise."

"Dad, you're not going to live forever. You won't always be here to run the business," she said. If she'd learned anything from the war, it was that no one, no matter their age, was immune to death.

"I'm aware of that," he said evenly.

"Do you think I wouldn't be capable of running it?"

George shook his head. "On the contrary. I think you're capable of doing anything you put your mind to."

"There's a 'but' in there somewhere," Grace said. "I can hear it." She stared at her teacup, half filled, the tea gone cold.

"Grace, it doesn't matter what I think. It's simply not done. Women running businesses."

"What about Coco Chanel?" She was the first person that popped into Grace's head.

"A woman running a business is an anomaly," he said. "They should be home, married and having children."

Grace sat back in her chair, looked up at the ceiling, and groaned. Her napkin slid off her lap, but she ignored it. "Dad, please don't say that. That's terrible."

"Hopefully, someday it won't be the case."

"Why does it have to be someday? Why can't it be now?" Grace asked. Before her father could respond, she said, "When you started making jelly in your mother's kitchen, you didn't look like someone who could run a big company either. You took on the establishment."

"I had determination," he said, smiling.

Grace tilted her head to one side and said, "You don't say."

"We are cut from the same cloth," her father admitted.

"We are," she agreed. "And you have no sons, so who better to someday run the family business than me?"

George pushed his plate of unfinished breakfast away, sighing. "You've made up your mind on this, haven't you?"

"Yes," she said simply.

"Historically, you do tend to do what you want. You always manage to get your way," he said. It was not an accusation. It was merely pointing out the truth. George Gibson knew he was partly to blame; he'd overindulged his daughter as he had his wife. But he had so much love for them both it was impossible for him to say no to them.

He clapped his hands so loudly, it was like the report of a rifle, startling Grace.

"Sorry about that. All right. Let's test your mettle. Let's see how serious you are."

Grace perked up, her back ramrod straight.

George pushed the stack of newspapers toward her. "There's *The Wall Street Journal*, *The New York Times*, and *The Lavender Bay Chronicles*, among others. You can't run a business if you don't know what's going on in the world, especially in the business sector."

Unable to mask her disappointment, Grace said, "You want me to read newspapers?"

"Yes. Every single day. And tomorrow, we leave here at seven sharp. I like to visit my grape growers a couple of times a year, to see if they need anything, how the crop is getting on, and if there are any problems. I don't like surprises."

Grace nodded.

"Then, we'll spend one day in the kitchen here, and I'll show you how I make grape jelly, just like I used to in my mother's kitchen."

"When was the last time you made a batch of grape jelly?"

"Doesn't matter." He tapped his forefinger against his temple. "It's all up here." He regarded her thoughtfully and said, "If you're serious, Grace, and I think you are, you'll need to work in the business from the ground up. It's the only way they'll respect you."

"Got it."

"You'll start on the floor of the factory," her father continued. "Canning, lids, packaging. Let's start there first."

She knew this was a test to see if she could handle it. She was determined not to fail. She didn't want to disappoint him or herself.

"You'll need to commit yourself," George said. "You won't only be spending a day there. It'll take months if you want to truly understand the business." With a certain gravitas, he added, "There will be no special treatment because you're a Gibson."

"I would expect nothing less," she said.

CHAPTER THIRTY-TWO

The following morning, Grace was up early, and once she finished her breakfast and read all the newspapers, she waited in the front hall, glancing at her watch.

"I see you're ready," her father said by way of a greeting. The two of them went out to the garage and George explained that he would be driving his car that morning.

"I don't like showing up in a chauffeured car when visiting the growers. In their eyes, it's arrogant. And besides, sometimes I like to drive myself."

The morning was warm and pleasant. The sky was a light blue, and the early morning sun was a pale white orb coming up over the horizon. They chugged along, heading north until they reached an area where rows and rows of grapevines hung on low fences on either side of the highway.

They pulled into the first vineyard. It was half a mile in from the highway, and the crops continued as far as the eye could see on both sides of the dirt road. They soon emerged into a clearing with what looked like a hastily constructed three-sided barn.

An elderly man stood near an aged pickup whose color was once red but had since been dulled by dust. Next to him was a young man not much older than Grace. The back of the pickup was crammed with all sorts of things, from crates to chicken wire to tools. Both men were dressed in light-colored short-sleeved shirts and pants. The old man wore a floppy wide-brimmed hat on his head. The young man's head was bare, and his face was tanned. Both men had the look of someone who spent a lot of time outdoors.

Grace and her father stepped out of the car, the dust from the dirt road coating their shoes.

George stepped forward, hand extended. "Alvin, how are you?" He then shook the young man's hand.

"Mighty fine, Mr. Gibson. It's been a good summer for grapes."

"That's what I like to hear. This is my daughter, Grace, who's learning the business."

They shook her hand, and the old man introduced his son, Alvin Jr. If they were surprised to see a woman there, they didn't let on.

The son spoke up first. "Miss Gibson, were you a Red Cross volunteer in the Philippines?"

Surprised, a smile grew on Grace's face. "I was. I was over there for almost two years."

Alvin Jr. laughed. "I knew you looked familiar. My ship anchored off that island to drop off supplies. You and the other two girls did that take on *Snow White*."

Both of them laughed as their fathers stared at them with bemused smiles.

Alvin Jr. shook his head at the recollection of it. "That was hilarious."

"It was good fun, wasn't it," Grace said.

"It sure was. It was brilliant." Alvin Jr. remained smiling.

Grace caught her father's eye. "Perhaps you could show us the vineyard," she suggested.

Grace and Alvin Jr. followed behind the two older men. Grace strolled along with her hands clasped behind her back as she and Alvin Jr. spoke generally of their war experiences, both agreeing that they certainly didn't miss military rations.

The four of them stood in one of the many rows of grapes as the September sun cast a burnished light along the grapes, and there was the low drone of the bees and crickets.

George picked off a small cluster of purple grapes, popped a couple into his mouth, and handed the rest to Grace. As her father chewed thoughtfully, he nodded with approval. Grace tasted the grapes her father had handed to her. They were delicious. Ripe to the point of bursting.

George looked over the rows and rows of grapes and announced, "That's a great crop."

"We'll start harvesting tomorrow," the older Alvin said.

George nodded in agreement. "They're ready."

They walked along a few more rows, George stopping every so often to inspect clusters of grapes. When they returned to their starting point, they all shook hands, and Grace and her father got in the car and drove off with a wave.

As they headed down the long dirt road back to the highway, George said again, "It's a fine crop this year."

"They seem to be nice people," Grace said.

Her father looked over at her. "Half of this business is the relationships you build with your people, whether they be growers, drivers, or workers at your factory."

Grace nodded, trying to absorb everything he was saying.

"And you did it perfectly, Grace," he continued. "You don't realize it, but you've already started a business relationship with young Alvin by sharing your recollections of your time in the Philippines. That will serve you long after his father and I are gone."

Although they'd spoken about it, Grace couldn't truly imagine her father ever being dead. He was too full of life.

They headed to the factory, where her father gave her a tour. The place was big, and there was the smell of sweetness and grapes throughout. As they toured the factory, it became evident that the line had stopped after lidding. All the jars of jelly stood still on the conveyor belt, waiting to go off to be labeled.

"What's going on, Nelson?" George asked the line manager.

"I think we've got a problem with the belt." Nelson wore navy blue coveralls with the Gibson's Grape Jelly logo over his breast pocket. He wore black glasses, and his wavy gray hair was cut short.

"Let's take a look." George removed his suit jacket and handed it to Grace. He rolled up his sleeves, hitched up his trousers, and got down on the ground and crawled under the belt with Nelson.

When they emerged, Nelson stood and offered his hand to George to help him up. He brushed off his pants, took his coat from Grace, and winked at her. "Don't mention this to your mother."

"Noted," she said with a laugh.

He showed Grace a broken part. "Sometimes this happens. We keep a supply of parts on hand and hopefully, we'll have a replacement for this one. If not, it'll have to be ordered, and production will be limited until it arrives."

She knew that would be costly.

As they walked on, Grace decided that she'd be hands-on with the business, just like her father.

On John's return from his month-long spiritual retreat, he invited Grace to join him for an evening walk on the beach. She hoped this immediate meeting was a portent of good things. They walked along the shoreline, the sun dipping toward the horizon, the sky a lovely combination of lavender and pink. A warm, soft breeze blew over them.

"How was the retreat?" she asked.

"It was excellent. After a month of prayer and fasting, I feel like I have so much more clarity about everything."

She sighed, not liking what her gut was telling her. He'd returned different, more relaxed than she'd ever seen him. She could tell that he was no longer wrestling with anything. The lines of his forehead had all but disappeared and he walked with purpose, his stride confident and happy.

"I spent a lot of time in contemplation," he said. He smiled at her. "I haven't felt this good in years."

Grace stopped in her tracks, the breeze lifting her hair off her shoulders. "Please, John, put me out of my misery."

Before he spoke, he sighed and lowered his head. Funny, how one simple sigh could have such a devastating effect on one's future.

"I'm going to enter the seminary come September," he said.

"Oh."

"I've made peace with my decision, and I hope and pray that someday you will too."

Grace didn't say anything at first. She couldn't.

"Are you all right?" John asked.

"No, I'm not all right," she replied tightly. She clenched her fists at her side. "I'm angry. This is my future, as well, that we're talking about. And I feel powerless. As if I have no say in what happens here between us."

He took her words in stride, in that maddening, calm way of his. "I'm sorry, Grace, but my mind is made up," he said quietly.

Grace stomped her foot in the sand. "Did you take my feelings into consideration at all?" she asked.

Beneath his tan, he blanched. "Of course I did. What do you take me for? You've been foremost on my mind. I've prayed and prayed about this. I've prayed for you and me and us."

She looked away and he gently placed his hands on her forearms. "It wouldn't work, Grace, because I can't ignore my calling, my true vocation. It's the reason I was born. And I wouldn't want to hurt you with my regret later in life. This is something I must do."

So many emotions flooded her. Anger at her powerlessness. Envy at his conviction about his life's purpose. But most of all, an overwhelming sense of sadness and loss. She burst out crying.

John pulled her into his arms, and she slid her hands around his waist, buried her head in his shoulder, and sobbed. His familiar masculine scent, a combination of sweat and soap, did not comfort her as it usually did.

"I love you, John," she said into his shoulder.

"I know. I love you too," he whispered against her hair.

She lifted her face toward him, tears running down her cheeks. "There's no way you'll change your mind?"

He shook his head. She laid her head against his chest and closed her eyes, wishing that the outcome had been different.

John went off to the seminary in September. She continued to visit his parents weekly. He'd asked if he could write to her, and she couldn't refuse. Although she'd wanted him for a husband, she wouldn't refuse his friendship.

Over the next five years, Grace devoted herself to learning the family business inside and out. She worked in every department of the factory: production, canning, lidding, and crating. She spent time in the shipping and logistics department. She worked in the office, learning accounting and doing the books. She made it her business to learn the names of every one of the employees and by the time she was thirty, she was working at the corporate level alongside her father.

CHAPTER THIRTY-THREE

1952

Grace arrived for her annual ten-day visit to Bernie's home in Kansas, on a large wheat farm not far from the Oklahoma border. Bernie Powers was now Bernie Katz, having married her boyfriend after the war. Grace always enjoyed seeing the different parts of the country on the train ride out, but she particularly loved Kansas, loved the endless prairie and the big red barns. Despite the distance, she and Bernie had remained great friends and kept in touch regularly.

Bernie had never fully recovered from her bout of malaria. It amazed Grace that she'd had a child, and Bernie had admitted to her that there would be no more. The arrival of a baby had come as a shock to her as well. She'd been married for years before Ada was born.

Grace sat on the porch of the two-story farmhouse with Bernie, who held Ada in her lap. Bernie had aged and was thinner than Grace remembered.

"Are you still writing to the priest?" Bernie asked.

"I am," Grace said.

"Do you see him?"

"Only occasionally. I went to his ordination last year, and I see him when he comes home for a visit. Now that his parents have passed away, I suppose he might sell the house."

"Won't he be a priest in Lavender Bay? Have a parish?" Bernie asked, bouncing Ada on her lap.

"No. He'll go where his order sends him."

"Have you been dating anyone?" Bernie asked. She'd encouraged Grace to put herself out there. Things hadn't worked out with John, but that didn't mean they might not work out with someone else, Bernie had reasoned.

Grace shrugged. "Here and there." She'd had her share of dates and little romances, as she liked to call them. But she'd soon grown tired of it. The problem was she always compared them to John and eventually, usually sooner rather than later, they all came up short. And then there were the ones that had annoyed her to no end. One had told her as soon as they got married, he would expect her to give up working and stay home and raise their children, because that was her job as a woman. Another had told her that after they were married, he would take over the running of Gibson's Grape Jelly, because after all, he was the man. Now that she was over thirty, she'd more or less given up on marriage. She was okay with that. She loved working, and she loved the family business. Her father, now well into his seventies, had semi-retired.

"And how are you getting along running the business?" Bernie asked.

Grace nodded. "As well as can be expected considering I'm a woman. Sometimes, the other members of the board question my decisions, and they go behind my back and run things by my father." This made her sour.

"What does your father think of that?"

Grace smiled. "He usually tells them that everything is up to me now. And that he wants to concentrate on his golf game."

The summer air was thick, heavy, and hot. But Grace always felt relaxed out here, looking out over the rows and rows of golden wheat as far as the eye could see. She thought it was beautiful, and told Bernie as much.

Her friend snorted. "It wasn't so beautiful two years ago when the locusts descended."

"I suppose not."

"After a while, you take it for granted, the wheat. Do you, with the lake?" Bernie asked.

Grace tilted her head to one side, thinking. "I guess so. You know it's always there, going nowhere. Yes, I guess we do take it for granted."

Despite several invitations to come up to Lavender Bay, Bernie had always refused. Grace tried again. "I'd love it if you and Ada came up for a couple of weeks and stayed with us."

"There's nothing I'd love more," Bernie said. "But Mr. Wonderful would never let me go. Who'd wash his dirty drawers while I was away?"

They both laughed.

"I don't think he likes me," Grace said honestly. She figured that Bernie's husband would prefer she wasn't there. He was always polite but never engaged her in conversation.

"Don't worry about him. I don't think he likes me either," Bernie said. They started laughing again, and the baby looked up at her mother and gurgled. Bernie scrunched up her face and said to Ada, "Isn't that right, honeybun? Mr. Wonderful doesn't like me. But he likes you, though. He thinks you're the bee's knees."

The baby laughed and gurgled some more.

"Bernie, why did you marry him?" Grace asked. They'd been through too much and had been friends for too long to shy away from asking personal questions.

"Look around, Grace, what do you see?"

Grace didn't have to look around to know the answer. "Lots of wheat."

"That's right, and nothing else. And no one else. There weren't a lot of takers for me, if you know what I mean. I've got a big mouth, a big nose, and big feet. And well, Harold showed some interest, and it was a plus that he was taller than me and his feet were bigger than mine. Most of all, he doesn't talk with his mouth full of food. At the time, I felt it could work."

Grace supposed other people had gotten married for less. She felt compelled to ask, "Are you unhappy?"

Bernie immediately shook her head. "Not on your life. Harold gave me Ada and for that, I'll always be grateful." She kissed the top of her baby's head. "Don't get me wrong, Harold isn't the love of my life or anything like that. There's no romance, but there was never any from the beginning. It's just how he's made."

"Would you like romance?"

"I'd like more laughs," she admitted.

"Do you ever talk about your experience in the war?" Bernie's husband had served, and Grace figured that would give them common ground.

Bernie shook her head and her eyes dulled. "Harold has never mentioned it. I brought it up once when we were first back, and he kind of downplayed my contribution. Said what I did was nothing compared to being in a foxhole."

"Oh, Bernie, I'm so sorry," Grace said. What an awful thing to say. She was offended on her friend's behalf. Granted, they never saw battle, and never once did they think they'd made the sacrifice that the troops had made, but Grace liked to think they'd made a difference.

"Harold is no Cary Grant," Bernie said, "and knowing that, I accept him at the level he's at." There was that spark of mischief in her eyes as she added, "Somewhere down in the cellar."

Grace burst out laughing. Visiting Bernie was always the highlight of her year.

CHAPTER THIRTY-FOUR

1995

G race sat on the edge of the bed in the hotel room in San Francisco and read John's letter again.

Dear Grace,

I'm delighted to hear that you've decided to attend the island reunion. I think you'll enjoy yourself. I agree, it is a shame that Bernie isn't with you, but I'm sure she's there in spirit. It's hard to believe that the war ended fifty years ago!

I was also surprised that you've shelved the idea of retiring from the family business. As long as you feel you can do it, why not. Like you've said, you'll reassess when you turn eighty. How is it possible that we're as old as we are? It went by in the blink of an eye.

I miss working, but I do what I can when I'm able. I don't know if I necessarily agree with the mandatory retirement age of seventy-five for priests. I was in tip-top shape at seventy-five. Now, not so much. Unfortunately, my most recent scan shows extensive metastatic disease, and I'll meet with the oncologist again to see what kind of treatment plan they have in store for me this time. If I'm even a candidate. To answer the question I know is coming in your next letter, I've made peace with it. Everything is in God's hands. I trust Him completely. Please don't fret over this.

I can't wait to hear all about your trip.
Have fun and enjoy yourself.
Yours in friendship and affection,
John

She carefully tucked the letter back into its envelope. His news about his health had weighed heavy on her heart since she'd received the letter more than a week ago. She was so upset she almost canceled her trip. But she knew John well enough to know that he wouldn't want that. They'd been friends for so long she couldn't imagine a world without him. It was the same when Bernie had passed away. She'd been distraught then, hating the change in the landscape after her friend's death. It was John who'd counseled her at the time. She'd leaned heavily on him then. But who would she lean on when he was gone? She put the letter into her suitcase and sat down again, staring out the window and trying to muster the ambition to go downstairs.

Grace, what you need is a good kick in the pants, she told herself. She stood and brushed her hair, put on a pair of clip-on earrings, and applied some lipstick before retrieving her handbag and heading out of her room, double-checking to make sure the door was locked.

As she walked through the hotel lobby, she was filled with a mixture of excitement and apprehension. She had no idea what to expect or who would be there, if anyone. What if no one remembered her? Would she be consigned to a corner, alone?

Fifty years! Sometimes, she couldn't believe how much time had passed. And yet, the memories were vivid and vibrant in her head. When she closed her eyes, she could still feel the wet heat of that island in the Philippines and see the precise shade of blue of that sky. She'd been there less than two years, and yet it was probably the most significant event of her life. After the war, she continued her involvement with the Red Cross, eventually serving on the board.

Outside the ballroom was a big sign announcing the fiftieth-anniversary reunion of those who served on the island. When she stepped inside, she was greeted by women much younger than herself, who manned a table. She gave them her name and was handed a name tag, which she stuck to her blouse.

She looked around, her eyes widening at the size of the crowd. There had to be hundreds of people there.

"Grace Jelly, is that you?" boomed a voice.

Her head snapped up and her mouth fell open at the sight of Buster Baines. His hair was now snow white, and he was heavier. On his head was a VFW cap pinned with small medals. He wore two prosthetic hands.

Grace hugged him. "Buster! I can't believe it. How are you?"

"I'm doing great! You haven't changed a bit." he said. He stepped back and put his arm around the smiling woman next to him. "This is my wife, Sarah. We've been married forty-seven years!"

"That's wonderful," Grace said.

"Is Bernie with you?" he asked.

She shook her head. "Bernie passed in 1979."

Buster removed his cap. "I'm sorry to hear that. She was great fun."

Grace laughed. "She sure was." Grace had continued to visit Bernie every year up until her death. Afterward, she'd convinced Ada to come to Lavender Bay every year to visit her.

"Come on, Grace, Ziggy and Timid Tim are here. They've got a table."

Grace felt the familiar prick of tears in her eyes as nostalgia rolled over her. "Ziggy and Timid Tim are here? Well, let's go, we've got a lot of catching up to do!"

Smiling, she stepped forward, following Buster and Sarah, ready to reconnect with people from a long time ago.

PART THREE

DeeDee

CHAPTER THIRTY-FIVE

As summer ended and autumn arrived, so did the cooler weather. DeeDee had forgotten how much she loved the vibrant colors of the season: the reds, the oranges, and the yellows. She even enjoyed the seasonal pumpkin-spice coffees and lattes Angie had on offer at Coffee Girl. The air was damp, and leaves continued to fall until the trees were bare and stark silhouettes against a gray sky.

When she visited Grace, they were no longer able to sit out back in Grace's sunroom, instead moving inside to the living room at the front of the house. It was painted in a shade of blue so pale that depending on how the light hit it, it could appear as a muted gray. It was a large, comfortable room with overstuffed furniture in various shades of cream, pale blue, and navy.

"This room is lovely," DeeDee said, settling onto the sofa across from Grace, who sat in a recliner with her feet up, a blue plaid blanket laid over her legs. A small fire crackled in the fireplace.

"Thank you. This was always my mother's favorite room. While she was alive it was done up in yellows. But I've since changed it."

"This shade of blue appears very soft."

"That's what I thought. Peaceful."

The room darkened as a cloud passed overhead outside.

Grace glanced out the window. "It looks like we're in for some terrible weather." She turned back toward DeeDee. "Why don't you turn on that lamp next to you so you can see what you're doing?"

Over the course of their meetings, DeeDee felt as if she'd really gotten to know Grace, the *real* Grace. She'd developed a genuine fondness for the elderly woman. Despite her wealth and age, she was very down to earth. Although she'd had a comfortable life, she'd had her share of heartache, proving that no one was immune.

Ada appeared, asking if either of them would like tea or coffee and a slice of cake.

They both decided on tea.

When Ada disappeared, Grace remarked, "Ada loves to bake and I love to eat, so we work out well together." She appeared thoughtful. "I don't know what I'd do without her."

The interviews were drawing to a close, and it saddened DeeDee that she'd no longer have an excuse to visit. She'd enjoyed their conversations.

"You've had a fascinating life, Grace," she concluded.

Grace shrugged. "I've had ups and downs like anyone else. Funny, how those two years in the Pacific changed my life forever."

"In what way?"

"I was a different person when I returned home. It was as if the girl who left Lavender Bay, determined to do her part for the war, died in the Pacific. When I came home, I knew I was a different person. How could I not be, with everything I'd seen and done in those few short years."

"How was it when you did return to Lavender Bay?"

"Honestly, I felt like a stranger in a foreign land, almost the same way I felt when I arrived in the Philippines. Everything was so different from what I'd become used to."

She looked off in the distance, and her eyes were hazy with memories. "When I returned, I had to start all over again."

Ada returned with a tray bearing two mugs and a small pot of tea. She left and reappeared with two plates of cake, handing each of them a slice.

"Yellow cake with chocolate frosting, my favorite," Grace said.

"Do you ever regret not getting married or having children?" DeeDee asked. It was a question she'd wrestled with herself. Hurriedly, she added, "I'm sorry, I didn't mean to pry."

Grace waved her hand around. "I would have liked to marry John and have some children." She shrugged. "But it wasn't meant to be."

"It must have been difficult," DeeDee said gently.

"It was. I was heartbroken for a long time. Despite his becoming a priest, we remained very good friends right up until he passed away. But now at my age, I have the benefit of hindsight. I have loved and been loved by many people. When I think about the work I did for the Red Cross during the war, I can honestly say that I have loved a thousand men. I consider myself very lucky."

DeeDee thought of the people in her own life. She was lucky too.

Grace continued, "It would have been impossible in those days to run a business and have a marriage and a family. Women worked, don't get me wrong, but they didn't often run companies. And they certainly didn't do both: family and career. It just wasn't done then. I was considered an anomaly, but I didn't care. I did what I wanted."

"Can you tell me what the most difficult thing in your life was?" DeeDee asked, setting up her phone to record.

"When you've lived as long as I have," Grace started, "There are many difficult situations. It's inevitable. There was disappointment in love, difficulties with readjustment to civilian life, and then of course the challenges inherent with trying to run a business, first as a woman and second, during economic downturns." She paused as if gathering her thoughts, steepling her gnarled hands in front of her. Although she looked out the window, her gaze appeared to be fixed inward.

"I would definitely say the most traumatic thing was the first time we were bombed on the island. The memory of that remains vivid, even after all these years. It was pure, violent chaos." She shook her head. "It ripped me out of the cocoon that my parents had so carefully crafted around me." She paused and then picked up her train of thought. "Looking back, I think it affected me more than I realized at the time. I had nightmares about it for years."

DeeDee's heart rate shot up and her mouth went dry. With a shaking hand, she picked up her mug and took a sip of her tea.

"You know, for the longest time," Grace said, "every time a siren went off—ambulance, police, whatever—I broke out in a cold sweat and palpitations. At the time, post-traumatic stress disorder had no name, but I'm sure I had it."

Fine beads of perspiration appeared above DeeDee's lip. Her hand continued to shake as she set her cup down.

"When I stood in that medical tent and saw Buster with his two bloody stumps, I froze. It was like the saying: I became a deer in the headlights. I was surrounded by carnage. Young men, men younger than me, with their limbs ripped off or missing half their face. Or worse, dead." She stopped and after a few moments, resumed speaking, "I didn't know where to look first. I didn't know how to help. I felt helpless and useless. To be witness to that was an awful feeling."

DeeDee absorbed what the older woman was saying and was forced to confront the parallel of her own life.

"There was so much going on, so many horrible things at once, and I think the brain has difficulty processing that in real time. It's almost as if it shuts down and goes into survival mode. But then when the event is over and the brain is operating at full capacity, it forces you to deal with those horrible things you saw." Grace paused before saying, "Anyway, that's my take on it."

DeeDee's thoughts led her down a narrow alley, one she didn't want to go down. It was almost like she couldn't help it, as if she were being propelled forward. Grace's relatable narrative triggered something she wanted to bury deep and forget. But it burst forth, unable to be contained. It startled her.

She gasped and lowered her head.

"DeeDee?" said Grace from her recliner.

But DeeDee didn't hear Grace. She was back there. That day. The bright sunshine. The way the palm trees looked against that endless blue sky. Three weeks before the play was to open, she'd been driving along a four-lane highway lined with one strip mall after another, had been singing along at the top of her longs to "Walking on Sunshine" on her car radio. She was in a great mood. She loved her part in the play, and her relationship with Brad was going well. She felt on top of the world.

There was a long strip of grass in the center meridian of the four-lane road. She remembered thinking how green the grass was and that someone must be watering it regularly in that heat. An SUV came up from behind her in the left-hand lane and flew by DeeDee's car, apparently trying to make the left-hand turn signal up ahead at the traffic light. But the sedan in front of DeeDee pulled over to the left-hand lane, unaware that the SUV was fast approaching. The SUV plowed into the sedan, spinning out of control and hitting the median with such force that the driver was ejected from the car, bursting through the windshield like a rocket. The SUV continued to spin, hitting the curb and rolling over, the top of it crumpling like it was made of cheap plastic. DeeDee had stopped singing, though the radio continued to blare. Her mouth hung open as she stared. The sedan immediately pulled over ahead, its hazards on and its back end smashed in.

Although it happened so fast, in the blink of an eye, it played out in slow motion in her memory. The car hitting the curb, the man being launched from the vehicle, the SUV flipping over and spinning like some out-of-control toy. All traffic came to a stop. Behind her, she heard another car being rear-ended by another vehicle.

Some kept driving. Some pulled over. DeeDee was closest and somehow remembered to throw on her hazards as she parked her car against the outside curb. She got out of her car and ran over to the SUV. All traffic had come to a complete stop. An older man wearing an orange Hawaiian shirt with a Miami Dolphins baseball cap ran toward the grassy verge where the driver had landed. As he ran, he pulled out his cell phone from his pocket. DeeDee hoped he was calling the emergency services. She glanced back at the driver. From where she was, she couldn't tell if he was alive. But she noticed something on the grass next to him. With horror, she realized it was his arm, which was no longer connected to his body. Her stomach roiled at the sight of it, and she forced her gaze away. She turned her attention to the upside-down SUV.

No one emerged from the car, and she hoped the driver was the sole occupant. She knelt down, ignoring the broken glass all over the asphalt. Peering inside, she spotted a woman in the passenger seat. Her hair and face were blood-soaked. Blood flowed from her ear. She moaned and mumbled incoherently. She was upside down, still strapped in her seat belt. The top of her head was against the crushed top of the car.

DeeDee thought, *Oh my God, Oh my God. Oh. My. God.*

"I've called the police," said someone behind her.

"So did I," said someone else.

A crowd had gathered. A young woman knelt on the other side of DeeDee, peered in, swallowed hard, jumped up, and took a few steps back, her hands over her mouth.

The woman in the car lifted her hand, and DeeDee took hold of it. "I'm DeeDee," she said. "Help is on the way." Off in the distance, sirens wailed, and she was never so grateful for anything in her life.

A man behind her said, "The driver's dead. He's a mess. Arm is gone. Legs are busted. You should see him."

The injured woman moaned louder.

DeeDee's head snapped up. "That is not helpful."

"Frank . . ." the woman moaned. She tried turning in her seat. "Frank." The moaning continued against the rising volume of the approaching sirens.

"Shh," DeeDee said, trying to comfort her. She gently stroked the woman's hand. It was delicate. Feminine. The nails were polished a coral color. "Should we try and get her out?" she asked out loud over her shoulder, over the woman's moans.

Someone behind her said, "No. We don't know the extent of her injuries."

That made sense. DeeDee continued to hold the woman's hand and speak reassuringly to her. She didn't know what else to do.

The area was soon filled with police, the fire department, and an ambulance. DeeDee looked over her shoulder as a police officer and several firefighters ran toward her. She was filled with relief. She felt the woman's hand go slack in hers, and she returned her attention to her. The moaning had stopped, and the woman's eyes were closed. Her chest wasn't moving.

"No," DeeDee said, blinking. "Don't go. Help is here."

But it was futile. The woman was dead. She looked different than she had only a moment ago, as if the soul had escaped the confines of the corporeal form, leaving only a shell behind.

A firefighter knelt beside her, and she looked at him, helpless.

"Ma'am, if you could please step aside," he said. He was young. Younger than DeeDee. Too young to have to deal with this.

DeeDee didn't move. She couldn't. She was frozen to the spot, still holding on to the woman's hand, looking from the dead woman to the firefighter, who was now leaning into the broken window and assessing the woman.

"Come on, miss," said a police officer at her side. Gently, he removed the woman's hand from DeeDee's. He helped her up.

Without a word, DeeDee stood, brushing broken glass from her knees, ignoring the bleeding where she'd been cut.

She followed the police officer and gave a witness statement before she was allowed to leave. Shaking, she walked back to her car, almost staggering, as if she'd had too much to drink. Inside, she went through the automatic motions of buckling up and turning off her hazard lights. The radio blared as she started the engine, frightening her. She reached over and shut it off. Somehow she made it back home, her errand forgotten. But later, when she reviewed the events of the afternoon, she came up blank with regard to the route home. She couldn't remember passing certain landmarks. Of the accident itself, she had perfect recall.

And that had been her undoing.

Back in Grace's living room, DeeDee leaned back against the sofa cushions and let out a cry.

Across from her, Grace asked gently, "Are you all right?"

DeeDee shook her head. She buried her face in her hands and cried.

Grace pressed a few buttons on the remote control of her recliner, and the chair lifted itself until Grace was in a standing position. Gingerly, she got her bearings, and walked around the coffee table and sat next to DeeDee. She took hold of her hand.

For the first time, DeeDee poured forth her story. She'd never told anyone. She'd kept it inside, burying it deep, not wanting to relive it or look at it too closely. Witnessing that accident had left her shattered. She'd walked around like a zombie in the months afterward, resulting in her disastrous performance in the play.

Grace listened patiently.

Finally, embarrassed at her outburst, DeeDee lifted her head. Grace handed her a box of tissues from the end table. DeeDee pulled one out, wiped her eyes, and blew her nose. Mortified, she said, "I am so sorry, Grace."

Grace waved her away. "Nonsense."

"I've never told anyone."

"I understand. How long ago did this happen?"

"It happened last spring." DeeDee said, blowing her nose again. "I've had difficulty moving forward from it."

Grace surprised her by putting a frail arm around her shoulders. "It must have come as a great shock to witness such a terrible thing."

DeeDee nodded. Her eyes filled up again. Here she was, eating a lovely piece of cake, and that man and woman were dead. Too young to die. They had lives. People who loved them. Plans.

"I felt so useless," DeeDee said quietly. "I didn't know how to help her."

"You might not have been able to help her," Grace said.

"But I wanted to."

"Of course."

DeeDee wiped her nose and looked at the older woman. "How did you deal with all the things you saw and experienced on the island? My goodness, you've seen a lot in your life."

Grace sighed. "I have. After that first bomb dropped, Bernie, Charlotte, and I were a little shell-shocked. But we had each other to lean on, and we were determined to help the boys."

"I realize I haven't experienced the types of things you have," DeeDee said. She didn't want to come across as a whiner.

"It's all relative. Who's to say what you witnessed was easier or harder than what I witnessed? Death outside the natural order of things is traumatic for anyone. Have you seen a therapist? A professional who can help you unburden yourself and get yourself unstuck?" Grace asked.

DeeDee shook her head. "No."

"That might be your first stop," Grace suggested gently. "They might be able to advise you on healthier coping mechanisms than the ones you're using now. That sort of support wasn't available to us after the war, but I wish it had been. We were just expected to get on with things. I threw myself into work, and I found that helped."

DeeDee poured more tea for the both of them.

"For my friend Bernie," Grace said, "it was humor. She would go out of her way to be happy, even when she had to find things to be happy about. The contrast between the laughs I had with her on the island and the war going on around us has never been lost on me. She was probably one of the funniest people I've ever met. She was our comic relief, and she made that whole experience so much better, more palatable, just by being herself." Grace's fond laughter was like the twitter of a bird.

"I've found that idleness is the worst thing," she went on. "For me, at least. It leads to too much thinking. It's too easy to be sucked down the rabbit hole of the past." She paused. "I'm closing in on one hundred years old. Most, if not all of the people I've known and loved, with the exception of Ada, are gone. Some for a very long time. Sometimes, I feel like God forgot about me."

"Does it feel lonely?"

"Sometimes it does. But then I get busy doing something productive. Having a purpose is important. At any age. Even at my age."

DeeDee nodded in understanding.

Grace patted DeeDee's knee. "You must throw yourself into something you love. And maybe it sounds trite, but you have to find some way to process what you've witnessed. As your friend, I would strongly advise seeking out the guidance of a therapist."

"Thank you," DeeDee said. "For everything. This has been a meaningful experience for me."

"Especially when I dozed off in the middle of that first interview." The elderly woman's eyes shone with glee.

DeeDee laughed and stood. "I've taken up enough of your time now. I'll go."

"Not at all. There isn't much I can do at my age. But I can listen," Grace said.

And DeeDee thought that might be more important than anything.

Chapter Thirty-Six

DeeDee and Louise walked along the beach. DeeDee couldn't remember the last time she and her mother had been to the beach together. Certainly not in recent memory. And most definitely not in November.

That particular morning was dry but damp, and the sky was a dull gray. Large foamy whitecaps roared toward the shore. There was a breeze that was bitter and bracing.

DeeDee was glad she'd worn a winter hat and a heavy pullover sweater beneath her coat. Her mother was similarly attired, but she'd added a fleece jacket over her turtleneck.

"How's it going with Grace Gibson?" Louise asked as they walked side by side along the shore, where the sand was wet and flat and easier to walk on. There was no one else on the beach. Some people found the waterfront depressing in the winter with all the gray and brown, but not DeeDee. She liked the lake in all its seasons.

"We finished last night," DeeDee said. "She's had an amazing life! She's done so much."

"I suppose if you lived to be one hundred, you'd get a lot done too," her mother said.

DeeDee disagreed. "Not necessarily."

"Maybe not," her mother conceded.

"I mean, she was one of the first female CEOs in the country. She was way ahead of her time."

"Funny, but I think the town took it in stride when she took over after her father. The townspeople figured she was a Gibson, why shouldn't she run the place?"

"Really?" DeeDee asked. Grace had told her that it wasn't until the sixties that a woman could open up a bank account, and even then she had to have her husband or her father's name on it. It wasn't until a decade later that women could have their own bank accounts and credit cards.

It boggled DeeDee's mind how much Grace Gibson had seen and experienced in her life. Her own paled in comparison.

"Oh boy, you've gone quiet on me. What's wrong?" Louise asked.

"Why do you say that?" DeeDee asked.

"Because I'm your mother and nobody knows you better. Ever since you were a little girl, when something is bothering you, you go quiet. My girl with the microphone in her throat goes silent when she's troubled."

A light drizzle started to fall and they turned around, heading in the direction of Heather Lane before it started to rain in earnest.

"When I look at Grace's life and then look at my own . . ." DeeDee's voice wavered.

"No, no, don't do that, DeeDee," her mother said. "That's not fair. You were born at different times. You're different people. You can't compare yourself to Grace."

"That's because there is no comparison," DeeDee said. "I'm a very selfish person."

Louise was quick to refute that. "I wouldn't say that. I suppose we're all selfish in some way when it comes to our own lives. Although being the youngest, Grammie did spoil the hell out of you." Louise smiled. "We all did."

"Grammie sure did. So did Pop-Pop before he passed." They walked a little further before DeeDee added, "I feel as if I don't have much to show for my life."

Louise stopped in her tracks and her expression transformed into one of sorrow. "Don't ever say that, DeeDee. Please. You might only be feeling like this after talking to Grace. Please remember, she's been alive sixty more years than you."

But DeeDee couldn't let it drop. "I know, but by the time she was my age, she was already a CEO."

The two of them had reached the parking lot and cut across it, heading toward Louise's home.

"Don't forget, she inherited the business from her father, so in a way, it was a ready-made position," Louise said.

DeeDee appreciated that her mother was trying to make her feel better.

The wind whistled and DeeDee's eyes stung. "I had so many dreams when I was eighteen."

"We all do. And life rarely turns out the way we think it will."

"I thought my career would be better. Farther ahead than it is." The recent setback remained a predominant thought.

"We all feel that way about various aspects of our lives," Louise said.

"Do you?"

"Sure. I had dreams of being a stewardess—er, flight attendant," her mother explained. "But then I met your father, and I had you girls. I wanted to see the world, but money was always tight in the early years, so your father and I couldn't really travel like we wanted to. And then your father died, and that was the end of that."

"Why didn't you go and travel yourself?" DeeDee asked.

Louise shrugged. "I didn't want to go without your father."

"Do you have regrets?"

"I think everyone has regrets to some degree. But overall, I'm happy with my life. Because if there's one thing I've learned, it's that people and relationships, especially family, are the most important things. More than anything."

It was good to hear her mother say she was happy with her life. DeeDee hoped it was contagious.

Louise reached out and put an arm around her. "Everything is going to be all right. You'll see."

CHAPTER THIRTY-SEVEN

DeeDee worked on the play into the winter, sitting at her mother's kitchen table, putting Grace's life story into three acts. As she worked, she listened again and again to the recordings of their interviews, drawing from them what she hoped was a fitting tribute to Grace. She sat bundled up in heavy sweaters, drinking one mug of coffee or tea after another. One day, she heard a chirp across from her.

"Peaches!" she said, pleased. She jumped up from her chair and approached him as he hopped around in his cage. "Did you just chirp?"

The reply was a second chirp.

"You've found your voice! Good for you!" She cooed at him for a minute or two, and got back to work with a smile on her face. Every once in a while, he emitted the odd chirp.

It was a start.

She continued her shifts at Coffee Girl, finding she was enjoying being with people. On the days she wasn't at Angie's café, she was over at Nadine's inn on Pearl Street, doing housecleaning. In the afternoons, she walked Rufus. Doing these jobs wasn't making her rich, but it was nice to have some pocket money, and it allowed her to keep her utilities on in her condo for when she returned, which she thought would be after the play.

After Christmas, she set about getting things up and running for the production. She booked the little theater inside the community center. She put out a call for volunteers to help with various tasks. She decided she herself would take the part of Grace at middle age. She had a moment of self-doubt about whether she could pull off the young Grace, the one who went away to the Philippines, but then decided she'd go ahead and do that too. It would be a great role, and she was looking forward to exploring it. Since speaking with Grace, she felt she had a good understanding of how the character should be played.

As the celebrations were due to kick off in April, the play had to be ready by then. The premiere was booked for April 19th, Grace's birthday, and there'd be a matinee as well as an evening show. Grace would be there for the opening performance, along with Ada. Two center seats in the front row had already been reserved for them. The play would run for several nights as there was not enough seating to hold all the townspeople, and proceeds from the ticket sales would go to a charity of Grace's choice.

At the end of January, on a Saturday morning, DeeDee trudged through the snow to the open casting call. The winter air was sharp and brisk. Before she'd left the house, her mother had given her a piece of advice: "Remember, they're amateurs. Go and have fun."

She'd put up flyers throughout town and had run an advertisement in *The Lavender Bay Chronicles* for the preceding two weeks. She'd made the mistake of including her phone number, and the calls were incessant. Edna Knickerbocker and Edith Bermingham were frequent callers, inquiring about the role of the older Grace. When DeeDee commented about it to her mother, Louise said seriously, "I hope a scuffle doesn't ensue."

There was a crowd at the community center, and DeeDee was pleased with the turnout. A quick glance around told her it was mainly women. There weren't a lot of men there, and that could be a problem.

She pushed through all the people as whispers rippled through the crowd. "She's here!" Like she was some kind of celebrity. DeeDee found this odd.

She pegged Mrs. Knickerbocker and Mrs. B as being the oldest auditionees. The biggest surprise was the appearance of Brett Jovanovic, the town's vet. She approached him, smiling. He shifted on his feet.

"I didn't know you were interested in acting," she said.

"I belonged to a drama group in college," he said. "How's Peaches?"

"He's been doing well. He's not singing yet, but he's started to chirp again."

He nodded. "Maybe he's starting to settle in."

She didn't want to think what returning to Florida might do to her poor canary in late spring when they went back. Would he go mute again?

The vet went quiet, and the air grew awkward around them. DeeDee excused herself. Curiosity filled her as to what his acting style might be. Could he even act?

She waved them all into the theater, instructing them to separate into two groups, male and female, and then breaking the groups down further by age group. Once she had everyone sorted according to the parts they were auditioning for, she handed out the sides, small portions of the script used specifically for auditions. She'd kept them to two pages.

DeeDee took a seat in the second row and was surprised to see her cousin Suzanne approaching her. Like her sister, Esther, Suzanne was a dark brunette, but she wore her hair long, just past her shoulders. DeeDee had always thought Suzanne was a gentle soul.

They hugged. "What are you doing here?" DeeDee asked, unable to hide her delight at Suzanne's arrival. "Did you want to try out for one of the parts?"

"Gosh no," Suzanne said with a laugh. "I thought I might be able to help. Do you need an assistant?"

"I wouldn't say no, but it would be an unpaid position, like mine," DeeDee said.

Suzanne shrugged. "I don't mind. It's not like I have anything going on at the moment. My youngest is in kindergarten and I'm bored. I might not be able to be here in the evenings, but I'll be here during the day."

Suzanne's husband didn't like her working outside the home. She said she didn't mind, that she preferred to be home with her children. But this aspect of Suzanne's marriage, and some other parts as well, were the subject of frequent conversation among DeeDee's mother, her aunt, Esther, and her own sisters. Suzanne's husband was not a popular person within the family.

"That would be fine," DeeDee said.

"I could take notes or something, or whatever you need me to do."

"Perfect!"

They were interrupted by the joint approach of Mrs. Knickerbocker and Mrs. B, who kept a distance of three feet from each other, just outside of the other's personal space.

"I'm here to try out for the role of Grace Gibson. The elderly Grace," Mrs. Knickerbocker said, casting a side-eye at her sister.

Next to her, Mrs. B raised her voice. "I would also like to *audition* for the role of the elderly Grace."

Edna was about to say something smart when Mrs. B said to her, "Nice coat." Edna wore a smart navy coat that looked vintage to DeeDee. Caught off guard, Mrs. Knickerbocker said through gritted teeth, "Thank you."

Mrs. B continued to speak. "I used to own a coat *exactly* like that one, but I recently donated it to thrift shop."

Edna's face went the color of puce. Immediately, DeeDee and Suzanne stood up. *I need to get us referee shirts, caps, and whistles*, DeeDee thought. *And maybe a few red and yellow flags for good measure.*

Before either of the sisters could orbit into space, DeeDee handed them the appropriate sides and said, "Go memorize these lines, and you can do your audition shortly."

"Mrs. Knickerbocker," Suzanne said, "why don't you go backstage, and Mrs. B, why don't you practice at the back of the theater."

Without a word, both women went off in the direction they were instructed.

When they were out of earshot, DeeDee confided to Suzanne, "I don't want to have to pick one over the other."

"Definitely not. We don't need World War III in town. The two of them are each like a keg of dynamite with an extremely short fuse."

"It's been that way for as long as I can remember."

"I think it goes back to when they were young women," Suzanne said.

"At their age, they should think of burying the hatchet."

"Before they bury each other," Suzanne quipped.

DeeDee shook her head. She couldn't imagine not speaking to her sisters, even if they tended to get on her nerves.

"Of course, each will be disappointed if they don't get the role. They'll want to be involved," Suzanne observed.

"We can find something else for them to do," DeeDee said.

In the end, neither woman was suitable for the role. Edna overacted, and not only did Mrs. B play Grace too coy, her voice could not reach the back of the theater.

"Could you speak a little louder, Mrs. B?" DeeDee had prompted her. "We're having trouble hearing you."

"Pretend you're shouting at me," Edna quipped from the fourth row, where she'd parked herself to watch her sister's audition.

To soften the blow of not being chosen, DeeDee asked Edna if she would like to be in charge of the lights.

"Is it hard?" Edna asked. To which her sister chortled. Edna shot her a look of daggers.

"Not at all," DeeDee explained.

"Sign me up."

Suzanne made a note of it on her list.

"Mrs. B, would you like to be in charge of costumes?" DeeDee asked. "They'd be from different time periods, of course."

"I always had an interest in fashion. I think I would be well suited to it," Mrs. B replied.

Behind her, Edna snorted.

In the end, DeeDee awarded the role of the elderly Grace to Kay Bright of the Lavender Bay Historical Society. She had a good grasp of Grace; it helped that she knew her personally. With a little direction, DeeDee thought she'd play the role perfectly.

When it came time for Brett to audition, he got up onstage and recited the lines for the role of John McNamara. Initially, his performance was flat. But as he got into it, he began to show signs of promise. There was some ability and talent there, and that was all DeeDee needed to see. She decided to give him the part, thinking she might be able to work with him and coax out a better performance.

CHAPTER THIRTY-EIGHT

Most of the roles were cast, except the roles of Bernie and some of the young soldiers on the island. For expediency's sake, DeeDee had written only three soldiers into the script: Ziggy, Timid Tim, and Buster. The problem of who was going to play these soldiers was solved by a quick call to the teacher over at the high school who headed the drama club. She promised to send her students over Saturday morning to audition. If necessary, DeeDee would have women play those parts. If Shakespeare could use men to play the roles of women back in his day, then she could do the reverse. But the role of Bernie remained elusive.

She walked from the community center over toward Coffee Girl, passing her aunt's antique shop, where Rufus sat in his usual spot in the front window. Passing by, DeeDee wrapped on the window and said, "Hi, Rufus!" and the dog thumped his tail slowly and looked at her with his doleful eyes.

There was a nip in the air, but the sun was bright. Snow crunched beneath her feet. She pulled a tissue from her pocket and wiped her nose, which had started running. She couldn't remember the last time she was home for winter. Although she missed the warm, sunny weather of Florida, the cold air was invigorating.

DeeDee pulled off her hat as she entered the café. There was a lull at Coffee Girl. Breakfast and lunch were over, and the tables were only half occupied. She was closing today, which meant she wouldn't get home until seven. But she didn't mind. It was better than sitting around all day doing nothing now that she'd completed the final draft of the play. During her off times, she tended to overthink, grappling with the question of what she was going to do with the rest of her life. It scared her to think her time in Florida might be over after those terrible reviews. It was better to stay occupied and keep herself from spiraling. She'd also noticed that on those days when she was very busy, she was less likely to have nightmares when she went to bed.

She said hello to Iris and Erica behind the counter and pushed through the Employees Only door to hang up her coat and put her purse in one of the lockers. She spotted Debbie standing in the doorway to Angie's office.

"Hi, Debbie."

"How's my favorite actress?" Debbie asked.

"I'm great. Almost finished casting the parts for the play." She joined Debbie in the doorway.

"How exciting!"

DeeDee nodded and looked at Angie. Now that her hair had grown back, she was beginning to look more like her old self.

"What's new?" she asked her sister.

"I have to leave early. Tom's taking me out to dinner," Angie said. She could barely contain her smile.

DeeDee was happy for her sister. Tom was a great guy and knew exactly how to handle her prickly sister. Her own ill-fated romance came to mind, and she thought maybe romance was not in the cards for her. Of course, she'd mainly dated other actors or directors or stagehands, because those were the circles in which she moved. Maybe she needed to enlarge her circle a bit more.

"Have a nice time. I can lock up and put the alarm on."

"You don't mind?"

DeeDee shook her head. "Not at all."

"So you said you're *almost* finished casting?" Angie asked.

"Yes. I have one part left to cast. It's a comedic part." She looked from one woman to the other.

"Nope, not a hope," Angie said, throwing up her hands. "Don't even think about it."

Debbie immediately shook her head. "No way."

"You should get someone who's naturally funny, like Esther," Angie suggested.

"Esther?" DeeDee repeated.

Angie nodded. "Esther is hilarious if you can get her off the subject of bowling."

"I think so too," Debbie agreed.

"Sure, she's funny, but I wonder how well she can act," DeeDee said. A throwaway comment Esther had made to her a while back floated around the periphery of her mind, just out of reach. "What's new with you guys?"

"Deb was just telling me she's still looking for a home for Peter," Angie said.

"The one-eyed and three-legged cat?" DeeDee asked.

Deb nodded. "Yes. He's coming along. Slow but sure. Litter-trained now."

"She had a cat once who wasn't. Have you ever seen a cat wearing a diaper?" Angie asked with a laugh.

"I can't say that I have." DeeDee laughed.

"Let me tell you, it's something you can't unsee," Angie joked.

"I think you'd make a great cat-mom for Peter, DeeDee," Debbie said.

DeeDee shook her head. "Nope. I don't think he'd be a good match for Peaches."

"How is he doing?" Angie asked.

"He's chirping from time to time."

"Progress, not perfection," Debbie declared.

DeeDee thought those were wise words and could possibly be applied to any situation in life.

Chapter Thirty-Nine

The first day of rehearsals was like herding cats. DeeDee still hadn't filled the role of Bernie, so she had Suzanne read the lines for Bernie during rehearsals. Students from the drama club at McKinley High were recruited for the parts of the troops on the island.

Suzanne walked around with a clipboard, making sure everyone was where they needed to be. And most importantly, she kept Mrs. Knickerbocker and Mrs. B as far away from each other as possible. Edna was at the back of the small theater, learning the lights along with her neighbor Hal from a few of the students from the drama club. And Edith was backstage, organizing costumes. Where she'd sourced them, DeeDee did not know, and she did not ask. She left her to it.

DeeDee assembled the actors onstage to talk about her vision for the play. She wanted to convey her artistic vision for the production.

"Although we all know who Grace Gibson is—in Lavender Bay, you'd have to live in a cave not to know who she is—most of us don't really *know* her," DeeDee started, looking around at each cast member. "I can tell you firsthand after spending time with her and talking about her life, she is someone worth knowing."

Some of them had blank stares and others nodded, and she wondered if her words had any impact. She spoke for a few more minutes and finished with, "But most importantly, we're here to have fun. We're not looking for accolades or perfect performances. The only thing you need to concentrate on is memorizing your lines and trying not to upstage anyone else. But I will help you with all that."

She handed out diagrams of the stage labeled with directional terms: center stage, upstage, downstage, right stage, left stage, up left, up right, down left, and down right. Everyone looked confused. "Memorize them," DeeDee said, "and it will help with your position and movement on the stage." To assist them, she'd taped off the floor of the stage in nine squares with the names of each area marked in the square. Walking from block to block, she explained it all. She had every confidence that they were directable.

Rehearsals were broken into two parts. The years that concentrated on the elderly Grace, starring Kay Bright, were held in the afternoon as most of the people in those roles were retired. The younger years were rehearsed in the evening. This kept DeeDee busy, and it also gave her no time to think. In the mornings she was either working a shift at the café or over at the inn, doing the cleaning. Always, at the back of her mind, she was anxious about being ready for April 19th.

DeeDee set up her chair at the front of the stage to watch all the rehearsals. Later, she'd move to the audience to watch the flow of the play. But until everyone's positions and movements were nailed down, she'd remain onstage. "Kay, could you step forward a bit, to where I've taped an X on the floor?" DeeDee said.

Kay, a sprightly retiree, did as she was asked. "I keep forgetting about that, don't I?"

"It's not the end of the world, Kay," DeeDee reassured her. Actually, Kay was pretty good. Her delivery of lines was near perfect. She only needed some guidance with voice delivery and blocking—her positioning and her movements. Sometimes, she stood in one spot as if reciting lines. It was difficult to coordinate speech, placement, and movement, but DeeDee was determined to help them all.

Suzanne was a big help. She oversaw all the minor details, which allowed DeeDee to focus on the bigger picture. She'd never directed a play before, and it surprised her to find that she really enjoyed it, from being backstage with Mrs. B going over costume choices to explaining different types of lighting to Mrs. Knicker-bocker to teasing out the best performance from each of the actors. She visited the art department several times, discussing ideas for set decorations, and that was fun too. The whole process of directing was a pleasant eye-opener for her.

DeeDee scratched her forehead. She was currently rehearsing one of her scenes with Brett. They'd done the run-through and were at the part where John McNama-ra was telling Grace that he was torn between his love for her and his calling to become a priest.

They were still in the early days of the rehearsals, and she hoped with time and some gentle guidance, Brett's performance would loosen up and become more natur-al. He was a bit standoffish, but it only seemed to be with her. He was friendly and chatty with the other perform-ers, and she wondered if she'd done something to offend him during that first visit with Peaches. Maybe he held it against her that she'd traveled over a thousand miles with her canary in a bird carrier. Finally, she concluded it was none of her business what he thought of her. She didn't have to be the popular girl. She couldn't take on one more thing to worry about.

During early rehearsals, it was all about learning their lines, and Brett had come prepared, for which she was pleased. But his lack of emotion worried her. From her interviews with Grace, she'd concluded that John Mc-Namara was the love of Grace's life, and most likely she was the love of his, even though he'd answered to a higher calling. If there was one thing she wanted to convey emotionally onstage, this was it.

Gently, she broached the subject with him. They were sitting in the first row of the theater seats. Other members of the cast were going over their lines onstage, and Mrs. Knickerbocker and Hal were practicing with the lights, which was punctuated by their howls of laughter, causing DeeDee to smile and shake her head. She was glad they were enjoying themselves.

"Brett, how are you finding the part?" she asked. She kept her voice low, not wanting to call attention to their conversation.

"Great," he said. "It's a role with a lot of depth."

"It is."

"I mean, he's in love with Grace, that's obvious, but he also recognizes his call to be a priest."

"He's really torn," DeeDee agreed. "How do you figure on playing him?"

"With great emotion, hopefully."

Gently, she said, "Are you happy with your performance?"

He laughed. "No, not really. I'm having a hard time conveying that emotion."

"Is it due to anything in particular?"

He opened his mouth, hesitated, then closed it. "Nothing I can put my finger on." He avoided meeting her gaze.

If he was hesitant around her, there'd be no way they'd be able to convey the chemistry between Grace and John that DeeDee wished to highlight. "May I make a suggestion?" she asked.

"Sure."

"I don't know if you have a girlfriend or are in a relationship—"

Quickly, he interrupted her. "No, I'm single. Haven't been in a relationship for a while."

It was a little more information than was called for, but she could work with it. "But at our age, we know what it feels like to be in love with someone," she prompted.

Surprisingly, he reddened.

She continued. "You know, those heady emotions of crushing on someone, and then those first throes of being in love," she said, watching his reaction. His gaze met hers. She wasn't sure if she was reaching him or not. "Do you know what I mean?"

He nodded quickly. "Yes, I do. And then sometimes those feelings are unrequited, which can be painful."

"True. But could you channel that feeling that it's reciprocated, so we're very clear that John and Grace have fallen in love?"

"I'll give it a try," he said. Uncertainty tinged his voice.

She gave him a reassuring smile. "I'll be more than happy to help you, Brett. We'll get there in the end, trust me."

He smiled warmly at her. "All right, DeeDee."

CHAPTER FORTY

As rehearsals for the play continued, DeeDee had many things on her mind, none more pressing than casting the part of Bernie. Not one audition seemed to fit Bernie as she envisioned her. And many people had tried out. Circling the back of her mind was Angie's suggestion to ask Esther.

She had just finished making one of the beds in the guest rooms at Nadine's inn, using hospital corners on the sheets to give it a neat, crisp look and tucking the duvet over it. She laid a plush velvet runner across the foot of the bed to add some pizzazz. She'd already cleaned the bathroom and emptied all the garbage cans. She ran the cordless vacuum, then put it on its charger in the utility closet in the upstairs hall. After she put all her supplies away, she pushed bundles of laundry linen down through the wall chute to the canvas laundry cart waiting below. She'd run down the two flights of stairs to start the washing machine.

As she reached the first floor, she spotted Esther through the window, standing on the front porch. Her cousin knocked and opened the door.

"Knock knock," she called.

"Hey, Esther, how are you?" DeeDee asked.

"Great."

Nadine and Herman appeared from the kitchen. The dog trotted along at Nadine's side but when he reached the doorway to the front hall, he paused, turned around, and backed into the room.

Esther laughed. "You know, that never gets old." Herman approached her and she bent to pet him. "Hey, boy, how are you?"

Herman wagged his tail in response.

Esther straightened and said to Nadine, "I've got your bowling shirt for the tournament." She held up a bag.

"Hold on," Nadine said. "I'll grab my wallet."

"Don't you want to try it on?" Esther said.

"Nope. I'm a medium all the time," Nadine said, disappearing back into the kitchen.

"How's the play going?" Esther asked.

"Great. We're getting there." That was the truth. Brett's performance was improving, and DeeDee was almost satisfied. A thought occurred to her. "Hey, can you meet up for lunch? To catch up?"

"Sure, I've got a half day on Friday if that works for you."

"Perfect."

"The Annacotty room is my favorite place. Would that work?" Esther said.

"I love it there as well."

"I'll make a reservation."

"Let me know what time. See you Friday," DeeDee said, and she waved goodbye and headed down to the cellar to start the wash.

DeeDee wasn't in the door for a minute when Louise greeted her, all excited. "Peaches is singing again!"

"What?" DeeDee ran to the large cage in the kitchen that housed her peach-colored bird. Peaches hopped from perch to perch, warbling and chirping. "Oh, Peaches." DeeDee's relief was palpable.

Louise joined her and said, "I had the radio on, and Barbra Streisand came on, and you know that song from *Funny Girl*, 'Don't Rain on My Parade'? When DeeDee nodded—of course she knew it, it was her favorite musical—Louise continued, "Well, Barbra really belts that song out. And I heard this noise. And let me tell you, I wouldn't have believed it if I hadn't heard it with my own ears! All of the sudden, Peaches was warbling like he had nothing to lose."

DeeDee pulled up the song on her phone and turned up the volume. Immediately, the bird let out a string of notes. She clasped her hands to her mouth.

"You and your bird have that in common," Louise said. "You used to love that song when you were a little girl. Remember you'd stand at the top of the staircase and belt it out as you made your way down the stairs? Grammie loved that."

With a wince, DeeDee looked at her mother and said, "I was really over the top at times, wasn't I?"

Louise wrapped her arm around her daughter and gave her a squeeze. "I wouldn't have you any other way."

CHAPTER FORTY-ONE

DeeDee met Esther at the Annacotty Room at the agreed-upon time. She saw her cousin regularly at the get-togethers that were a mainstay of the Cook family. Every Sunday was coffee morning at Louise's house, which she could hardly escape as she was living there. But she wanted to talk to Esther alone.

When she was shown her seat by the hostess, DeeDee looked around, aware that her sister Maureen had decorated the place. She loved the combination of lime, grape, and silver colors. Her sister certainly had an eye for color and design.

She had no sooner sat down than Esther appeared. Esther was the oldest of the cousins, and DeeDee was the youngest. Pop-Pop used to call them bookends.

Esther pulled out the chair across from DeeDee, and it occurred to DeeDee that this is what Aunt Gail must have looked like thirty years ago.

"How've you been?" Esther asked.

Before DeeDee could respond, the server approached them to take their drink order. Then Esther asked what the specials were.

"I might as well have my dinner now," she said, even though it was only one in the afternoon. "Then I won't have to worry about what to cook later."

They both glanced over the menu before choosing: pan-fried sole with lemon butter sauce for DeeDee and a strip steak with onion rings and mashed potatoes for Esther.

"How's everything? What's new?" DeeDee asked.

"Not much. Work is the usual." With a sigh, Esther added, "The guy I've been seeing wants to take it to the next level. I hate that term. It makes it sound like a video game and we're trying to get a high score."

"What does he want?"

"He wants me to move in with him," Esther said, clearly displeased. After a painful breakup in college, Esther preferred to keep relationships on a superficial level.

"What are you going to do?" DeeDee asked.

"What can I do? I'm going to have to break up with him. I'm not moving in with him."

"Why not?"

Esther shook her head. "No, no, no. I'm happy living by myself."

Deciding to play devil's advocate, if only for the fun of it, DeeDee said, "It may enrich your life."

Esther snorted. "My life can be enriched by him staying over at his house and me at mine."

"You've been going out with him for a while, haven't you?"

She nodded. "I have. And I like him. We get along great. He doesn't get on my nerves. Well, not until now. And he's a great cook, which works out really well because I don't like to cook."

Their meals arrived and Esther said, "Don't you find living alone freeing?"

DeeDee shrugged. "I don't know. Sometimes, I think I'd like something permanent." It would be nice to have companionship, someone to talk to daily. She was aware that at times, she could be an incredibly naïve dreamer. In her last relationship, Brad had fed her all sorts of lines, and she'd fallen for them. At her age, she really should have known better. Would she ever learn?

Esther picked up her fork and knife and began to cut up her strip steak. "How's it going with the play? It's all anyone is talking about."

DeeDee figured this was as good a segue as she was going to get. "It's going great." *For an amateur production*, she thought. It wasn't without its hiccups but overall, they were getting there. "But that's the reason I asked you to meet me for lunch."

Esther paused, chewing, hands holding utensils poised above her plate.

"I have one part that I'm having trouble casting—" DeeDee began.

Esther shook her head. "Nope. Nope."

"Hear me out," DeeDee pleaded.

Esther resumed eating her meal. "Sure, I'll listen, but my answer is already no."

"I've got a role that has your name written all over it."

"Is that so?" Esther did not look up, forking another piece of her steak and popping it into her mouth.

Her cousin was going to be a tough sell, but that only made DeeDee more determined that Esther was going to play the part of Bernie.

She explained the role and added, "Remember, I've got to cover one hundred years, and Bernie was only in the Philippines for eighteen months until she got malaria and was sent home."

"It's still a no from me."

"Grace said she was really funny."

"Again, no."

"Aw, come on," DeeDee pleaded. "You said yourself that you used to belong to the drama club in high school."

Esther leaned forward. "That was twenty-five years ago."

"It'll be fun!"

"It'll be torture, that's what it'll be," Esther said. "Besides, how do you know I can even act?"

DeeDee laughed. "It's an amateur production. It's not a Broadway play, and you have some experience."

"That was back in high school when I was laboring under delusions of grandeur," Esther said with a grin. "I am much more sensible these days. I don't fancy getting up onstage and making a fool of myself."

"Who's to say you'd make a fool of yourself?"

"Me! That's who."

DeeDee finished her pan-fried sole, which was delicious. She must remember to text her mother that she wouldn't have any dinner that evening. Undeterred, she realized she had to make an offer. A trade of sorts. And she'd have to use Esther's kryptonite, which was bowling.

"All right, I'd be willing to join your bowling team if you play the part." There, she'd said it.

Esther did not say anything at first. She studied DeeDee before declaring, "You must be desperate."

"I am, actually, but I can so see you as Bernie."

Esther pushed her plate aside and leaned forward on the table, lowering her voice. "I don't remember anything about acting."

"I'll help you," DeeDee promised. "Besides, you're not alone. Like I said, this is an amateur production. No one knows how to act. It's not like Lavender Bay has a community theater. This is from the ground up."

"If it wasn't for the fact that Maureen and Allan are going away on a two-week cruise, I wouldn't even consider this," Esther said with a sigh. "The league is wrapping up, and your sister will be away during the tournament." She huffed. "Who books a vacation during a bowling tournament? Who does that?"

A thought occurred to Esther, and she tilted her head and asked her cousin, "DeeDee, do you even know how to bowl?"

"Actually, I took bowling lessons from a pro in Florida."

Esther's mouth fell open and she blinked several times. "What? And how did I not know this?"

DeeDee raised her eyebrows. "Because I never told anyone."

"Why did you take bowling lessons?"

"I had a minor, minor part in a film that required me to be able to bowl well."

Esther grinned. "You little sandbagger. I love it." Amused, she thought for a minute before asking, "Are you any good?"

"I am—er, I was then. It was ten years ago."

"It'll come back to you. Do you often do that? Take lessons to prepare for a part?"

DeeDee rattled off a list of classes she'd taken. "Fencing, kickboxing, tap dancing, ballet—"

Esther held up her hand. "I get it. You show up prepared. That's a family trait."

"I suppose it is."

"All right, I'll do this, but only on one condition."

DeeDee braced herself.

"If I stink," Esther said, "please take me out. Don't let me make a fool of myself in front of the whole town. I have to live here in this community. I have a reputation to maintain."

DeeDee immediately put her cousin's mind at ease. "Of course. But in the meantime, I'll teach you the basics. Like a mini master class."

"Whatever. When is this play?"

"End of April," DeeDee said.

They went their separate ways after lunch, Esther promising to show up for rehearsals the following evening. DeeDee promised she'd email over the script, assuring her cousin that it was a small part. She added that she was looking forward to bowling on Saturday night, which might have been a little white lie.

Buoyed, DeeDee left the restaurant, satisfied that the final piece of the puzzle had been secured.

Hopefully, Esther could act. Or at least take direction.

CHAPTER FORTY-TWO

It was the last dress rehearsal before opening night. DeeDee had butterflies in her stomach. Her mother and her aunt sat in the fourth row, eager to get a sneak preview, and she was curious as to what their opinion would be. They'd be the first members of the public to view the production. They'd been rehearsing all weekend, starting with one of DeeDee's favorite exercises, an Italian run-through, where the actors said all their lines and did their actions and movements quickly to help them with pacing, cues, and remembering lines. She herself knew every line by heart. During the past week of rehearsals, Suzanne had sat in several spots throughout the theater to view the play through the eyes of the audience members, advising and adjusting the movements of the actors or their delivery of lines.

Esther, with some guidance, was a natural as Bernie, and Brett as John had come a long way. DeeDee didn't know who his crush was that he was channeling, but it got the job done.

When it came time for the scene where John told Grace he'd chosen the priesthood, DeeDee could so easily feel Grace's hurt at being dumped. It was an easy emotion to access. As she acted out the scene with Brett, everything seemed to fall away. She was no longer aware of her mother and aunt sitting in the theater or the sounds coming from backstage or even the misplaced lighting, courtesy of Mrs. Knickerbocker and Hal.

"There's nothing I can do to change your mind?" DeeDee said as Grace.

Brett shook his head and DeeDee, on cue, began to cry, covering her hands with her face. Brett pulled her into his arms, his voice on the verge of breaking as he said, "Please don't cry, Grace."

As she sobbed, he rubbed her back until the lights were dimmed onstage.

As soon as the scene was over, the curtains drew to a close, and DeeDee pulled away from Brett.

"You're doing great, Brett," she said truthfully.

"Thanks, I had a good teacher," he said.

They finished the dress rehearsal, and DeeDee was satisfied. When they gathered on the stage at the end, she joined her mother's and her aunt's applause and said to the cast, "Well done! You're all going to be great tomorrow night."

At that moment, one of the spotlights swung wildly around on the stage. DeeDee turned to peer at Edna and Hal in the shadowy darkness at the back of the theater.

"Sorry about that, everything's all right," Mrs. Knickerbocker shouted. And then to Hal, she said, "Now stop that, you rascal, and behave yourself."

DeeDee rolled her eyes, and Louise and Gail burst out laughing in their seats.

April 19th turned out to be a sunny and beautiful spring day. The first blooms of tulips and daffodils had appeared, and the trees had tiny mossy-green buds on their bare branches. It looked hopeful. DeeDee thought it was a perfect day to turn one hundred years old. She tried to call Grace several times to wish her a happy birthday, but the line was always busy. She supposed she wasn't the only well-wisher that day.

She met Suzanne at the theater early that morning to do some last-minute preparations. Her cousin hugged her clipboard to her chest and looked around the dimly lit theater.

"I can't believe it's already here. The last couple of months have gone by fast, haven't they?" she asked.

"A little too fast," DeeDee agreed. "I wish we had more time."

"It's ready," Suzanne said. "Mom loved it. Said it was great."

Despite this, doubt filled DeeDee.

Suzanne, sensing this, reached out and laid a gentle hand on her arm. "It's ready. It's good. You've done a great job here."

"Thanks."

"I was so happy to be a part of this," Suzanne admitted. Her smile wavered. "This has been good for me."

"I'm glad," DeeDee said.

DeeDee buzzed around the theater, double-checking everything, making sure everything was in order. She gave a pep talk to the cast and crew and thanked them, wrapping it up by telling them to go and have fun. Edna and Hal seemed to have a grip on the lighting. The mics were all working, and the costumes were ready.

DeeDee had never been as nervous as she was for the opening of this play. She'd invested so much emotionally into the production. She stood backstage, which was a hive of activity. Students from the drama club were getting the set decorations in place, and one of them wheeled a rack of costumes past her to the small cubicles behind the stage that served as dressing rooms. Brett approached her as she peeked out at the audience. Every seat was full. Grace and Ada were front and center. DeeDee drew in a deep breath.

"Are you nervous?" Brett asked.

"Surprisingly, I am," she admitted.

"It's going to be great," he said.

"Do you think so?"

"I do. We had a superb director."

She laid her hand on his arm. "Thank you for that, Brett."

"Sure. I better get backstage and get ready," he said, but he hesitated for a moment before leaving.

Right before the start of the play, she gathered everyone backstage and spoke for a few moments, reminding them that they were there to have fun. Again, she talked about the fourth wall, advising them to look past the audience to the back of the theater and envision the scene they were in playing out on that back wall.

She looked around at them excitedly. "All right, I think we're ready. Break a leg!"

The curtains opened, and the first act began.

All went smoothly until the man playing George Gibson dropped one of his lines during the scene at the train station when Grace was leaving for the American University in Washington, DC, but DeeDee improvised and got them both back on track.

One of her last scenes with Brett was poolside, when John told Grace he was going away on a spiritual retreat to make a decision. They stood center stage, a backdrop showing Grace's house behind them. As scripted, DeeDee flung herself at Brett the same way Grace had done when she kissed John on the lips. Brett responded in kind, pulling her close, wrapping his strong arms around her waist and returning her kiss. She had to remind herself that this was only acting, even though her body was tingling in response to his touch. When he lingered longer than scripted, she whispered, "Pull away."

He did so abruptly, in a way that was even better than what they'd rehearsed. Brett as John took a step back, looking gutted. *Bravo*, she thought.

Throughout the production, the energy was amazing, with the performers and the audience seeming to feed off of each other's excitement.

She couldn't believe how fast the night went by. Before she knew it, she was standing in the middle of the stage, holding Brett's hand on her left and Kay Bright's hand on her right. The whole cast took a bow, and a large bouquet of roses was delivered to Grace in the front row. Grace handed the flowers to Ada and turned in her seat to wave at everyone in the theater. The audience got to their feet and rewarded her with a standing ovation.

It was as beautiful and rewarding a moment as DeeDee had ever known in theater.

CHAPTER FORTY-THREE

DeeDee made her way up the long drive to Grace Gibson's home. The play was over, and she was beginning to make moves to head back to Florida. Although she was dragging her feet. Over the last eight months, Lavender Bay had seeped back into her soul, and she'd gotten comfortable there. She liked the camaraderie with her sisters and cousins and being a part of their lives once again. And Peaches was singing. She'd brought down the record player from the attic along with some old vinyl albums. He warbled and sang along with the soundtracks to *Hello, Dolly* and *On a Clear Day You Can See Forever*. Peaches had become a big Barbra Streisand fan. The thought of the long drive and him going mute again stalled her return.

But now as she stood on the front step of Grace's home, hesitating to ring the bell, her concern was that on the other side of the door, there might lie a rebuke over the play. Maybe she hadn't portrayed Grace or her life story the way the elderly woman had wanted. Overall, DeeDee thought it had gone well. There were rave reviews in *The Lavender Bay Chronicles* and as she went through town, everyone congratulated her. But now she wasn't so sure. It was tricky telling the story of a real person and real-life events, especially when said person was still alive.

Finally, after drawing in a deep breath, she pressed the doorbell. While she waited, she stretched her neck to work out a kink that had developed. A headache wouldn't be far behind. Best to work that out.

Ada answered the door, all smiles. Having seen many of Grace's old photos, DeeDee had come to appreciate how Ada bore a strong resemblance to her mother, Bernie, with the same dark hair and remarkable height.

"Come in, DeeDee," Ada said, stepping aside to allow her in. As they walked to the back of the house, she said, "I really enjoyed the play. You did a wonderful job. And Esther, who played my mother, was spot-on. It made me realize how much I miss my mother and her marvelous sense of humor."

DeeDee thanked her and noted she'd said "I" enjoyed the play instead of "we." She swallowed hard, hoping against hope that Grace hadn't brought her here to dress her down. It wouldn't matter if the whole town loved it or if she were celebrated and praised for her efforts if the subject, Grace Gibson, didn't like it. How horrifying that would be. Remembering advice from her Grammie, she decided not to borrow trouble.

Grace was back in the sunroom. Although the sun was out, it was still only April, and the heat was on. Grace sat in a recliner with a fleece blanket thrown over her legs.

"There she is!" Grace crowed on seeing DeeDee, holding out her hands.

DeeDee went over to the now one-hundred-year-old woman and clasped her hands, which were cool. "How are you doing, Grace?"

"Considering my age, I think I'm doing pretty good," Grace joked.

"I think you're doing terrific," DeeDee said.

"Me too," Ada agreed, her smile warm.

"Sit down, DeeDee," Grace said, waving her toward the chair next to her.

"Grace, would you like lemonade or something warmer?" Ada asked.

"Tea is fine, Ada."

"DeeDee?" Ada asked.

"Tea is also fine for me," she answered.

Ada disappeared.

Grace leaned over the side of her chair in DeeDee's direction. "Now tell me. Are you in the spotlight of adulation after the play?"

DeeDee blushed.

"Don't be shy about it. It was wonderful!" Grace gushed. "I thoroughly enjoyed it. Actually, I was tickled."

"I'm relieved to hear that," DeeDee admitted with a laugh. "I thought I was summoned to be chastised."

"Oh goodness no, why would you think that? You must think more of yourself and your abilities. I do."

DeeDee nodded, tucking that piece of advice away for future reference.

"And Esther's portrayal of Bernie was spot-on. She didn't know she could act, did she?"

DeeDee laughed. That had turned out to be the biggest surprise of all. "No, she didn't."

"The acting gene must run in your family."

"Apparently."

"There is a reason I wanted to see you," Grace said, getting down to business.

Ada reappeared with a tray bearing three cups of tea. She set the tray down and put one mug on a coaster for Grace on the small table between Grace's and DeeDee's chairs. Then she took the seat across from them.

"I have a proposition for you," Grace said, lifting the mug with a shaky hand and sipping from it. Ada watched the older woman carefully.

DeeDee sipped from her own mug and waited.

"After the play, I realized what this town needs is a community theater. It's such a shame that we can't have more performances like that in Lavender Bay, that we have to travel outside of town to see a play or a performance."

"I agree," DeeDee said. "Any kind of art is important to a community."

"Hear, hear."

There was a slight pause before Grace continued speaking. "Anyway, I've given this great thought." With a nod toward Ada, she said, "And Ada and I have discussed it at length."

DeeDee waited, unsure of where Grace was heading, but certainly curious.

"I'd like to put up the funds for a community theater program," Grace said.

DeeDee blinked her eyes several times and said nothing.

Grace continued. "There'd be a season of performances from September to May every year. And I'd like you to be in charge."

DeeDee placed her hand on her chest. "Me? I don't know the first thing about running a community theater."

Grace leaned toward her. "You just *think* you don't. Look at what you've managed to accomplish in a short period of time. You can run it, be on the board, whatever you need to do, and in the off-season you could hold workshops on acting. We don't have anything like that in town, and I bet there'd be a lot of interest."

DeeDee agreed with her, but she wasn't sure she was the one to take charge. Surely there was someone more experienced, more qualified.

"It would be a salaried position for you, DeeDee, although I realize most of the parts would be volunteer. But maybe we could work out a small stipend for staff, including actors."

"Gosh, Grace, that's very generous."

Grace laughed. "My money will outlive me. There's more than plenty of it to go around. And I like to invest it in Lavender Bay, just as my father did."

"I don't know what to say."

"Don't say anything yet. But please give it serious consideration."

"I promise I will seriously think about it."

They made small talk and when DeeDee finished her tea, she stood, thanked Grace and Ada, and went on her way.

This was a life-changing opportunity. Although she would give it due consideration, her instinct told her to jump at it. It meant moving back to Lavender Bay long-term and as she thought about it, she realized that staying in her hometown, permanently, was something she'd very much like to do.

CHAPTER FORTY-FOUR

DeeDee retrieved Rufus's leash from the back room of Aunt Gail's shop. Her aunt was busy with a customer, so they exchanged a wave and DeeDee clipped the lead to Rufus's collar and coaxed him off the couch. He rolled off, righted himself, and waddled out the front door. The first time she walked him, she'd chosen to go down Main Street, and that had been a colossal mistake because everyone stopped to pet Rufus, who thoroughly enjoyed being the town's celebrity. Now she made a quick right onto Pine from Main and headed in the direction of Pearl Street. They didn't go far because he walked so slow—half his fault and half not. His legs were so short there wasn't much of a stride there, and he sniffed everything along the way. *Everything.*

DeeDee stood there on the sidewalk, staring at the sliver of lake visible between the houses on Pearl Street, thinking of nothing specific, waiting for Rufus as he thoroughly investigated a shrub.

A car turned from Pearl onto Pine and slowed in front of her, parking next to the curb. DeeDee recognized Brett and waved at him. He emerged, smiling, and approached her, leaning over to pet Rufus. "Hey, Rufus, how are you doing?"

She hadn't seen him since the last run of the play. More than once, her mind had drifted back to that kissing scene on opening night.

"How are you, Brett?" she asked.

"I'm well. You're the talk of the town, DeeDee," he said with a smile. He'd certainly loosened up since she first met him.

She shrugged. "I don't know about that. Everyone was easy to work with."

Rufus, sensing they might be a while, sank to the ground and closed his eyes.

"I really enjoyed myself," Brett said.

"I'm glad to hear that. And you did so well in the end. I don't know what crush or past girlfriend you channeled, but you played John just the way I envisioned. Grace was pleased."

"I'm glad to hear that."

"I hope your crush knows how you feel about her," DeeDee teased.

He tilted his head slightly. "Do you think I should tell her?"

She nodded enthusiastically, thinking that was one lucky lady.

"All right then, I will." He smiled. "When I first met you, that day you brought Peaches in, I'd heard about you."

DeeDee arched an eyebrow.

He was quick to reassure her. "Not like that. I'd heard that you were an actress. And when you came into my clinic, I was tongue-tied."

"Because I'm an actress?"

He shook his head. "No—well, maybe a little, but also because you were very pretty. I felt like a teenager again." He paused and added, "I guess I was starstruck."

DeeDee blinked, realizing that *she* was his crush.

"And then you turned out to be kind, too, which was why I was flailing in the beginning of the rehearsals."

"Why?"

"Because I really liked you. But I realize that I came off as standoffish and that made things worse."

"You did seem that way, a bit," DeeDee admitted. "Everyone told me you were a great guy, and I was having a hard time believing it."

Brett grimaced. "Was I that bad?"

"Yes," she said, laughing. "I thought you were haughty!"

"I've got my work cut out for me."

"I think you might be able to redeem yourself," she said. Beside her, Rufus let out a loud snore.

"Can we start over? Maybe go out for dinner?" he said.

"I would really like that," she said truthfully.

He was all smiles. "That's great! I'll call you."

He got back into his car and drove away with a wave.

"Come on, Rufus, let's go," she said, unable to suppress a smile. She and the dog headed off, and DeeDee had a definite spring in her step.

Things were looking up.

"It's perfect," DeeDee said as she finished her tour of the small single-story cottage on Primrose Street. It was a two-bedroom home with a small backyard and a front porch. The windows and doors had recently been replaced, and there were hardwood floors throughout. A faint smell of Murphy Oil Soap and lemon-scented cleaner hung in the air. The house was empty except for a stove and a refrigerator.

"I'll require the first and last month's deposit," said Mrs. Knickerbocker, who was about to become her new landlady.

DeeDee had already flown down to Florida with her nephews, Everett and Lance, and put her condo up for sale. The three of them packed up her belongings, and her nephews loaded them into the rented U-Haul truck, which they then drove back to Lavender Bay. She'd left Peaches in the safe hands of her mother, who had purchased a new album for him to listen to. It was the soundtrack of Barbra Streisand's film *Funny Girl*.

DeeDee nodded at Mrs. Knickerbocker and added, "I have a canary." It was best to be upfront. She didn't want to be evicted later because of her singing bird.

"That's fine. Does he sing?"

"He does. He loves show tunes," DeeDee told her.

"I like him already." Edna narrowed her eyes at DeeDee. "You're not bringing a dog or a cat, are you?"

DeeDee shook her head. "No, it would just be me and the canary."

Mrs. Knickerbocker nodded and whipped out a lease agreement from her purse. "Read this over, sign it, and get it back to me with the deposit."

"Will do."

DeeDee would be moving in on the first of the month. She looked back over her shoulder as she walked away. It was a welcoming little home, and she thought it would be perfect for her as she started her new life in Lavender Bay.

It was the first day of summer, and DeeDee walked along Main Street, thinking she might go to the beach later on. Rehearsals for her new play didn't begin until

August for the scheduled opening at the end of September. She was excited about that. She was still working at the café in the mornings, and in the evenings she worked on the play at her kitchen table, right next to Peaches's cage, as the music played and the bird sang.

She looked back at the red brick building with the white trim where she'd just finished her scheduled appointment. She wished she'd done this a long time ago. Although the nightmares hadn't stopped completely, she wasn't having them as frequently anymore. This was her second counselor. The first one hadn't worked out, but Grace Gibson had encouraged her not to give up. Dora Delaney was middle-aged with black hair with a great white streak on the right side of her face. She had been instrumental in helping DeeDee process things relating to the accident and death she'd witnessed.

DeeDee didn't turn down Primrose Street toward her new home, instead, choosing to pop in and see her mother. She knocked on the front door and when there was no answer, she tried the door handle. Finding it unlocked, she stepped inside.

She could hear her mother in the kitchen, talking to someone in an affectionate tone. DeeDee wondered if one of the grandchildren was there.

"Mom?" she called out.

Louise poked her head out of the kitchen. "DeeDee, come on in, I made a strawberry-rhubarb pie."

"I haven't had that in years," DeeDee said. "Who were you talking to?"

Louise crooked her finger and beckoned. "Come on, I want you to meet the new man in my life."

DeeDee froze. Her mother was dating? She'd always said no one could ever fill her late husband's shoes. Curiosity propelled DeeDee into the kitchen, where she expected to see a man her mother's age sitting at the table, devouring a slice of pie. But there was no one there.

"Mom?"

It was worse than dating; her mother had an imaginary friend now.

Louise stretched out her arm, and DeeDee looked in the direction she pointed. Peter, the one-eyed, three-legged ginger cat, sat hunched over a small blue dish on the floor, nibbling some wet cat food.

Her mother was all smiles. "This is Peter Cook."

"I know him. How did you end up with him?"

"I dropped off a birthday cake and a present for Debbie—as you know, her family would never think to give her a gift," Louise said with a huff. "Anyway, she was quite upset because Peter was going to have to be put down because she couldn't find a home for him, and one of her cats—I think it was the one that used to wear the diaper—was tormenting him. So, I offered to take him."

"Mom, you don't even like cats."

"That's true. But with Peter, it was love at first sight," Louise gushed. "Just look at him. How can you not love a face like that? He hasn't had an easy life." The cat, as if knowing he was being talked about, walk-hopped over to Louise and rubbed up against her leg.

Louise looked tenderly at the cat. She reached down and rubbed his head. "You're a good boy, aren't you?"

"He's a lucky cat," DeeDee said. From living rough to being pampered. It was a beautiful thing.

"Sometimes, all you need is a new beginning," Louise said.

"I agree!" DeeDee said wholeheartedly.

ACKNOWLEDGEMENTS

As always, I'm grateful for all the help during the research of this book. It's always fun to go down the rabbit hole.

Erica Lansberg from the National WW2 museum, who provided me with a comprehensive list of resources about women and their contribution to WW2, especially non-medical workers, and Red Cross volunteers. Many thanks.

To my friend, Courtney Bahr, who graciously and with great detail answered all my questions about acting. It turned out to be a mini-master class in the art. I realize that I've only skimmed the surface of this profession.

Any mistakes are mine.

SIGN UP FOR MY NEWSLETTER

To stay up to date with new releases and receive exclusive bonus material, sign up for my newsletter at www .michelebrouder.com

ALSO BY MICHELE BROUDER

The Lavender Bay Chronicles
The Inn at Lavender Bay
Lost and Found in Lavender Bay
Second Chances in Lavender Bay
New Beginnings in Lavender Bay
Looking Back in Lavender Bay (Coming in June 2025)
Hideaway Bay
Coming Home to Hideaway Bay
Meet Me at Sunrise
Moonlight and Promises
When We Were Young
One Last Thing Before I Go
The Chocolatier of Hideaway Bay
Now and Forever
Escape to Ireland
A Match Made in Ireland
Her Fake Irish Husband
Her Irish Inheritance

A Match for the Matchmaker
Home, Sweet Irish Home
An Irish Christmas
The Happy Holidays
A Whyte Christmas
This Christmas
A Wish for Christmas
One Kiss for Christmas
A Wedding for Christmas
Audiobooks
Coming Home to Hideaway Bay
All books available in ebook, paperback, and large print paperback. Audiobooks coming soon.

www.ingramcontent.com/pod-product-compliance
Lightning Source LLC
Chambersburg PA
CBHW031741180726
48283CB00005B/1610